TALES OF THE RIGHTEOUS

Tales of the RIGHTEOUS

Retold by
SIMCHA RAZ

Translated by RABBI DOV PERETZ ELKINS
Foreword by ELIE WIESEL

Originally published in Hebrew as *Sipurei Tzadikim* © Kol Hamevaser, 2000

Cover Design: Leah Ben Avraham / Noonim Graphics
Typesetting: David Yehoshua

Cover painting: Shoshannah Brombacher, Ph.d.
shoshbm@gmail.com

ISBN: 978-965-229-540-8

1 3 5 7 9 8 6 4 2

Gefen Publishing House Ltd.
6 Hatzvi Street
Jerusalem 94386, Israel
972-2-538-0247
orders@gefenpublishing.com

Gefen Books
11 Edison Place
Springfield, NJ 07081
1-800-477-5257
orders@gefenpublishing.com

www.gefenpublishing.com

Printed in Israel

Send for our free catalogue

Library of Congress Cataloging-in-Publication Data

Raz, Simcha.
[Sipurei Tzadikim. English]
Tales of the righteous / retold by Simcha Raz; foreword by Elie Wiesel;
translated by Dov Peretz Elkins.
p. cm.

ISBN 978-965-229-540-8

1. Hasidim--Legends. 2. Jewish legends. I. Elkins, Dov Peretz. II. Title.

BM532.R38413 2011 • 296.1'9--dc23 • 2011034180

Contents

Foreword by Elie Wiesel

"The Deliverance of the Almighty Is Swift"

I have a warm regard for the Hasidic tale. It summons me back to a world that has been engulfed by time; only its echo still resounds in our ears. Is it possible that this world has invested us with the power to carry on? Or do we live in its shadow? I feel certain that it imbues us with a vital life force. Just as a God-fearing Jew feels the need to regularly read the Book of Psalms, a Hasid longs to listen to and to tell Hasidic tales and legends.

Without them he would feel impoverished and alone.

What is that unique quality contained in the Hasidic tale? The tools of literary analysis will not do here. For a Hasid, such scrutiny has no relevance. For the non-Hasid, the special flavor is lost. Whereas a Hasid lives the tale with the telling, one who is not a Hasid peers through the texture of words from the outside looking in.

In the eyes of a Hasid, every act is "a fearful and amazing act" and each tale "a wondrous tale"; sublime and remote from the understanding of man, occupying the realm beyond the rational. Deposit your demands of logic at the door; if you wish to enter the realm of these tales, you must open your heart to faith in the Almighty. His dynamic alone can alter the scheme of nature through the channel of His chosen envoys.

One thousand and one legends have been told far and wide of the great Hasidic figures. Actually, all the legends are one, for we find a single dominant recurrent theme: there is a Jew in need of assistance, he prays and weeps, the tzaddik rushes to his aid. Thus, each tale offers the elements of drama, conflict, crisis, and resolution. And the conclusion is always optimistic: the poor man becomes rich, the sick man recovers, the evil man is punished. Good triumphs over evil.

Impossible? It doesn't happen in our corporeal world, where the textures of light and darkness are interwoven? Well, in the Hasidic tale all things are possible and, therefore, we are intrigued. Here we find the charm of innocence, benevolence, righteousness, and compassion. The tzaddik is always ready to hear out a person in trouble and offer him the understanding of a compassionate heart. For a vital principal of Hasidism is that one must not fall into despondency. It is sufficient that an individual simply ponder repentance, think a single thought of atonement, for one's eyes to be opened and to see that all of creation is in God's hands. The natural result of this is that the individual is blessed with the comprehension that the Almighty can come to his assistance in the following instant. The impossible becomes possible.

On occasion, the Almighty's help tarries. The tzaddik speaks and the meaning of his words becomes clear only several weeks or several years later. What of it? The salient point is that there exists a link which refutes the likelihood of a world of pure chance. In the Hasidic tale, time is not an absolute dimension: the tzaddik uses time as he wishes, and even the angel of death must obey.

Make no mistake, the telling of the Hasidic tale is a special skill and one that Simcha Raz knows well. It is truly a pleasure to observe how he has regenerated and restored legends and tales drawn from the wellspring of Hasidic lore.

Congratulations to the author. He presents us with the fair, literary, and humane countenance of Hasidism. The reader will sail off to the most lofty horizons on a voyage of legend; his whole being will be enthralled. This book contains stories both short and long, sad tales and happy ones; narratives simple and complex. What then do they have in common? The reader is drawn to these tales because of an inner yearning to believe that even today one can be visited by the prophet Elijah. In other words, miracles can still happen. The heart wants to be reassured that prayer has the power to deliver from the pitfalls of life.

We who inhabit a world so devoted to its enhancement of the material will find that the reading of Simcha Raz's book offers us the opportunity to embark on a journey of discovery into another, more sublime world.

Preface by the Author of the Hebrew Edition

At the outset it is appropriate to point out that the authors of the stories did not intend, by and large, for the fruit of their muse to be put into writing. And as such it was not their intention to have their language flow smoothly. Rather, their objective was to tell and retell their stories in order to impart lessons to their audiences in varied locations and circumstances, and at different periods of time.

Therefore, when these stories were transmitted from a small group to a wider public, it was but natural that many elements and components were added, and many alterations and additions were made. Nevertheless, the essence of these tales retained their spirit, which returns in the course of generations, in one form or another, in the mouths of tzaddikim and maggidim, who preserve and inherit their message.

In the rich folk literature of Hasidut, many are the stories that are associated with the actions of the tzaddikim, of their battle with the evil within them. Some stories are passed down exactly as they happened, and others have elements that are read between the lines, embellished by the imagination. Some stories emerge from grim reality, and are transmuted into the world of simple faith which does not need any explanation or surprises. Both kinds excel in their simplicity, in their accessibility, in their direct expression, in their flexible framework – and above all in their ethical, spiritual, and social message.

This wide range of stories and tales, with their unique characterization, are laid out in their varied forms in this book. They embrace the entirety of existence, whispering of this world and the World to Come, of the life of matter and of spirit, of the experience of the individual and that of the collective. It is my hope that by reading these stories and tales readers will uncover new landscapes which will deepen their consciousness and bathe them with grace and kindness.

The essence of the stories lies in the oral tradition that was passed down from the mouths of the tzaddikim themselves or which was retold, person to person, by their students and admirers. It is natural that in the course of years an aura of mystery enveloped these looming personalities. Nevertheless, the story has the power to bring down to us the giants of Israel from their high place of honor, to teach us that even you and I are able to reach their level. The tzaddik is only flesh and blood, but he was able to purify his character and restrain his native urges. And there are those among them who did not pass the test and were not ashamed to relate their failings. Undeterred, they strove to acquire anew each sterling character trait, arduously climbing the ladder of moral integrity – always aware that no inheritance comes free.

It is in regard to this powerful struggle, replete with both failure and soaring success, that the Hasidic tale comes to instruct us.

Let not a simple story seem unimportant in your eyes. Rabbi Yisrael of Rizhin, one of the giants of Hasidic storytellers, taught:

> Once Rabbi Yisrael Baal Shem Tov (the Besht) was traveling with his students, discussing matters of godliness and worship. Night was falling. When they passed by a tree, the Besht got down from the wagon, stood near the tree, and became deeply engrossed in prayer.
>
> A short while later the Besht told his pupil Rabbi Leib ben Sarah to bore a hole in the tree and place in it a lit candle. Rabbi Leib ben Sarah did so, and while standing next to the lit candle the Besht prayed fervently. He continued until the fire went out.
>
> The Besht then lifted his eyes to Heaven and called out in a voice filled with joy: "Thank you, Holy One! Thank you, Master of the Universe!"
>
> When he returned to the wagon the sun had set and the moon shone brightly. After a lengthy period of silence the Besht roused himself from his musings and said, "Blessed be God Who saved our people, Israel, from the evil decree, Heaven forbid."
>
> The students understood that due to the merit of the burning candle an evil decree had been cancelled.

> The Besht and his students alighted from the wagon and broke out in a lively dance by the light of the moon, singing, "Salvation and comfort for our fellow Jews; salvation and comfort!"

Rabbi Dov Ber, the Maggid of Mezritch, related the following story to his circle of friends:

> On one of my trips I got down from my wagon, stood next to a tree, and had a hole bored in the tree to place in it a burning candle. Then I began to plead strongly and recited this prayer: "Master of the Universe! It is well known to You that I am not able to express eloquent appeals as did Rabbi Yisrael Baal Shem Tov. Therefore I ask You that due to his merit I may be worthy to pray before You, and that You will remove from the holy people of Israel the wicked decree about to come upon us."

The same tale was told by Rabbi Moshe Leib of Sassov when he was traveling with his entourage. He stopped alongside a tree, and after he told his students the story of the burning candle in the tree, which cancelled an evil decree in the days of the Baal Shem Tov, and in the days of the Maggid of Mezritch, he concluded: "My friends, the holy Baal Shem Tov knew the secret of the fire, and he had great powers with prayers and entreaties. Rabbi Dov Ber also knew the secret of the fire, but he did not have the power of prayer and entreaty. We, the generation whose hearts have shrunk, orphans of orphans, we understand neither the secret of the fire nor of the special prayers and entreaties with which our holy teachers were able to cancel the evil decrees over the Jewish people. Please, from Your place in Heaven, have mercy upon us, and may the merit of our great rabbis bring about the power to cancel the evil decrees...." (Adapted from *Knesset Yisrael*, Warsaw, 1896)

~

If we were to ask Rabbi Dov Ber, the Maggid of Mezritch, "This passion for God – how can we access it?" he would answer: "One must search for a spark amid the ashes." This is hinted at in the injunction to resemble dust and ashes, which became a central tenet of Hasidic thought: the spark is hidden within the ashes!

In today's world people either are not prepared to become like dust and ashes, or they are not ready to bend down to search and find the embers and the spark in the ashes. Today people need assistance and persuasion and enticement – in the best sense of that word – and this is what a good story can provide; a story that describes the giants of Israel in their integrity and wisdom, their greatness and humility.

The young generation – and perhaps also the older and wiser among us – who will peruse this book, will become closer to these tzaddikim who are so full of passion and empathy. But for those who negate the power of a story, seeing in it merely miracles and wonders which are suitable only for young children or passionate Hasidim – for them the book will be worthless. As the Maggid has taught, there are two kinds of dancing: One lifts the dancer up from his place and raises him to a higher level, even if only a few inches off the ground. The other consists merely in jumping and bouncing in place – accomplishing little more than wearing out the man's shoes.

As for me, in my writing I focus on the former.

Simcha Raz

Preface by the Translator

I am delighted and honored to have a part in bringing this book to the English-reading world.

I hold a deep respect and admiration for my friend and teacher Simcha Raz, a distinguished Israeli scholar and writer. This is the third book of his that I have been privileged to have translated into English. The first two were *Hasidic Wisdom* (translated with my son, Jonathan Elkins), and *The Torah's Seventy Faces*. All three books are the product of Simcha Raz's lifelong study of the sacred literature of the Jewish people.

Simcha Raz has the unique ability, like a bee, to gather honey from many places and deposit the sweetness and beauty of Jewish wisdom into a series of outstanding collections on many themes.

I particularly enjoyed translating this book, titled in Hebrew *Sippurei Tzaddikim*. The stories reflect the powerful ideology of the Jewish people's leaders in the eighteenth, nineteenth, and twentieth centuries. Figuring prominently in the book are tales of the beloved Hasidic masters, which reflect the deep moral and spiritual heritage that they have bequeathed to future generations.

Hasidism has added a great deal to Jewish life, and is today enjoying a renaissance, with stories and music à la Rabbi Shlomo Carlebach. It is easy to understand why. The Baal Shem Tov's revolution opened the hearts of Jews to something they had lost: the joy of life, vibrant faith in God, satisfaction with the simplicities of spiritual life, and the independence of one's own heart and spirit to attain spiritual satisfaction. Despite terrible external conditions of persecution and anti-Semitism, Jews could now find all they needed to develop a flourishing spiritual life, inside their own hearts.

As Simcha Raz points out in his preface, learning about Hasidic tzaddikim, these giants of the spirit, can infuse Jewish life today with a much-needed renewal of commitment to the Jewish way of life – to the beauty of its observances, to the soundness of its theology, and to the joy of its celebrations.

In closing I want to thank my devoted wife, Maxine (Miryam), who tolerated my obsession with the computer during our wonderful six-month stay in Jerusalem in the first half of 2010. Working on translating this amazing book has brought me great joy and renewed appreciation of the Jewish tradition to which we have together devoted our lives.

Rabbi Dov Peretz Elkins
Lag baOmer 5771

Anger

TWO *TALLITOT*

For a long time Rabbi Mordekhai of Neshchiz longed for a *tallit katan* made of cloth from Eretz Yisrael. When the special fine wool finally arrived, he asked one of his favorite students to honor him by sewing for him a *tallit katan*. The student agreed. But unfortunately the student accidentally folded the cloth twice and instead of one neckhole he cut two, creating a tear that could not be repaired.

The student was mortified about this, and feared that his teacher would be angry with him. After all, the Mishnah states (Bava Kama 2:6) that humans are always fully responsible for the consequences of their actions.

But Rabbi Mordekhai did not reprimand his pupil, and did not even show anger toward him. Just the opposite. He smiled at him and said, "Good job, my son! You carried out the task according to Jewish law. I really need two pairs of the *tallit katan*. One to fulfill the mitzvah of *tallit katan*, and the other to put Reb Mordekhai to the test, to see if he can overcome his *yetzer hara* (evil inclination) to get angry."

HAVE PITY

A woman once brought her case before a court headed by Rabbi Hayyim Halevy Soloveitchik, only to have the court rule against her. The woman became arrogant and angry, to the point that she scorned the dignity of Rabbi Hayyim, and one of the judges became angry with her. "Shut your mouth, you arrogant woman!" he shouted.

Rabbi Hayyim silenced the judge, saying, "Why is she subject to your anger? This is a fine Jewish woman, but she is worried about her finances, and her soul is embittered since she believes that she had justice on her side. Therefore she is screaming and furious. Let her yell and ridicule me until she settles down."

YOU ARE FORGIVEN

As leader of the Jewish community in Jerusalem, Rabbi Yosef Zundel of Salant was entrusted with giving out the *halukah* (charity that was sent from overseas). While Rabbi Yosef Zundel was walking in the streets of Jerusalem one day, one of the usual recipients began to harass and badger the rabbi for depriving him of his share of the funds. Several people who were standing around gathered together in amazement. A Jerusalemite would insult Rabbi Yosef Zundel? It became apparent that the man did not know Rabbi Yosef Zundel at all, and had thought he was one of the charity collectors of the school. The people standing around wanted to attack the man for affronting the dignity of such a tzaddik. But Rabbi Yosef Zundel did not permit them to do so.

Toward evening Rabbi Yosef Zundel went to the house of the man, and asked him for forgiveness, since it was because of him that the man suffered such aggravation.

FEAR NOT!

Rabbi Leib ben Sarah arrived in a particular city to collect money for redeeming captive Jews from prison. He sent his assistant to a certain wealthy man to request a large donation for this holy purpose. The assistant was very reluctant to perform this mission because the wealthy man was well known in the city for his stubborn and angry character.

Rabbi Leib told him, "Come and I'll explain something important to you. The ground on which we tread is made of mere dust. The table around which we sit is in essence from dust. The house in which the rich man lives is built from dust. All his silver and gold were quarried from the dust, and the prosperous man himself was originally from dust. His wealth is certainly dust of the dust. So are you really afraid of dust?"

IN MY ANGER, BE MERCIFUL

At midnight a sound of alarm and crying was heard, emanating from the walls of the beit midrash in Radin.

The people on the street walked toward the window of the beit midrash, and saw that it was Rabbi Yisrael Meir Hakohen, author of the *Hafetz Hayyim*, screaming from the depths of his heart. "Master of the Universe! I want so much to distance myself from anger. But I am afraid that I, Yisrael Meir, a kohen, will be one about whom our Sages taught that 'kohanim are an irate brood.' Therefore, please God, strengthen and fortify me, that I shall be able to conquer the anger implanted in me; 'a pure heart, God, please create within me' (Psalms 51:12)."

WORDS OF WISDOM

ANY OLD EXCUSE

We get up in the morning, and immediately get angry. And we look for any excuse to cast our anger and fury on someone.

Rabbi Gershon Henokh of Radzin

CAREFUL WHAT YOU WEAR

Never wear a garment whose top part is made of pride, and whose bottom part is made of anger, and is sewn with threads of dark gall.

Rabbi Naftali of Ropschitz

HUMILITY

"The study of the Torah is good when combined with a worldly occupation [*derekh eretz* – literally, the way of earth]" (Pirkei Avot 2:2).

This counsels us to learn from the earth: The ground gives life to every living thing, and from it all existence emerges. Yet even though everyone treads on it, it does not get angry or annoyed.

Rabbi Avraham "the Angel"

Authors and Books

BORROWED BOOKS

Rabbi Hayyim of Zanz had very few books. When he needed a certain book he would borrow it from someone. His son asked him: "You give so much to charity that there is nothing left for you even to buy books?"

His father answered him: "Yes, a book I can borrow, but the mitzvah of *tzedakah* cannot be borrowed."

MEDITATE UPON IT DAY AND NIGHT

Though Rabbi David Halevy was among the giants in halakhah and author of the commentary on the *Shulhan Arukh* known as *Turei Zahav*, he held the position of rabbi in a small town and his salary was meager. Despite this he was content with his lot, and he was sorry about only one thing – that it was impossible for him to buy books that he needed for his studies.

Once a bookseller came to Rabbi David's city with his wagon full of holy books, and as was his custom he displayed the books on a table in the beit midrash. The rabbi perused the different books, but as it happened there was not one book with which he was not already familiar.

The bookseller noticed this and told Rabbi David, "There is one very important book which, due to its rarity, I have not placed on the table. If the honorable rabbi is interested in the book, I can bring it out and show it to you."

"And what is the name of the book?" the rabbi asked. The bookseller replied: "*The Book of Compilation*. Its author is the gaon Rabbi Alexander Zuslin Katz, who was one of the great scholars of halakhah, and died a martyr in Germany in the year 1349. Until recently this book was only available in manuscript, but only a short while ago it was printed."

The rabbi, who had heard about this important book but had never seen it, asked to look it over.

When the bookseller brought him the book, the rabbi perused it and saw that the book was overflowing with new interpretations of Torah. Longing to buy the book, he asked about the price. But when he heard the required amount, he realized he did not have enough money to buy the precious book. With deep regret he placed it back on the table and walked away.

The bookseller noticed the rabbi's sadness and suggested a discounted price, but even this amount was too much for the rabbi to pay. Nevertheless he still longed for the book, and before he left the synagogue he asked the bookseller if he could borrow the book overnight. The merchant reluctantly agreed and handed the book to the rabbi.

Rabbi David returned to his home, closeted himself in his room, and read the book the entire day. He did not budge from his desk except to daven Minhah and Maariv, after which he immediately returned to the book. By the next morning he had finished reading the entire book. He then went to the synagogue, and happily returned the book to the bookseller as he had promised.

"You should know," said the rabbi, "that I read the entire book, and I know it almost by heart. And even though I was careful with the book, and did not cause any financial loss to you, nevertheless I do not want to benefit from it for free. You make your living by selling books, and thus I want to pay you a portion of the price of the book as a 'reading fee.'"

The bookseller saw how much the rabbi enjoyed studying books of deep wisdom. Impressed with the rabbi's honesty and depth of soul, he did not want to accept any gain from him at all. "I am giving you this book as a present!" he exclaimed. But the rabbi refused to accept the gift.

From that day on Rabbi David never saw the book again, but every time he mentioned the author of *The Book of Compilation*, he recalled the impressive events of that day.

GRATEFUL FOR A REPRIMAND

One of the students of the Holy Jew tells this tale:

I came once to the home of my teacher, my master, and he was very surprised at how sick at heart I appeared. "What's going on?" he asked me.

"I am humiliated," I told him.

"Who caused you this humiliation?"

"Someone humiliated me," I replied.

My rebbe asked me to tell him the person's name, but I didn't want to. He pressed me strongly, since he wanted to admonish the person who had caused me such pain, but I still refused.

"And what did you do to the person who insulted you?" my rebbe asked.

"I kissed him," was my unexpected reply.

My rebbe was understandably shocked, and demanded that I reveal to him the name of the person who had humiliated me.

I explained to him: "Rebbe, is it not written in the Jerusalem Talmud that one who teaches must stand before his student while he teaches? Today I studied the book *Sheivet Musar*, and saw that the author was standing before me and gazing at me with an angry mien. I asked him, 'What sin, what fault have I that you should stare at me in such anger?' 'Study the book very diligently,' the author replied, 'and you'll understand.'

"I studied the book, and I realized that I still did not worship the Creator fully, and I still have not attained the required qualities of one who is of the stock of Avraham, Yitzhak, and Yaakov. I do not have appropriate fear of Heaven, nor humility with other people. And when I realized this, I became extremely mortified. I took the book, kissed it, and placed it on the bookshelf, but it still did not cease staring at me."

BRINGING SERENITY

Among the Hasidim of Anapol the following tale was widespread:

In the Upper World their teacher Rabbi Zusha met with Rabbi Avraham Azulai, author of *Hesed l'Avraham*. Rabbi Avraham said to Rabbi Zusha: "Zusha, my beloved friend, I have written ten holy books, and every one of them is studied in the Upper World. Nevertheless no one ever mentions my name here. But when your honored name is mentioned, there is much commotion in Heaven. You have written no books, what indeed have you accomplished in that world?"

"It is true that I have not written any books," Rabbi Zusha replied, "but this is what I did: Every Friday evening, when Shabbat arrived, I would go into the kitchen in my home and say '*Shabbat Shalom*' to the women who helped prepare the Shabbat meal for the visiting Hasidim. Immediately the women in the kitchen would hug one another and ask forgiveness from each other, as if it were Yom Kippur. All this was due to the great love and holiness of Shabbat that I brought them."

Rabbi Avraham fell deep in thought. "If so," he said, "all is as it should be."

IS IT WORTH IT?

Rabbi Menahem Mendel of Kotzk was asked why he did not write any books. He replied: "Let's pretend that I wrote a book. Who would buy it? Naturally, people who know me. And when would my friends, who are always busy with concerns for making a living, have time to turn to reading a book?

"Naturally, on Shabbat. But a Jew on Shabbat must do many things – go to the *mikveh*, pray, review the weekly Torah portion, eat three meals, sing Shabbat hymns, fulfill the mitzvah of "*shaynah b'Shabbat taanug*" (taking a nap). So when will one have time to peek into my book?

"Naturally, only in the few brief minutes before falling asleep after a big afternoon meal – after filling his belly with fish and meat and all kinds of delicacies, when he is tired and ready to fall asleep. By the time he peeks into my book, sleep will snatch him, and my book will fall from his hand and land on the floor. Now think about it! For this is it worthwhile for me to write a book, that it should help someone drowsy fall asleep?"

LOOKING FOR BUYERS

Rabbi Yisrael Baal Shem Tov (known by the acronym "the Besht") had great admiration and respect for his student Rabbi Yaakov Yosef Hakohen of Polnoye. He asked God: "Master of the Universe, remember me for good, since I raised and educated and prepared for You my student Yossele."

Rabbi Yaakov Yosef, it is told, would travel around many Jewish communities in order to sell and distribute his book *Toldot Yaakov Yosef* (The generations of Yaakov Yosef), the first book on Hasidism, published twenty years after the death of the Besht. The price of the book was a guilder, a large sum in those days.

In one of his travels Rabbi Yaakov Yosef visited the city of Berditchev, where he sat in one of the local inns and waited for buyers. Because of the book's high price, however, he was dismayed to find that there were not many in that Jewish city who were jumping for the book. When Rabbi Zev of Zhitomir, who happened to also be visiting Berditchev at the time, entered Rabbi Yaakov Yosef's room to pay him a visit, he found him burdened with sorrow and anger.

"Why are you so upset, my friend?" Rabbi Zev asked.

"I came here to sell my book, which is constructed entirely on the Torah ideas of our teacher, Rabbi Yisrael Baal Shem Tov. But there are no buyers, so how can I not grumble?"

"So what," laughed Rabbi Zev. "Even the Blessed Holy One, in all His Glory, offered the Torah to many nations, and they refused to accept it."

Body and Soul

WHICH COMES FIRST?

Rabbi Shneur Zalman of Liadi and Rabbi Levi Yitzhak of Berditchev married off their grandchildren to each other. Amid the rejoicing, Rabbi Shneur Zalman lifted his glass and made a toast to his new relative. "*L'hayyim*, my dear friend! May it be God's will that we both find success, materially and spiritually."

"How can you, my dear friend," asked Rabbi Levi Yitzhak in surprise, "precede material success to spiritual success?"

Rabbi Shneur Zalman replied, "I have proof from our Torah. Our forefather Yaakov vowed (Genesis 28:20–21): 'If God remains with me, if God protects me on this journey...and gives me bread to eat and clothing to wear...the Lord shall be my God.' From this you see that Yaakov put material comfort before spiritual fulfillment."

THE BLESSINGS OF POVERTY

Rabbi Yehiel Mikhal of Zlotchov was extremely poor. Once he asked himself, "I am so poor that I do not even have my simple daily needs. So why do I, who have absolutely nothing, recite the daily morning prayer in *birkot hashahar* thanking God for supplying all my needs?"

He reflected a while and said to himself, "If the Blessed Holy One bestowed poverty on me, then that must be what I need." Immediately he began to bless God with great joy: "Blessed are You, God, Who provides me with all my needs."

DOUBLE BLESSING

When Rabbi Hayyim of Volozhin parted from his teacher, the Vilna Gaon, he asked his teacher for a blessing.

The Vilna Gaon replied, "May it be God's will that you merit two *tamids* [always], according to tradition." A smile of joy crossed Rabbi Hayyim's face, and he parted from his teacher.

The students who were nearby did not understand their teacher's meaning. When Rabbi Hayyim left the Gaon's study, the students followed him and asked him to explain the meaning of the blessing.

"The interpretation is clear and simple," Rabbi Hayyim explained. "Our teacher referred to the words of the Rama [Rabbi Moshe Isserles], who began his commentary on the *Code of Jewish Law*, the *Shulhan Arukh*, with the biblical verse 'I am conscious of God's presence always [*tamid*]' (Psalms 16:8), and concluded his commentary with this verse: 'Contentment is a feast without end [*tamid]*' (Proverbs 15:15).

"So this is what our teacher referred to in his blessing, that these two biblical verses with the Hebrew word *tamid* should be fulfilled: 'I am conscious of God's presence always,' and 'Contentment is a feast without end [*tamid*].'"

THE REAL WORLD

Once during the third Shabbat meal Rabbi Yitzhak Isaac of Zhidachov spoke about spiritual awakening in a way that penetrated the hearts of his listeners. The next day not one person who had been a Shabbat guest approached him to say good-bye. It did not occur to the merchants or laborers to return home to their work.

When Rabbi Yitzhak Isaac saw that no one was leaving, he sent his son to ask several of the guests the reason for this. Their explanation was that on Shabbat the rabbi had preached about the wasted time in this world, and as a result they were embarrassed to return to their daily chores.

Rabbi Yitzhak Isaac sent word to them: "Shabbat is one thing, and the days of the week are another. As it is written, 'The heavens belong to God, but the earth God gave to humans' (Psalms 115:16)."

The merchants and artisans folded their *tallitot*, said good-bye to the rabbi, and returned to the real world.

WORDS OF WISDOM

WHERE IS SPIRITUALITY?

There is nothing material in this world that does not have some sparks of spirituality.

Rabbi Elimelekh of Lizhensk

THE IMPORTANCE OF THE BODY

God deems the human body to be extremely important. Did God not place upon it so much Torah and so many mitzvot?

Rabbi Menahem Mendel Schneerson

WHO IS FREE?

Whoever possesses the soul of a slave is a slave even when there is no master. One who possesses the soul of a free person is enslaved neither to a master nor to oneself.

Rabbi Simhah Bunim of Peshischa

TO HONOR MY SOUL

In past times I would punish my body in order to accustom it to tolerate my soul. However, I learned from my rebbe, the Maggid, that what I really need is to accustom my soul to tolerate my body, and not to run away from it.

Rabbi Shmelke of Nikolsberg

INNER SANCTUARY

"And they shall make me a Sanctuary, that I may dwell among them" (Exodus 25:8).

Every person must create a place for a sanctuary inside his soul, in which the *Shekhinah* (Divine Presence) can dwell.

Rabbi Menahem Mendel of Kotzk

ALWAYS RISING

"The soul of a person is the lamp of God" (Proverbs 20:27).

Just as the flame of a candle always reaches upward, so the inner spirit, or soul, of a person rises upward.

Rabbi Shneur Zalman of Liadi

WHO IS TRULY RICH?

"Ben Zoma taught.... Who is rich? The person who is satisfied with his lot" (Pirkei Avot 4:1).

Spirituality and materialism are opposite in their essence. When one rises in materialism, he descends in spirituality. In material things, one who is "satisfied with his lot" is a great person. And if he works on himself to improve his spiritual qualities, he rises to even higher levels.

With regard to spirituality, if one is "satisfied with his lot" – his spiritual level – that is the greatest fault, and such a one continues to descend in spirituality, God forbid.

Rabbi Menahem Mendel Schneerson

Character Traits (Midot)

MERITING A SON

Rabbi Avraham Yehoshua Heschel of Apt told the following story:

"Rabbi Eliezer was beloved in Heaven and adored on earth. He lived in a small village in Podolia where he hired a young boy, one of the farmers' sons, to sit at the gate of the village, and instructed him that whenever a stranger would pass by the village, he should bring him to Rabbi Eliezer's home. Whenever the boy brought a guest, Rabbi Eliezer would immediately give the guest enough money that he could eat a good meal before he left."

Rabbi Avraham further said of Rabbi Eliezer that in the highest heavens Rabbi Eliezer was praised greatly for his fulfillment of the mitzvah of *hakhnasat orhim* (hospitality), and especially for his love of every single Jew in Israel. He did not distinguish between rich and poor, he made no difference between a righteous person and a wicked person, between one who was devoted to God and one who was not. He would receive all of them warmly. He loved humanity and reached out to them, and would share all that he had with everyone.

Rabbi Avraham continued the story: "Satan arrived, sat down among the heavenly choir, and asked that they permit him to go to the home of Rabbi Eliezer and test his sincerity. However, just in time, Elijah the prophet got there first. He disguised himself as a poor man, entered the house of Rabbi Eliezer one Shabbat afternoon, with his staff in his hand, and his pack on his back, and greeted the host and his wife Sarah with a blessing of *Shabbat Shalom*.

"Rabbi Eliezer saw that the poor man knew that it was Shabbat and was deliberately violating its prohibitions, yet despite this Rabbi Eliezer did not chastise him. Instead he greeted the guest pleasantly, inviting him to feast with them at both Shabbat meals. After Shabbat he invited the man to attend the *melaveh malkah*, the post-Shabbat celebration, and generously supplied him with food and drink – all without ever mentioning a word about his having violated Shabbat, in order not to embarrass him.

"At that very moment the prophet Elijah revealed his true identity to Rabbi Eliezer. 'I have been sent by the heavenly angels in order to test you,' said Elijah, 'and to find out how far you fulfill the mitzvah of *hakhnasat orhim*. As a reward for having passed the test I bless you with this blessing: very soon your wife Sarah will give birth to a son who will enlighten the eyes of Israel, and his heart will be full of love and compassion for every Jew.'

"About a year later," concluded Rabbi Avraham Yehoshua Heschel of Apt, "a son was born to Sarah and Rabbi Eliezer, and he was named Yisrael. He was Rabbi Yisrael Baal Shem Tov, the founder of Hasidism."

HOLY SERVICE

As a young man the Baal Shem Tov was a servant to Rabbi Yitzhak of Drohovitch. One day after the Besht served his master a cup of coffee, he waited until the rabbi finished the drink and then removed the empty cup.

Rabbi Yitzhak smiled and said, "You brought me a cup of coffee with the thought that you were indeed doing service for a scholar. But what mitzvah do you think there is in removing an empty cup?"

The Besht replied, "Even returning the ladle full of incense in the service of Yom Kippur was considered an important part of the service."

Rabbi Yitzhak was so impressed with the answer that he told the Besht, "From now on I am obligated to serve you!"

COME BACK AND VISIT AGAIN

A meeting of community leaders took place in the home of Rabbi Tzvi Hanokh Hakohen Levin, the rabbi of the city of Bendin. They met to deal with the problems of their community. At the head of the group sat, naturally, their respected rabbi, whose personality and wisdom made a deep impression on the leaders' discussions.

Suddenly, in the middle of the discussion, the door opened and an unknown Jew entered the house. Rabbi Tzvi Hanokh noticed the stranger, who was standing hesitantly by the door, and immediately got up from his seat and welcomed the man with obvious joy.

"*Shalom Aleikhem, Shalom Aleikhem*," he said as he greeted him with heartfelt warmth. As he was ushering the guest to the table, he turned to the community leaders and said, "Excuse me, please wait a short while because I must deal with my dear guest."

After the guest was seated, the rabbi called his wife who was standing in the kitchen. "Please look, we have a dear guest who has come to visit us."

He joyfully offered the guest a glass of liquor and some honey cake. While this was happening, the rabbi's wife prepared a meal for the honored guest.

The guest finished the meal, and left with deep thanks from Rabbi Tzvi Hanokh. The rabbi accompanied him to the door of the house and said to him, "Whenever you happen to be in Bendin, come to our house. You brighten up my day!"

The community leaders saw the great affection that their rabbi felt toward the guest, and asked with curiosity, "Is this gentleman a relative to our rabbi, or a neighbor?"

To their great surprise Rabbi Tzvi Hanokh answered them in all sincerity, "I don't know him at all! But when a Jew comes to my house, it is my duty to honor him and to take care of him, since the mitzvah of *hakhnasat orhim* (hospitality) is a mitzvah for which there is no measure."

EMULATE THE MORAL QUALITIES OF OUR FATHER AVRAHAM

Rabbi Hayyim Halevy Soloveitchik, an acknowledged giant in Torah, was also known for his compassionate and kind heart. Once a pious-looking Jew came to the rabbi's home, and was received by Rabbi Hayyim with great warmth. The rabbi extended his normal gracious hospitality, giving him food and drink and making up his guest's bed himself.

Early in the morning the man awoke, placed in his bags everything from the room that would fit, and left the house. When the members of Rabbi Hayyim's family awoke, and saw what the "honored" guest had done, they turned to Rabbi Hayyim and lectured him about his foolish acts: "Why do you bring into our house unworthy people? How can you welcome every strange guest, without distinguishing between good and bad people?"

Rabbi Hayyim replied, "When the Blessed Holy One wanted to bring merit to our father Avraham with the mitzvah of *hakhnasat orhim* (hospitality), he sent him angels who resembled desert wanderers who bowed down at the dust of their feet, people who were grimy idol worshippers. This was to teach us that with regard to *hakhnasat orhim* one does not check the visitor's credentials, to decide whether he is worthy of being given hospitality. In future we can lock up our valuables, but our home must be open to everyone."

Another story of Rabbi Hayyim: A guest who was staying with the rabbi was very uncomfortable with the fact that one of the great rabbis of the Jewish people was himself taking personal care of him, preparing his meals, making his bed. Occasionally he would say to the rabbi, "Why does the honorable rabbi trouble himself?" But Rabbi Hayyim would not reply.

One morning during prayer services the guest was honored with the privilege of *hagbah*, lifting the *Sefer Torah*. When the man approached the bimah to lift the *Sefer Torah*, the rabbi said to him with a gentle smile, "Why do you trouble yourself? Why do you trouble yourself?"

NEVER EMBARRASS

Rabbi David Halevy Segal, known as the "Taz" after the initials of his book *Turei Zahav*, had a custom not to recite Kiddush on Shabbat by memory. He would follow it in the siddur word for word. The reason for this was that in the event that a guest attending the Shabbat meal did not know the Kiddush by heart, he would not be embarrassed when he had to turn to the siddur.

A SERENDIPITOUS GIFT

Already as a youth Rabbi Eliyahu Raguler became famous as a giant in Torah, as well as for his qualities of righteousness and piety. Shortly after he celebrated his bar mitzvah his father arranged a marriage for him to the daughter of a great scholar, who was also one of the wealthy people in the city. When he stood under the huppah (marital canopy) and broke the glass, as is the custom, he bent over and by himself gathered the shards of glass and put them in his coat pocket. When asked why he did that, he answered, "I was afraid that, Heaven forbid, someone would cut himself, and then I would be responsible for causing harm to another."

Another story about his piety: When Rabbi Eliyahu was twenty-seven years old he was appointed rabbi of the city of Ragula. Despite his meager salary, his door was open wide to all poor wanderers, and even the tramps who passed by. It happened once that a beggar came to Ragula, and the rabbi invited him to his house and gave him food and drink and a place to sleep. The next day the poor man left the house with blessings of appreciation and continued on his way.

After a while the rebbetzin noticed that her gold ring was missing. The ring, inlaid with precious stones, had been an inheritance from her distinguished mother. The rebbetzin suspected that the poor man whom her husband had invited to the house had stolen the ring. Without telling her husband, she went and notified the police, who were able to catch the man. Upon finding the gold ring in his pocket, the thief was arrested and the ring was returned to the rebbetzin.

The rabbi's wife told her husband the whole story, and scolded him for bringing unworthy people into the house. The rabbi listened silently to his wife's words, then went to the police chief, and requested that the imprisoned man be released.

The rabbi told the police chief that in order to avoid bringing trouble to such people, it was his custom every evening before he went to sleep to relinquish possession of everything in his house – golden jewelry, silver vessels, etc. "This custom of mine," explained the rabbi to the police chief, "is known to all the members of the city, and this poor wanderer who came to Ragula certainly knew about my custom, and it is that which prompted him to take this ownerless ring.

"Therefore," concluded the rabbi, "not only am I obligated to help release him, but my wife must return the ring to him, since it belongs to him now, and by doing so she will also appease him for the insult that she caused him."

The words of the rabbi, spoken sincerely from the heart, made a great impression on the chief of police, and the latter released the man from jail.

HARDER TO PLAY MORDEKHAI

In the *musar* yeshivah of Rabbi Yosef Yuzel Horovitz, a play was presented about Mordekhai and Esther. Rabbi Yuzel taught that it was easier to play the role of Haman than the role of Mordekhai. This is so because each of us has a little bit of the qualities of Haman, the pride and arrogance. But it is difficult to pretend to have the qualities and attributes of Mordekhai, which takes special talent and effort.

TURN IT OVER AND OVER

A friend of the rabbi of Kalish, Rabbi Hayyim Elazar Wachs, was a wealthy merchant and an honorable person. One day he came to the rabbi and revealed to him that he was about to conclude a large business transaction, and if the rabbi would help him in an act of fraud, the rabbi would stand to gain a great deal of money.

The rabbi replied, "The Torah in Parashat Ki Tisa teaches that the two tablets of the Ten Commandments were written "on both surfaces, on one side and the other side" (Exodus 32:15). Why does the Torah mention this? To teach us that whichever way we turn the Torah, 'You shall not steal' still stands firm."

JUSTICE FOR ALL

Rabbi Yisrael Salanter, founder of the *musar* movement in Lithuania, taught: "We learned in the Talmud, 'A judge must always see oneself as if a sword is hanging over his head, and Gehinnom (hell) is open before him' (Tractate Sanhedrin 7b). This Talmudic statement is not directed only to judges, people who are experts in deciding cases for others. Rather it is written as a warning to every person to be a judge of himself, and feel the weight of responsibility hanging over him in every deed he performs."

A GOOD-BYE BLESSING

Every time that Rabbi Simhah Zissel of Broida, the head of the Hevron yeshivah, left his house, he made sure to say to his wife, "*Shalom* and my best prayers and wishes to you." One of his students, who accompanied him on a trip, tells this story:

"It happened during the later years of Rabbi Simhah Zissel's life, when walking was already difficult for him, that suddenly the rabbi said that he wanted to return home because he had forgotten something.

"As we were already far from the house, I asked him if I could go back to the house instead of him to bring back what he had forgotten. It would be such a shame for the rabbi to undertake such a difficult task. However, the rosh yeshivah insisted on returning all the way home.

"When he opened the door, he asked forgiveness from his wife for neglecting to bid her *shalom*."

KILLING WITH WORDS

Rabbi Aharon of Karlin went to visit his teacher, the Maggid of Mezritch, together with a group of wagon drivers. As they rode along, the drivers passed the time by slandering the Jews of the city.

Rabbi Aharon heard this and involved himself in their discussion. He turned the topic of conversation to horses. The wagon drivers enthusiastically conversed with him all about horses during the entire trip, until they reached Mezritch.

When the wagon reached the city, a large number of Hasidim came to welcome their honored teacher. The wagon drivers were very surprised at what they saw, and asked Rabbi Aharon, "If you are a rabbi, why did you chat with us the entire trip all about horses?"

Rabbi Aharon answered them as follows: "I listened to the nonsense of your discussion in which you were killing people's reputations. So I said to myself, better that you should kill horses."

ASSURING DIGNITY

Rabbi Hayyim Ozer Grodzinski took a walk once in the streets of Vilna together with his students. Suddenly someone approached and asked if the rabbi was familiar with a certain street. Despite the fact that the street was very far, this well-known rabbi took the man by the hand and walked with him a half hour until they arrived at the exact location that the man was seeking.

The students asked their teacher, "Is it possible? Why did our master devote so much time to this stranger? Was it not possible to do as is the custom, namely, to point the man in the right direction and give him instructions how to get there? If he still did not find the place, he could have always asked someone else to direct him. Why did the rabbi feel obligated to trouble himself with this long walk?"

Rabbi Hayyim Ozer answered the students: "Did you not see that this Jew stutters? Did you notice how embarrassed he was to ask me for directions? Had I not gone with him, hand in hand, to the place in question, he would have had to undergo embarrassment again and again in order to arrive at his location.

"So in order to spare this Jew more embarrassment, it was well worth it to walk the far distance together with him."

ASK HER FORGIVENESS

Rabbi Barukh Ber Levovitz served as the rosh yeshivah of Kamenetz, near Brisk in Lithuania. Under his leadership the yeshiva grew to be one of the most prestigious yeshivot of Europe, until its destruction during the Shoah.

When Rabbi Barukh Ber traveled to the United States, he visited the home of his student Rabbi Koppel. When he entered the home, Rabbi Koppel's wife was listening to a lovely melody on a record. In honor of the presence of the distinguished rabbi, Rabbi Koppel quickly turned off the record player and pulled up a chair for Rabbi Barukh Ber.

However the rabbi did not sit down, but asked his student to go outside on the terrace because he wanted to tell him something in private.

When the two of them went outside, the rabbi castigated his student. "How did you permit yourself to turn off the record player without asking permission from your wife? You surely insulted her. I understand that you did this for my honor. However, is this the way you honor your wife, by turning off the music when she is standing and listening to it? Please go back in now and ask her forgiveness."

WORDS OF WISDOM

IT'S OUR CHOICE

"Rabbi taught: What is the proper way that a person should choose? That which brings glory to one's Maker and glory from other people." (Pirkei Avot 2:1)

Rabbi used the word "choose" rather than "walk," because people must choose for themselves the paths to go on, rather than conducting themselves according to what others do.

Rabbi Yehezkel Halbershtam

THE IMPORTANCE OF HOSPITALITY

"Welcoming guests is greater than welcoming the *Shekhinah* (the Divine Presence)" (Talmud, Tractate Shabbat 127a).

The *Shekhinah* is found at all times and in all places, and is always available to be received. But one cannot perform the mitzvah of welcoming at all times. Therefore, welcoming guests is a greater mitzvah.

Rabbi Moshe Leib of Sassov

The Coming of the Messiah

SALVATION IS COMING!

Rabbi Mendele of Rimanov used to say that the coming of the Messiah would resemble the Kabbalat Shabbat service in Lvov. One *erev* Shabbat Rabbi Mendele decided to spend the Shabbat in Lvov. On Friday, just after twelve noon, he began to have a strong yearning for the holy Shabbat, and his soul hungered for Shabbat's arrival.

He told his *shamash* to go out into the city and see if people were already preparing themselves for the coming of Shabbat. The *shamash* went into the street, stopped many Jews going about their duties, and asked them, "When will you greet the Shabbat?" They answered him that there were many worries on their mind, and there was ample time to be concerned with Shabbat.

About an hour later Rabbi Mendele sent his *shamash* to see if perhaps the Jews had yet started to prepare themselves for Shabbat, and he received the same answer. He did this several times, again and again. Rabbi Mendele sat and waited impatiently, until suddenly he heard from all over the town the sound of shop doors closing, and he saw Jews running and scampering in the streets. The holy Shabbat was about to arrive!

"Do you see?" said Rabbi Mendele to his *shamash*. "This is how the Messiah will come. The people of Israel will be busy with routine chores when suddenly, in a moment they will be aroused, and from every direction the stores will close, and they will all drop their customary chores, 'On that day they shall fling away their idols of silver and idols of gold…' (Isaiah 2:20). The Messiah will have arrived!"

DID YOU LONG FOR REDEMPTION?

The students of Rabbi Shmelke of Nikolsberg once asked him, "How is it possible to expect the coming of the Messiah in our generation, since we are poor in good deeds, and since many generations of Tannaim, Amoraim, Geonim, and other righteous scholars were not able to bring the Messiah?"

Rabbi Shmelke answered, "It is like an army that conquered a fortified city. After the conquest they must bring in simple workers to clear the heap of debris."

RICH IN LONGING

The Baal Shem Tov taught: "Every Jew must fix the piece of the stature of the Messiah that belongs to the root of his soul.

"What is our true purpose on earth? Perfecting life. We live in order to increase life. The more we increase our good deeds and fix the world, the more we usher in the Messianic age.

"And who has greater yearnings for good than those who are poor and indigent? Since the yearnings are prayers, it stands to reason that all the lives of the poor are prayers and longings for the Messiah. The smaller the spark, the greater are the yearnings for the flame."

THE PLEDGE

One Rosh Hashanah there was a gathering of saintly scholars in the home of Rabbi Aryeh Leib, the Shpoler Zeide: Rabbi Levi Yitzhak of Berditchev, Rabbi Zusha of Anapol, Rabbi Mordekhai of Neshchiz, and Rabbi Yehudah Leib, the preacher of Polnoye, were in attendance. After the meal these five pillars of the Jewish world arose and adjourned to a different room to discuss matters of the redemption and the pangs of the Messiah.

During the conversation Rabbi Zusha said to Rabbi Leib of Polnoye, "You, Leib, are guilty more than the rest of us for the absence of the Messiah. You are the preacher to the people of Israel, so why have you not been chastising them to repent?"

Immediately the Shpoler Zeide arose and said, "I understand the words of Rabbi Zusha." The holy zeide then raised his hands to Heaven and declared: "Master of the Universe, I hereby pledge to You, that by means of punishment and chastisement the people of Israel will not repent. So why do You punish them for nothing? Do You not understand, Our Father in Heaven, what will happen at the end of time? Ultimately the Messiah will come and the world will be redeemed. I therefore request that You should be only kind to Your people. As a father is merciful to his son, even if the son does not go on the straight path, so should You act mercifully toward us and toward all Israel."

The zeide spoke in a voice that kindled flames of fire and an outburst of tears. And all those who heard him cried with him.

THE TIME OF REDEMPTION IS CLOSE

After the death of the Seer of Lublin, his son Rabbi Yosef of Turtzin received his portion of the inheritance: some silk clothing for Shabbat, a belt, and a clock that always hung in the room in which the Seer sat.

On Rabbi Yosef's trip back from Lublin to his home, a torrential rainstorm began. It was impossible to travel further, and he was required to remain in a nearby village. For three days, the heavy rain pelted the area, during which time a Jew who lived in the village hosted the rabbi. When the rain stopped and the rabbi was able to continue his journey home, the villager asked for his fee for hosting the rabbi.

Rabbi Yosef told him that he did not have any cash, but he had some sacred property left from his father. He took out of his sack everything that he had inherited, and told that villager to choose whatever he wanted in lieu of the fee that he owed him.

The villager asked his wife to advise him what to choose. She said that the clothing and the belt were worth nothing to them, but it was possible to make use of the clock, in order to determine each morning the hour at which to milk the cows. They therefore accepted the clock.

Some weeks later, Rabbi Ber of Radoschitz was traveling in the same village, and because the hour was late in the evening he stayed in the same villager's home. The villager put him in the room where the clock had been hung. All night long the rabbi of Radoschitz did not sleep; instead he danced back and forth in his room. In the morning the villager asked him about his unexpected behavior. The rabbi replied, "Tell me, where did you get this clock?" The villager explained that he had acquired the clock in lieu of payment for lodging a traveler.

The rabbi of Radoschitz explained, "When I heard the ring of that clock, I immediately recognized that the clock is the one that had belonged to the holy rabbi of Lublin. Why? Because every clock has a special ring that informs its owner when his hour of death is near. And even though the sound is necessary to recognize, the sound brings sadness and sorrow. But this clock, that of the rabbi of Lublin, makes a sound of joy and celebration, because it announces the hour of the coming of the holy Messiah.

"Therefore I could not sleep out of joy, and instead I danced and danced and danced..."

MAY MESSIAH COME NOW

Rabbi Yehezkel Sarna, rosh yeshivah of Hevron, lamented: "The prophet Isaiah said, 'For one short minute I abandoned you, but in vast mercy I will bring you back' (54:7). Was it only 'one short minute'? The destruction of two temples, the long trek of pain the Jewish people endured through the exile, the years of the Inquisition, the dreadful pogroms, the bitter Crusades, the slaughter and the atrocities committed throughout the generations, the unprecedented genocide of the Shoah, and everything else that has plagued us until now – all this is encapsulated in 'a short minute'? How can one comprehend such a phrase?

"However, if these pain-steeped millennia are designated 'a short minute,' think about what the future will be like when 'in vast mercy I will bring you back.'"

Confession

PAY ATTENTION

It happened once that Rabbi Yisrael of Modzhitz went out with his Hasidim into the forest, and he heard the sound of a shepherd humming. He told the driver to stop, and listened attentively to the song of the shepherd until he had finished.

Rabbi Yisrael noticed that his Hasidim were surprised at his behavior, so he explained, "When someone sings, it is as if he is confessing. When a person confesses, whether the person is a Jew or not, one must pay attention."

HEAL ME, GOD, AND I SHALL BE HEALED

When Rabbi Dov Ber of Radoschitz fell mortally ill, he considered how best to deal with his situation. "One who is ill must confess his sins. But for me, what can I confess? Shall I say that I sinned? A person who is sick is especially bound to tell the truth. Shall I say that I diminished the amount of time of my prayers to the Blessed Holy One? This too would not be true. I did all that was in my power to do.

"Only this much can I say. That from this day on I accept upon myself to worship Hashem, the Blessed One, with a more clear mind, with no diversion of any kind – only to God alone, because a pure, clear mind is something of which there is no measure and no end, since the infinite God has no end. Whatever a person grasps of the greatness of the Creator has no limit.

"Therefore I accept upon myself that if God helps me, and heals me of my illness, I shall serve God with an even more pure and clear worship."

REGRET FOR THE PAST, PROMISES FOR THE FUTURE

Every night as he was retiring to sleep, Rabbi Levi Yitzhak of Berditchev would scrutinize his deeds, focusing on his faults and failures, and say to himself, "Levi Yitzhak will not do this again." A few minutes later he said to himself: "Did you not last night say the same thing, and yet you did not improve yourself!

"Ah, but last night I did not speak the truth, and tonight I say this in truth."

LET'S FORGIVE ONE ANOTHER

A certain Hasid came to see Rabbi Elimelekh of Lizhensk on the eve of Yom Kippur. He clung to the *shamash* and asked him eagerly that he be able to witness the actions of the rabbi when he visited various villages.

When Rabbi Elimelekh heard about this, he ordered to have the Hasid brought to him, and told him to take a wagon and travel to such and such a village, not far from Lizhensk, and there he should seek out a certain innkeeper, and stay at his inn.

When the Hasid arrived at the inn he found a room filled with drunken people. The Jewish innkeeper, a simple, burly man, and his wife, a clumsy Jewish woman, were busy serving their guests. The Hasid sat down quietly on a bench in the corner and pretended to fall asleep.

In the middle of the night, after all the guests had gone on their way, the Hasid saw the innkeeper walking around the room, sighing. Then he asked his wife to bring him his accounts record. She pulled out an old, torn notebook, and the innkeeper sat down at a table and began to leaf through the book, page by page. As he read each page he did so with tears in his eyes.

In this book he had written all kinds of transgressions that he had committed over the course of the year. One day he had received a guest in an impolite way, and had not fulfilled the mitzvah of welcoming guests. On another day he had listened to the foul language of drunken people. On another day he had thought foreign thoughts while praying. The list of failures went on and on, page after page. After reading each page of the book he sighed deeply, and when he was finished he cried bitterly.

The innkeeper then turned again to his wife and asked her to bring out the second book of accounts. She brought it out and gave the tattered journal to her husband, who began to leaf through it, page after page. In this book there were lists of all his problems, troubles, worries, and agonies that he had suffered during the year. It was a very long list. There was not one day on which he had not suffered aggravation or frustration.

After he finished reading the second book, he leaned his head on the table, and sank into deep thought. Then he lifted his eyes to Heaven. "I do not deny, Master of the Universe, the great debt that I owe You – a tremendous debt. However, You also owe me a great debt. I am not sure which debt is greater – mine to You or Yours to me. The calculation is very complex. And since it is the eve of Yom Kippur, the day of forgiveness and pardon, therefore, Master of the Universe, let us make a deal. I won't be indebted to You, and You won't be indebted to me. A notebook of transgressions in trade for a notebook of pain and anguish. This is a fair trade, and my exoneration – so I wish You *l'hayyim*, Master of the Universe."

The next morning the Hasid returned to Lizhensk, and when he visited Rabbi Elimelekh the rabbi welcomed him with a big smile.

"So, what did you see?" he asked. The Hasid related to him everything in great detail.

"You should know," replied Rabbi Elimelekh, "that the same thing that the innkeeper said to God, King David also said. This is the simple meaning of the verse 'Lord, You are aware of all my petitions; my groaning is not hidden from You' (Psalms 38:10). Yes, 'You are aware of all my petitions,' my heartfelt cries of repentance, but also 'my groaning is not hidden from You.' I give you credit, and You do the same for me, and we will pardon one another."

Desire

THE HEART COVETS

Rabbi Yitzhak Meir of Gur taught: "It is well known that at the time of the receiving of the Torah, God held Mount Sinai over the heads of the people and warned them, 'Accept the Torah or here will be your graves.' Why was this necessary? The people had already announced their willingness to obey the commandments by saying 'We will do and we will obey' (Exodus 24:7).

"However, when the people stood at the foot of Mount Sinai and heard the commandments 'You shall not murder,' 'You shall not steal,' the 'good Jews' shrugged their shoulders and stared at one another. The scholars asked themselves, 'For this Moshe brought us here? We assumed that we would hear some deep, original ideas. To people like us they have to say "You shall not steal," "You shall not covet" – *to us*?' They then prepared to turn away from Mount Sinai.

"It was at that moment that God turned the mountain over their heads and shouted, 'Do not dare move! These words apply to you scholars too! If you search far inside yourselves you will find that deep, deep inside every person there is hidden a little bit of the urge to steal, and a little bit of the urge to kill, and without doubt some degree of envious desire.'

"On the superficial level it may seem to you that you have none of these. The Ten Commandments that you hear will uproot every shred of an idea of theft which might be hidden far inside your heart."

WE MUST NOT TRANSGRESS – EVEN TO PERFORM A MITZVAH

The widow of a great tzaddik desired to sell the pair of *tefillin* of her late husband for a large fortune. These *tefillin* had been written especially for him, with particular holiness and purity.

Despite his poverty, Rabbi Menahem Mendel of Kotzk took every penny he had, and sent a messenger to go and purchase the pair of *tefillin*. When the messenger returned with the valued property, he reported to the rabbi, "For a pair of *tefillin* I transgressed the commandment, 'You shall not covet.' I could not resist wearing these *tefillin* even without asking your permission."

The rabbi glared at the messenger, and returned the *tefillin* to him, saying, "Take these as a gift. I have no need for them. A pair of *tefillin* that caused a Jew to violate 'You shall not covet' is of no interest to me."

YOU SHALL NOT COVET

Rabbi Simhah Bunim of Peshischa once came to a certain city, and they prepared for him a place in a beautiful inn. After he had alighted from the wagon, he wandered around the inn until his baggage was brought to his room. Suddenly he told his helper to gather his possessions and return them to the wagon, since he wanted to leave that inn. Perplexed, his helper nonetheless complied.

Rabbi Simhah Bunim and his helper made the rounds of the various inns in the city, but could not find an available room. The rabbi was forced to sleep in a simple room with the local *shohet* (ritual slaughterer).

Upon settling into his new room, Rabbi Simhah Bunim explained his actions to those standing nearby, who were amazed that he had left the lovely inn that had been prepared for him. "I did not find a single problem, Heaven forbid, with the inn," the rabbi said. "It was extremely beautiful. But I felt that I would be covetous in my heart for a room like that, and so I was apprehensive to accept it."

"WHAT'S MINE IS YOURS, AND WHAT'S YOURS IS YOURS" (PIRKEI AVOT 5:13)

The Baal Shem Tov, together with his young son Tzvi, entered the home of one of the wealthy Jews in Mezhibozh. There they saw beautiful vessels of gold and silver. The furniture was also very beautiful and lavish, causing little Tzvi to feel jealous.

When they left the house, the Besht said to his son, "I felt that you were covetous of the home and possessions of that wealthy Jew. In your father's house are only very simple things, nothing of gold or silver. Believe me, my son, if I had the money to buy beautiful furniture and silver and gold dishware, I would not buy them. I would distribute the money to the poor. And whatever was left over I would donate to charity, so that I would have not a dinar left."

"YOU SHALL NOT COVET YOUR NEIGHBOR'S WIFE"

An obese wagon driver riveted his eyes on a married woman, desiring her to the point that he was unable to stop thinking about her. When he realized how serious his sin was he visited a rabbi and told him that his evil inclination was getting the best of him.

The rabbi replied, "Leave the evil inclination to better men than you. You merely have a big appetite, and it has nothing to do with your evil inclination."

WORDS OF WISDOM

"DO NOT FOLLOW YOUR HEART AND EYES IN YOUR LUSTFUL URGE" (NUMBERS 15:39)

The order seems reversed. First the eye sees, and only afterwards does the heart covet. So why did the Torah mention the heart before the eye?

We cannot judge someone because of the first glance one makes. It is very possible that the first glance is a misstep. The punishment follows the second glance, when the person looks with malice at what he sees after the heart covets.

The Alshekh

Eating and Drinking

PRIMARY AND SECONDARY

Rabbi Yaakov Yosef of Polnoye used to say: "The act of fasting, in which one denies himself, resembles the tax of the community in our day, in which the wealthy, knowledgeable people assess the majority of the tax on the poor. Since the poor have nothing to give, they must bribe the tax collector with some money, which the latter may need for daily expenses. In this way the collector can stretch the time limit to collect the taxes, and the debt remains on the books. It would be better if the wealthy would pay the tax, and not burden the pauper.

"The parallel is the body, whose mouth and ears are the 'wealthy' among the parts of the body, and most sins are carried out by them. The belly has only one meal inside, and it is innocent of all sin. When a person regrets his sins, and wants to do repentance, he immediately punishes his stomach, which is poor and deficient, yet the sins of the wealthy are borne by it.

"It would be wiser to deprive the body parts which commit the sin – namely, to seal the mouth, shut the eyes, and close the ears."

GUARD THAT WHICH COMES OUT OF YOUR MOUTH

The Holy Jew of Peshischa instructed his student Rabbi Simhah Bunim to take a trip, but did not explain the purpose. Rabbi Bunim took with him several Hasidim and began the journey. They came to a certain village, and wanted to eat with one of the residents of the village. The resident informed them that he did not have any dairy products in the house, but had only meat. The Hasidim began to investigate the level of kashrut, such as who was the *shohet* (ritual slaughterer), whether the animal had been a kosher one, and whether the salting procedures had been carried out properly.

While they were questioning the resident in these matters they heard a beggar call out to them, "Hasidim, Hasidim! What you place in your mouth you inquire about – whether it has been kashered, and how it has been kashered. But what comes *out* of your mouth – the words you utter – about them you ask no questions, and do no intensive inquiry."

When Rabbi Simhah Bunim heard the words of the guest, he understood why the Holy Jew had sent him: in order to learn this important lesson from the passing stranger. He then returned home immediately.

SELF-DECEPTION

Rabbi Yisrael of Koznitz, as the Baal Shem Tov and the Maggid of Mezritch, was not pleased with those who fasted and afflicted their souls and bodies.

He used to say, "I respect the one who says publicly that he is fasting from one Shabbat to the next, yet secretly eats, more than one who truly fasts from Shabbat to Shabbat. The former only deceives the public, while the latter, who truly fasts and afflicts his soul, deceives himself!"

TEACHING BY EXAMPLE

A certain Hasid of Rabbi Elimelekh of Lizhensk was devout in matters of Hasidut, but he was addicted to eating with a huge appetite. So Rabbi Elimelekh invited him to have a light breakfast with him. The Hasid was delighted at the merit of sitting with his rabbi at a meal.

On the table were only a piece of black bread, salt, and a knife. Soon after reciting the blessing on bread, Rabbi Elimelekh began to speak to himself aloud: "*Oy vavoy*, Elimelekh, look at how you are eating, such a man of enormous appetite. You're so eager to swallow the bread in one gulp that you're even eating, as it were, with your eyes, glutton and drunkard that you are. Your appetite for food is greater even than a cow.

"Elimelekh, Elimelekh, stop it! Be a *mensch*! Remember that eating is permitted only for *pikuah nefesh* (saving a life), so that one will be strong enough to worship the Creator."

Rabbi Elimelekh took another crumb of bread and continued: "Elimelekh, Elimelekh, *oy vavoy*, you are only deceiving yourself. You act as if you are prepared and ready to break the habits of your evil inclination. You promised yourself that from now on you would exercise caution in your eating habits, and focus only for Heaven's sake, in order to have strength to study, to pray, and to serve your Creator.

"Look, Elimelekh, what a glutton you are! Every bone in your body cries out, eat! Your mouth consumes food, and all your 248 limbs gobble it up. And yet you still have the hutzpah to think that you are focusing all this effort for the sake of Heaven."

After all this Rabbi Elimelekh began to act as defense counsel for himself. "However, Elimelekh does want to change his eating habits. But he doesn't have a choice – after all, he is only flesh and blood. He eats against his own will. His body requires nourishment. His body tells him: If you don't feed me, I will perish. It says to him: You are my brother, and you must sustain me."

When the Hasid heard the words of his rabbi, his heart weakened, and he almost fainted from sadness and shame. From that time on the Hasid changed his eating habits and became a true Hasid in every way.

GENEROSITY

Rabbi Menahem Mendel of Rimanov and the members of his household used to bake bread to distribute to those in need. One day the rabbi noticed that the loaves of bread were smaller than usual. When he asked why this was, his family answered, "The price of flour soared in the market." Rabbi Menahem Mendel replied, "The way we measure is not according to the price of the flour in the market but by the needs of the families."

YOU SHALL EAT AND BE SATISFIED

The Gaon Rabbi Eliyahu of Vilna (known by the acronym, the Gr"a), was once invited to a *seudat mitzvah*, a religious feast. He noticed that there were two tables set up – one for the important guests, and another for the indigent.

Rabbi Eliyahu saw that the notables had already started to eat, but the underprivileged were still sitting and waiting. The rabbi asked the poor folks why they were not eating. They answered that the important guests should finish eating first, and then the others would take their turn.

The answer was not acceptable to the Gaon, and he said to them that they were violating a Torah command, namely, "Thou shall not plow with a donkey and an ox yoked together" (Deuteronomy 22:10). The Baal Haturim (Rabbi Yaakov ben Asher) explained the reason for the law is that it is the nature of the donkey to eat and swallow immediately, while the ox brings up its cud and chews the food all day, causing anguish to the donkey.

If the Torah has pity on an animal, how much more so must we have mercy on poor Jews and prevent them from the agony of watching others eat while they are hungry.

TORAH VALUES

Rabbi Naftali Tzvi Yehudah Berlin (the Netziv), rosh yeshivah of Volozhin, wanted to enlarge and broaden the boundaries of the yeshivah and increase the number of its students. It was also important to him that the Torah that the students absorbed in their souls would be a living Torah, and would not reduce their physical strength.

The rabbi himself had studied all day long as a child and had paid no attention to his health. Now that he was the rosh yeshivah he was careful and fastidious that his students would take good care not only of their souls but also of their bodies and health.

When a young man came to Volozhin in order to enter the yeshivah, the Netziv would carefully examine him to find out how much knowledge in Torah he had acquired. When he was satisfied that a young man was appropriately prepared in Torah to enter the Yeshivah of Volozhin, he would ask him, "Tell me the truth – has your soul longed for Torah knowledge?"

When the potential student answered positively, the Netziv would then ask another question: "Will you apply yourself diligently?"

The young man, naturally, answered that he was ready to apply himself to his studies night and day. At that point the Netziv would interrupt him, asking, "Do you know the meaning of applying yourself diligently? Diligence means eating on time, sleeping on time, and studying on time."

HARD ON HIMSELF, EASY ON OTHERS

It happened that guests arrived at the home of the Netziv on the seventeenth of Tammuz, the fast day commemorating the breach of the walls of Jerusalem before the destruction of the Second Temple.

Worn out from their journey, the guests turned to the Netziv and asked him, "Our master, we know that today is a public fast day, one of the four minor fasts, but we have been traveling from place to place and are a bit weakened; it will be difficult for us to fast."

"If that is the case," the Netziv instructed them, "it is permissible to eat."

The rabbi immediately set the table, and even served them himself, taking care of every detail of their meal. Then he said to them, "The mitzvah regarding hospitality is more important than the command of a public fast."

A CRUMB OF BREAD SHALL YOU EAT

Rabbi Akiva Eger heard that one of the young men in the yeshivah was living in poverty, and people had great pity on him. Every evening he would eat a slice of dry bread for dinner, recite *kriyat shema* (the biblical verses declaring the oneness of God and commanding love of God), and go to sleep.

"Whoever eats dry bread," said Rabbi Akiva Eger, "and recites *kriyat shema* and goes to sleep, I have no pity on him. I have great pity, however, on one who eats a delicious dinner of roasted chicken, and goes to bed without reciting *kriyat shema*."

WORDS OF WISDOM

FEASTING FOR GOD

It is harder to eat for Heaven's sake than it is to fast for Heaven's sake.

Malbim

FASTING

It is better to teach the heart, than to teach the stomach to fast.

Rabbi Menahem Mendel of Kotzk

WHEN DO YOU SEE GOD?

"And they saw God, and they ate and drank" (Exodus 24:11).

Even when you eat and drink, and engage in physical matters, still keep God in your vision.

Rabbi Dov Ber of Mezritch

THE BEST WAY TO FAST

"Fools suffered for their sins, and fasted because of their iniquities" (Psalms 107:17).

Those who say they will repent of their sins by fasting are fools. Better to have a fast of words than a fast of food.

Rabbi Moshe Leib of Sassov

Emotion

COUNTS AND RECKONS

Rabbi Elimelekh of Lizhensk was worried on the eve of Rosh Hashanah. With a deep sigh he thought to himself, "How can I dare go before the Omnipresent on the Day of Judgment? I have committed so many sins!" He thought about the matter in great detail, as he was accustomed to do. In the end he decided, "My broken heart will stand me in good stead on the Day of Judgment."

INSCRIBED IN THE HEART

Rabbi Mordekhai of Lechovitch was invited to meet with Rabbi Avrahamele of Trisk. They proceeded to discuss words of Torah and Hasidut.

Rabbi Avrahamele asked Rabbi Mordekhai, "Did your masters leave you their books?"

"Yes," answered Rabbi Mordekhai.

"Printed books or manuscripts?"

"Neither printed books nor manuscripts," answered Rabbi Mordekhai. "They left their books in the hearts of the Jewish people."

EACH HEART IS DIFFERENT

A Hasid approached Rabbi Avraham Yaakov Friedman of Sadigora and complained to him, "There is a certain wealthy Jew in town who is tightfisted. The cry of the poor does not touch his heart."

The rabbi replied, "Why should you complain about him? A good heart is a gift of the Creator, and this fellow did not merit such a gift. Give thanks to the Blessed Holy One that you were given a good heart. Who knows if your hand would be so open if your heart were like his? Our tradition teaches: 'Hate not your brother in your heart' (Leviticus 19:17). You should not think ill of him because you were given a good heart, and he was not."

HEALING THE HEART

Rabbi Yehiel Yehoshua Rabinowitz of Peshischa taught: "When I learned the detailed mechanics of a watch, I discovered that a watch that is perfect does not lack a single part. But if one tiny spring, as thin as a string of hair, is bent just a drop, it prevents the watch from working. If you straighten the spring, immediately the watch works again just fine.

"I reflected to myself: How does a watch resemble the heart of a human? If the heart is twisted even as much as the thickness of a hair, the person requires healing."

ENTERING THROUGH THE HEART

At the Pesah seder of Rabbi Menahem Mendel of Kotzk, the rabbi was about to recite the passage beginning *shfokh hamatkha*. One Hasid proceeded to open the door, as is the custom, and immediately he came back, shaken and pale.

The rabbi asked him, "Why are you so afraid?"

The Hasid explained, "At the rabbi's seder, I am certain that the honorable Elijah the prophet would enter the door, and I was frightened."

"Do you really think that Elijah enters through the door?" countered the rabbi. "Not at all! He enters through the heart!"

WORDS OF WISDOM

GOD'S PRAYER

"Open for us the gates even as You lock the gates." (Yom Kippur/Neilah liturgy)

Just as we entreat the Creator to open the gates of Heaven, So does God entreat us to open the gates of our heart.

Rabbi Menahem Mendel of Kotzk

Eretz Yisrael

PREPARING THE HEART

When the secular Zionist movement Hibat Zion (Love of Zion) was founded in the early 1880s, it encountered great opposition from Haredi circles. One of their arguments was that they did not like the fact that left-wing ideologues would be the ones to rebuild Eretz Yisrael.

Rabbi Shmuel Leib Zak of Biala pointed out to them that even King David himself prophesied that this would be the situation at the beginning of the movement of the return to Zion, as it says in Psalms, "The offspring of God's servants shall possess it; those who cherish God's name shall dwell there" (Psalms 69:37). It is not written that "God's servants shall possess it," but rather, "the offspring of God's servants," namely, the children of God's pious servants. In other words, even though the children will not be God-fearing, they will possess the land and occupy it, and then, later, "those who cherish God's name shall dwell there."

WITH LOVE AND RESPECT

After the Yeshivah of Volozhin had closed, the Netziv (Rabbi Tzvi Yehudah Berlin) settled in Warsaw. From time to time many of the great scholars of the city would visit him, among them Hasidic leaders, to discuss with him matters of Torah as well as issues of national import.

At one such discussion the topic turned to the Hibat Zion movement. One of the Hasidic leaders, who objected to the new movement, expressed his astonishment that the Netziv spoke with great love about those who were rebuilding and settling Zion – despite the fact that they were far from Torah and Jewish commitment.

The Netziv replied gently, with the following explanation: "The Torah records that 'Yaakov was greatly afraid and terrified' (Genesis 32:8). Our sages commented on this verse that 'The elect of the patriarchs was Yaakov, to whom God promised "Behold I am with you," and yet he was afraid. Why? Yaakov explained: "Since all these years Esav was dwelling in Eretz Yisrael, and he was approaching me with the merit of having lived in Eretz Yisrael"' (Midrash Bereishit Rabbah, Parashah 76). Yaakov, the elect of the patriarchs, who had said of himself, 'I dwelled with Lavan and still I kept the 613 mitzvot,' this tzaddik was afraid of such an evildoer as Esav, because Esav had fulfilled the mitzvah of living in Eretz Yisrael. How much more so should the righteous who live outside Eretz Yisrael be obligated to relate with awe and respect toward Jews who are settling Eretz Yisrael, even if their deeds are not up to par."

SHORT SPEECHES

Following the First Zionist Congress of 1897, Rabbi Shmuel Mohliver gathered the Zionist leadership together for a meeting in Bialystok. At the beginning of the meeting Rabbi Mohliver turned to all the gathered delegates and said, "My friends, I have two requests to make of you. Firstly, to sit with covered heads, and secondly, to speak in Yiddish." However, among the delegates were some whose native tongue was Russian. One of them, Dr. Kohen Bernshtein, arose and said, "Honorable Rabbi, regarding your request to be diligent about covering our heads, we can accommodate you, even though it will be a bit uncomfortable. However, we don't know how to speak Yiddish, and it is a language in which we cannot properly express our thoughts. If there is someone here who does not understand Russian, we will provide a translator."

"No," answered Rabbi Mohliver with a smile. "I requested that you speak Yiddish not because people do not speak Russian, but for the good of the mission. You well know that Moshe Rabbeinu was 'slow of speech and slow of tongue' (Exodus 4:10). From a logical point of view it is difficult to understand why God would send someone to Pharaoh who had difficulty speaking. For such an important mission, whose purpose is to persuade the king to free a nation, it would seem that it would be preferable to send someone who is eloquent, whose words would convince and persuade!

"The truth is, my friends, the opposite. If God had sent someone with unusual oratorical ability, a smooth talker, he would have presented himself regally and delivered an inspiring discourse on freedom, justice, and fairness – to the point that he may have forgotten the main topic: the redemption of the people of Israel. But since Moshe was 'slow of speech and slow of tongue,' he approached Pharaoh, and spoke in a few pithy words, 'Let my people go!'

"Such is the case with our meeting. I am certain that each of you, thank God, can deliver a gifted, lengthy oration. And I am fearful that if each person rises and addresses in beautiful imagery the wonders of Eretz Yisrael, we may never get to the main topic of our agenda.

"However, if you speak Yiddish, in which you are 'slow of speech and slow of tongue,' each person will speak only briefly and to the point."

HOW CAN I ANSWER?

The pupils of Rabbi Yisrael of Rizhin asked him, "Why did you not make aliyah to Eretz Yisrael?"

"If I settle in Eretz Yisrael," Rabbi Yisrael replied, "people will ask me, 'Why did you come without your congregation?' And for this question I will not have an answer."

ERETZ YISRAEL IS BUILT BY HARD WORK

Rabbi Barukh of Medziboz, grandson of the Baal Shem Tov, sent Rabbi Zev of Zavrizh to Eretz Yisrael in order to strengthen the settlement of Hasidim there. After a few years Rabbi Barukh sent Rabbi Yaakov Shimshon of Shepetovka to Eretz Yisrael to inquire as to the welfare of Rabbi Zev and of the community of Hasidim who took shelter in his shadow.

With great dedication Rabbi Yaakov Shimshon arrived in Akko, and from there he hired a donkey to convey him to Tiberias. When he arrived at the courtyard of Rabbi Zev he noticed women cleaning linens. He recognized among them the wife of Rabbi Zev. Distressed that the rabbi was so poor that he could not afford a servant, he immediately ordered his donkey to return to Akko.

Rabbi Zev's wife recognized what was happening and immediately ran to Rabbi Yaakov and explained to him, "Honored Rabbi! These sheets that we are washing are not ours. They belong to others, and we are washing them for a fee. Please get down from your donkey and stay awhile. Though we are not as comfortable as we were in Poland, we are privileged to be here. This is Eretz Yisrael and the efforts we expend are our pleasure."

Immediately Rabbi Yaakov Shimshon got down from his donkey and entered the home of Rabbi Zev, as tears of joy ran from his eyes.

GUARDING THE LAND'S REPUTATION

When Rabbi Yaakov Shimshon of Shepetovka made aliyah to Eretz Yisrael, he decided to go first by himself, and then at a later stage bring his family. On his journey back to his family, he stayed overnight in one of the inns along the way.

When he looked in the mirror that night, he noticed that because of the strain of the journey his body had become lean and gaunt, and his face was thin and bony. He thought to himself, "If I return now to my city, my friends will say, 'Eretz Yisrael consumes the blood and meat of its inhabitants, and removes the spark from their faces.' And I will ultimately, God forbid, bring a bad name to the Holy Land."

What did he do? He stayed in the inn several days, ate and drank very well, and lifted his spirits until he was strong again. By the time he returned to his town his appearance was healthy, so that all who saw him were impressed with the "land flowing with milk and honey."

Faith and Trust

OUR GOD AND THE GOD OF OUR FATHERS

Rabbi Yisrael Baal Shem Tov used to say: "There are two kinds of believers in God. One believes because he received the tradition from his ancestors; the other comes to his faith through his own searching. The difference between them lies in this: since the faith of the first is rooted in tradition rather than intellectual analysis, opposing arguments, God forbid, will be less likely to impact him. But the weakness of such faith is that it is based in routine and habit, without careful thought and analysis.

"The strength of the other person is that due to his careful thought he has acquired his faith on his own, but he is liable, Heaven forbid, to be seduced into heresy if he encounters arguments that contradict his faith.

"The person who believes because of both approaches has the strongest faith. Namely, he relies on the faith of his ancestral tradition, and he also includes his own thinking, analysis, and searching. This is the best and fullest kind of faith.

"We recite 'our God,' due to our own exploration, and also 'God of our ancestors,' due to tradition. Therefore, we say 'God of Avraham, God of Yitzhak, and God of Yaakov' – not once but three times a day – to enunciate our belief that Yitzhak and Yaakov did not rely on the tradition of Avraham, but sought out the nature of God through their own individual thinking."

MAY MY HEART WORSHIP YOU IN TRUTH

A student complained to his teacher, Rabbi Noah of Lechovitz, "I stand all day before my Creator and recite the sentence, 'I believe with perfect faith...' and yet I am never completely certain that my faith is absolutely sincere. If I ever discover, God forbid, that my faith is faulty, then I am lying before the Creator."

His teacher comforted him with these words: "'I believe' is not a pronouncement, but a prayer. A Jew prays to the Blessed Holy One, and says,

'Master of the Universe! I believe – I *want* to believe. Please help me to truly believe.'"

AT THE FAIR

Rabbi Leib of Rekesh was a saintly and pious man. In the city of Mir where he lived, he and his wife owned a store selling all types of cloth. His wife would mind the store while the rabbi sat and occupied himself with Torah and prayer.

Once his wife suggested to him, "Go see all the merchants who are traveling to the fair. If you go, you can buy merchandise for the whole year."

Rabbi Leib followed his wife's suggestion and prepared for the trip. His wife prepared for him a list of different kinds of cloth with their suggested prices. Rabbi Leib arrived at the fair and found out that it would last a whole month. He thought to himself, "What's the rush? In any case I have to linger here until the conclusion of the fair and then return home with the rest of the merchants. I think I will buy my merchandise on the last day of the fair, and then return home. Meanwhile, I can sit and study Torah."

The rabbi sat and studied Torah the whole month. On the last day of the fair, he went out to the market to buy the merchandise. But he found that every merchant told him that he had nothing left. It was all sold. Finally, he found one merchant who still had one red roll of cloth which could be used for high-level officials, but it was extremely expensive. The most successful of the merchants could sell about ten yards a year. Rabbi Leib purchased a considerable amount of this cloth, spending all the money he had, and then returned home.

As soon as he returned, he went straight to the study hall, and resumed his study and prayer.

When his wife discovered what had happened, she was stunned. How in the world could they sell such a large quantity of red cloth? And what would they do now with no money and no merchandise? She ran to her husband in the beit midrash and burst into tears. "What have you done to us? In twenty years we will never sell the amount of cloth you bought! How will we make a living?"

"Why are you crying?" said Rabbi Leib, unfazed. "Don't you have faith that our needs are fixed from one Rosh Hashanah to the next? So what's the difference between one cloth and another?" Rabbi Leib returned to his books.

It did not take long before a messenger from the mayor of Radzivil visited Rabbi Leib's shop to buy several hundred yards of red cloth. The mayor wanted to dress all his servants in red cloth. Rabbi Leib's wife sold all the cloth she had, and that whole year they were able to live comfortably with more than enough for their needs.

WORDS OF WISDOM

TRUE BELIEF

There are many who believe that there is a God in Heaven, but the true believer is one who believes that God also rules on earth.

Rabbi Hanokh Henekh of Alexander

FAITH AND PRAYER

Everyone prays to the Creator to have their desires fulfilled. But they don't realize that their faith requires them to fulfill God's desires.

Rabbi Menahem Mendel of Kotzk

PRAYER MUST NOT STOP

A child who is lost in the forest cries out bitterly, "Abba, Abba, save me!"

The anxious child knows that as long as he screams, the hope is not lost that his father will hear him and extend a hand.

But if he stops calling out, he is lost.

Rabbi Nahman of Breslov

UNITE OUR HEARTS

"Unite Our Hearts to Love and to Fear Your Name" (from the morning prayers).

In the real world love and fear are in opposition to one another. One who loves is not afraid, and one who is afraid does not love – with the exception of love and fear of God. In that case love and fear complete one another. The believer unites the two.

Rabbi Dov Ber of Mezritch

Fear of Heaven

A GOOD NOTE

Rabbi Yitzhak Meir of Gur, who was for a long time a devoted student of Rabbi Menahem Mendel of Kotzk, once entered the home of the senior master of the generation, Rabbi Avraham Yehoshua Heschel of Apt, and gave him a slip of paper bearing a request, as was the custom of every Hasid who entered the private room of his teacher. However, this slip of paper had just one sentence written on it: "Yitzhak Meir, the son of Hayah Sarah – for fear of Heaven and healing of soul."

The elder of Apt looked at the slip, and then looked again, and again. He sank into deep thought, and then whispered to himself, "Wonder of wonders! This is indeed a slip from the Baal Shem Tov himself! He does not pray for a healthy body, or to make a good living, but for fear of Heaven, for healing of soul. It's been a very long time that my eyes have seen such a holy slip of paper such as this."

GOD IS BEFORE ME

When Rabbi Avraham Yitzhak Hakohen Kook studied as a young man in the yeshivah of Volozhin, the other students noticed that during the daytime the lantern in the oil menorah was missing. Rabbi Kook would sit and study by its light until the late hours of night. When he finished studying, he would remove the lantern and put it away.

The other students were surprised at this, and were curious to know the explanation of the matter. They finally figured out the secret. On the lantern Rabbi Kook had written the words, "I have placed God before me always" (Psalms 16:8). In this way the important verse would be before his eyes at all times.

A SPARK IN THE ASHES

A certain man clung to the Maggid of Dubnow, Rabbi Yaakov ben Wolf Kranz, in order to mock him. The man said to the rabbi, "They say about you that you have such power that your speeches bring back the masses to the fear of Heaven. Perhaps you can influence me with your words of virtue to turn me into a *baal teshuvah* (one who returns to the tradition)."

Rabbi Yaakov replied with these words: "I'll give you a parable. A certain city dweller came to a large town and saw bellows being sold in the market. He bought one and brought it home to his wife and told her that he had an instrument to stoke fire in the stove. His wife took the bellows and fanned it in the pot, but nothing came up. Not even a tiny spark of fire from the coal.

"Immediately the woman called out in disappointment, 'Such a fool! You waste money on an instrument that has no use. Those who sold this to you are liars, and you are a fool for letting them mislead you. What kind of bellows is this? Where is the fire? I work and work, and get no fire, and not even a sign of a flame.'

"'The man was annoyed at his wife and let her know this in no uncertain terms. 'You are a fool,' he said, 'since you don't know that the bellows has no ability to strike a fire from nothing. It can stir up a flame when there is even a tiny spark, which it enlarges and brings to a large flame. But not when there is no tiny spark to enlarge.'"

The rabbi then explained the moral of the parable. "I am a bellows in the hands of the Almighty. Give me a heart that has a spark of Yiddishkeit, and I can arouse it to do repentance. But hearts that are empty, and void of any spark, hearts of stone, hearts of coal, what can I do?"

I MUST BE PERFECT

Rabbi Yaakov Yitzhak Horowitz, the Seer of Lublin, entered into a discussion with a simple Jew, a God-fearing man. "I am jealous of you," said Rabbi Yaakov, "since you are a greater saint than I.

"Why? Because a rabbi, by profession, must fear the Lord, or else the entire community will chase after him with complaints. If, Heaven forbid, I transgress one small point of halakhah, or violate one tiny mitzvah, or if for some reason I don't wash my hands and recite the proper blessing before a meal, immediately there will be a tumult. 'The famous Seer of Lublin did not wash his hands!'

"But you, an ordinary Jew, upon whom no one looks or cares how you act, yet nevertheless you conduct yourself with fear of Heaven and deep piety. You are a true tzaddik!"

HOW ARE YOU DOING WITH YOUR FAITH?

Rabbi Levi Yitzhak of Berditchev noticed someone running very quickly. He appeared very rushed to accomplish some mission. Rabbi Levi stopped him to ask, "Reb Yid, why are you rushing so?"

"I don't have time to talk right now with you, honorable rabbi."

Rabbi Levi Yitzhak continued to press him. "What is your mission, why are you rushing so?"

"I urge you, honored rabbi, not to slow me down right now. My time is extremely tight, I must take care of something immediately."

Rabbi Levi Yitzhak persisted. "OK, OK, your mission is very important and pressing. And your obligations are numerous. But I am asking you not about your many tasks, but about your main task, the one important task, what is it?"

The man stared at the rabbi in surprise. He did not understand the question.

Rabbi Levi explained, "I know that all your responsibilities are for the sake of the Blessed Holy One, to provide for your body that the Almighty gave you. But food is the job of the Holy One. Your mission is to fear God. So why are you neglecting the only true task of fearing God and instead running after the tasks that God will take care of?"

WORDS OF WISDOM

LOVE OR FEAR?

Fear – that's the job of man.
Love – that's a gift from the Creator.

Rabbi Yehudah Aryeh Leib of Gur, the "Sfat Emet"

WISDOM OR FEAR?

All my life I have been fearful that my wisdom will be greater than my fear of sin.

Rabbi Pinhas of Koretz

FEAR OF HEAVEN

Fear of Heaven is not something one can put in a box of tobacco to smell, or in a locked box....

Rabbi Simhah Bunim of Peshischa

Giving Advice

THE IMPORTANCE OF ANSWERING *AMEN*

A certain Hasid consulted the Maggid of Mezritch with regard to the question of whether he should uproot his dwelling from the village in favor of the city. There he would be able to pray in a minyan, which would enable him to publicly sanctify God's name with the recitation of "*Amen – yehei shmei rabba mevorakh*… (Amen – may God's great name be blessed…)."

The Maggid replied: "If you will take my advice, living in the village will be as good as living in the city. This is what you should do. When a guest arrives, first of all bless him with *Shalom*. Then ask him if he is hungry, and offer him some food. Next offer him a place to sleep. When he leaves give him money to ease his journey, and accompany him for a while and part from him with blessings of *Shalom* and other good wishes.

"Acts like this are as worthy in the eyes of the Blessed Creator as reciting '*Amen – yehei shmei rabba mevorakh.*'"

I KNOW THAT I DO NOT KNOW

This was the routine of Rabbi David, rabbi of Navardok: All day long he would sit in the beit midrash and occupy himself with Torah study. He learned and taught, instructed and judged, answered orally and in writing all the questions of Jewish law that came to him from near and far.

Once one of the important leaders of the community came into the beit midrash, approached the rabbi, and asked his advice on a matter relating to business. Rabbi David said to him, "In matters of business I know nothing."

Some days passed and the same man entered the beit midrash where the rabbi was sitting, deeply immersed in difficult issues of Jewish law. Again the man approached the rabbi and asked his advice in matters of matchmaking. The rabbi answered him, "In matters of matchmaking I know nothing."

The man pressed him. "Rabbi, I am amazed. Why do you receive a salary from the community treasury? Perhaps because you know nothing?"

Rabbi David answered him with a smile. "You are wrong. I receive the salary for the little that I do know. Were I to receive a salary for all that I do not know, all the treasures of the empire would not be sufficient to pay my salary."

THE VALUE OF *MUSAR*

A certain merchant came to Rabbi Yisrael Salanter to ask his advice. Since the merchant was so very busy, he had only about an hour a day available to study. What should he study in that hour: Talmud, Jewish law, or *musar* (Jewish ethics)?

"Study *musar*," answered Rabbi Yisrael, "and then you will be convinced of the need to find additional hours for study."

WISE ADVICE

Rabbi Menahem Mendel of Kotzk was asked how he was able to give advice to Hasidim in matters of business and other worldly matters even though he was isolated from matters of this world.

The rabbi replied, "One who is outside this world is able to see inside, since one who is outside a matter can penetrate the essence of the matter. But one who is in the middle of a matter cannot see as clearly."

REACHING THE DESTINATION

A certain Jew complained to Rabbi Avraham, the elder of Slonim, "I returned to tradition, but I don't feel any change for the better. What will be with me?"

Rabbi Avraham replied, "A person who gets into the mud and wants to get out makes the first step into mud with great difficulty. The second step is no better than the first – his foot is still stuck in the mire. Nevertheless his hard work is not in vain. He should continue walking, and each step will bring him a little closer to the shore of security."

WORDS OF WISDOM

PARTIALITY

A person who wants to give advice, yet has a vested interest in the matter, is worse than one who is blind.

A blind person does not see anything. A person who has a stake in the outcome sees things backward.

Rabbi Avraham of Sochochov

GRIEF IN MY HEART

"How long will I have cares on my mind, grief in my heart all day?" (Psalms 13:3)

As long as I have cares on my mind, there will be grief in my heart all day. Only when I lose all my cares, and have only God as my refuge, perhaps salvation will come.

The Holy Jew of Peshischa

Honor

THE ESSENCE OF HONOR

Rabbi Moshe of Savran was one who distanced himself from honor and pride. He had many devotees, however, and on one occasion the citizens of a city greeted him at the entrance to the city in a carriage harnessed to four horses. Against his better judgment, the rabbi felt obligated to get down from his simple carriage and climb into the fancy carriage that was prepared for him. Wishing to nonetheless distance himself from the offered honor, he began to give lengthy consideration to the matter. During the whole ride he repeated to himself, "What is really the essence of this honor? The sum total of it all is a few horses!"

HONOR THE HORSES

Before Rabbi Zusha of Anapol became well known, he was wont to travel through Europe anonymously to do holy work. Occasionally he would stop in Berditchev. There he would be housed in the home of one of the poor teachers.

After some time his reputation spread as a worthy scholar and teacher, and thousands of Hasidim were attracted to him. On one occasion he came to Berditchev, where he was welcomed with great honor and was driven in an ornate carriage pulled by three horses. Large masses came to the city boundary to greet him, among whom was one wealthy gentleman. The man approached the rabbi and invited him to please honor his table by staying at his home.

Rabbi Zusha replied, "I have been in Berditchev many times over the years. Why now do you invite me? Why not before? The only difference now is that there are horses bringing me. Before I came on foot, and now I arrived in a carriage. Therefore, invite the horses to your home, and I will go stay with one of my fellow teachers."

AN UNSELFISH DEED

At the time that Rabbi Aryeh Leib Hakohen Heller, author of *Ketzot Hahoshen*, served as spiritual leader of Stry, Galicia, there lived in the town a wealthy man who was very generous and gave much *tzedakah*. However, it was important to him that his good deeds would be well publicized.

Rabbi Aryeh Leib told him that when one does a mitzvah, one should be free of all selfish motives. "What's the difference?" asked the donor. "A mitzvah is compared to a candle in the biblical verse, 'A mitzvah is a candle; the Torah is light' (Proverbs 6:23). So what difference does it make whether one lights a candle with a match or with a burning stick?"

"There is a difference," answered Rabbi Aryeh Leib. "In Parashat Pekudei it is written, 'Moshe lit the lamps before God' (Exodus 40:25). One must light the lamp for God's sake, not for personal, selfish motives."

Humility

HUMILITY COMES FROM THE HEART, NOT THE BRAIN

Rabbi Yisrael Baal Shem Tov taught: "Our early sages in the Talmud and midrash, and also later Jewish scholars in homiletical and ethical texts, strongly emphasize the importance of humility and the potential harm of pride. Why, then, do we not find in the entire Torah, in any of the 613 commandments, a mitzvah to be humble?

"The answer is simple. A person who became humble because it is a mitzvah is in fact not humble at all. Such a person is essentially thinking to himself, 'It is true that I am better than my associates in knowledge of Torah and in the performance of good deeds, but what can I do since the Torah decreed that I be humble and self-effacing, and I am duty bound since the giving of the Torah at Mount Sinai to fulfill this mitzvah.'

"Humility such as this, which does not come from the depths of the soul, is insincere and empty. The source of true humility is from the heart, and not from the brain. It must pervade our entire being out of full genuineness, lacking any calculation or consideration of being commanded.

"The greatness of a Jew is not measured by how much Torah one knows or the number of mitzvot one performs, but rather according to one's integrity, authenticity, and sincerity in the study of Torah and fulfillment of mitzvot."

WHO AM I?

Rabbi Shimon, son of the Hatam Sofer, was sitting and reading to his aged and infirm father some of the questions in halakhah which were sent to him from all corners of the Jewish world. One day he read to his father a letter from a certain rabbi, repeating all the words of praise with which the rabbi began his letter. The Hatam Sofer heard the admiring words and heaved a deep sigh.

His son turned to him with curiosity and asked, "What is there to sigh about? Are you not aware, Father, that you are considered today the giant among scholars in this generation?"

"That's why I am sighing," answered the Hatam Sofer. "Because our generation is so bereft of great leaders that I am considered such a giant of the generation."

It is also told of Rabbi Akiva Eger that he received a letter with a question from one of the great scholars of the age, in which the writer began the letter with titles of honor such as "the great Gaon," "the crowning glory of the Jewish people," and "the master and teacher of the entire Diaspora community." Rabbi Akiva read these grandiose encomiums several times.

His students were surprised at this, and one of them got up the courage to ask the rabbi about his behavior. The rabbi answered, "This great rabbi, who referred to me with such honorable titles, certainly believes that if I wanted to, it would be in my power to really achieve these qualities. I read these things and examined my soul and my abilities, and it is very clear to me how far I am from being such an elevated person."

Rabbi Akiva Eger despised all these words of praise and adjectives of acclaim, and while he was in truth one of the great masters of the generation, as well as serving as rosh yeshivah and chief judge of the court in his city – nevertheless, in his letters and in his responsa, he would sign only his first name, "Akiva," without adding any degrees or titles.

HONORING SCHOLARS

Rabbi Akiva Eger and his friend Rabbi Yaakov Luberbaum of Lisa, author of *Netivot Hamishpat*, arrived in Warsaw for a major conference of rabbis. The Jews of Warsaw came to the gate of the city to welcome these two giants of the generation. With great honor they led them in a beautiful carriage tied to two horses, and brought them to the city center with the sound of rejoicing and celebration. Out of their great enthusiasm in honor of these two Torah leaders, the crowd loosened the horses from the carriage, tied themselves to it in place of the horses, and pulled it forward.

When Rabbi Akiva Eger realized what was happening, he asked, "For whom is all this honor and glory, if not for Rabbi Yaakov of Lisa?" He descended from the carriage and was swallowed up into the crowd. Because the area was so crowded no one noticed who he was, and he, along with the rest of the enthusiastic crowd, joined them to pull the carriage.

Rabbi Yaakov asked himself, "For whom is all this honor and glory, if not for Rabbi Akiva Eger, Torah leader of the generation?" He too descended from the carriage and joined the crowd that was pulling the carriage. In this fashion they pulled and pulled until they realized that no one was in the carriage.

"MAY MY SOUL BE TO ALL LIKE THE DUST"

Two emissaries from Eretz Yisrael, followers of Rabbi Avraham of Kalisk, came to Rabbi Shneur Zalman of Liadi, and poured on him words of insult regarding the controversy that had broken out at the time about funds from the *halukah*, the charity sent from abroad.

The rabbi listened to all the insults and did not reply with even a word. His friends asked, "Why is it that you, a Torah scholar of such high caliber, do not defend your honor?"

Rabbi Shneur Zalman answered, "Every evening and morning I recite in my daily prayers, 'May my soul be to all like the dust.' Now that I have the opportunity to fulfill these words, why shouldn't I?"

HONORING THE PLACE

As the Hasidim in the court of Rabbi Yehezkel of Kozmir were enjoying their *seudah shlishit* (the traditional third meal of Shabbat), a young man noticed that an elderly Hasid, a person widely honored as a learned scholar, was sitting near the door because the table was so crowded.

Believing that the elderly Hasid should sit at the head of the table, the young man asked the *gabbai* to communicate this to the rabbi.

The rabbi replied in a loud voice, "The mezuzah, which is very holy, nevertheless has a place at the door."

GOOD TRAITS

"One should not be frivolous with the trait of humility," said Rabbi David Twerski of Tolna. To illustrate the point he told this tale: After the death of his father, a wealthy man came to him and gave him a large sum of money.

"Why do you give me so much money?" asked Rabbi David.

The wealthy benefactor replied, "It was my custom to give it to your father, and I wish to continue the custom also with you."

"How can you compare me with my father?" asked Rabbi David. "My father was a very holy man, a giant in Israel, and what am I?"

"Is that so?" answered the generous donor. "I thought that you too were a great man. But since you yourself tell me that you do not equal your father's greatness, I do not have to contribute to you." He then took back the gift.

"From this Jew," concluded Rabbi David with a smile, "I learned that it is forbidden to insist too much when discussing the quality of humility."

DUST AND ASHES

The Maggid of Mezritch once asked his student, Rabbi Yehiel Mikhal of Zlotchov, "How is it that you, honorable rabbi, have so many Hasidim?"

Rabbi Yehiel Mikhal replied, "Because people know that I study Torah from one of the great tzaddikim of the generation."

The Maggid of Mezritch answered, "This man that you think is one of the great tzaddikim of the generation, I deem him to be but dust and ashes."

"Precisely because of this I think of him as one of the great tzaddikim of the generation," countered Rabbi Yehiel Mikhal.

He was not the only student to be impressed with the Maggid's humility. The first time Rabbi Nahum of Chernobyl visited the Maggid of Mezritch, he asked the Maggid to give him some good advice – namely, how to avoid the quality of pride.

The Maggid replied in sincerity, "The honorable rabbi should believe me that I cannot offer him any advice on this matter. With regard to the matter of pride I have no knowledge, and I don't understand at all how anyone can be proud."

SMALL-MINDEDNESS

Rabbi Yisrael Baal Shem Tov taught: "All sadness comes from pride. The root of pride is small-mindedness. A small person wants to be great, and a simple person jumps to the top. 'Every haughty person is an abomination before God' (Proverbs 16:5). A proud person walks around empty, since he wastes time on thoughts of pride, and has no time left to study Torah. One who worships God has no time to be proud. The proud person worships oneself.

"There are those who consider themselves scholars, people of repute; they feel that they perform good deeds, fear God, and act with gentleness and kindness. From their perspective, they are so great that it would not be proper for them to become friendly with everyone. But since it is a mitzvah to be humble, they lower themselves to converse with others. But those who are humble because it is a mitzvah commit a transgression. Sometimes humility is negated because it comes from pride. The problem is that the urge to be proud is a master at deception. It dwells in small crevices of the heart, and attacks people without their knowing it."

Once the Besht had a conversation with Rabbi Yaakov Yosef of Polnoye. The Besht said to Rabbi Yaakov, "I hear from time to time from those who oppose my views, most of whom are important rabbis and outstanding scholars, that they spread rumors about me, saying that I disparage, Heaven forbid, the honor of those who study Torah.

"I value the great importance of those who study Torah for its own sake, as well as those whose deeds are for the sake of Heaven. I am but dust under their feet. But I object to those students who take pride in their Torah knowledge and in their fear of God. In my view one who is evil and knows he is evil, is greater than the righteous person who considers himself righteous, and brags about his righteousness.

"The wicked one who admits that he is wicked is truthful. The seal of the Blessed Holy One is truth. The one who is righteous and knows he is righteous and takes pride in it – such a one clings to falsehood. The proud person should know that 'there is no tzaddik in the world who does good and does not sin' (Ecclesiastes 7:20). And since the Blessed Holy One says of such a one, 'He and I cannot live together in the world' (Talmud, Tractate Sotah 5a), how can I be friends with such a one?"

WHAT ANSWER CAN I GIVE?

Rabbi Yehiel Mikhal of Zlotchov once said, "When I reach 120 years, and it is my time to enter the world of truth, they will ask me, 'Why did you not study the entire Torah, the Babylonian and Jerusalem Talmuds, all the midrashim, and all four sections of the *Shulhan Arukh* (*Code of Jewish Law*)?' I will reply, 'My small mind is not able to grasp so much material.'

"And if they will ask me why I did not fast every Monday and Thursday, even though it is written in the *Shulhan Arukh* that one is obligated to fast on those days in memory of the destruction of the holy temple, I will explain to them that I had many physical ailments and was not able to fast. And if they will ask me why I gave so little to charity, I will tell them that I am a stingy person. But if they then demand, 'OK, you have a small mind, you have many ailments, you are stingy – so why are you so arrogant?' For that I will have no answer."

WHO AM I?

When Rabbi Moshe Sofer, author of the *Hatam Sofer*, was seeking to remarry, the matchmaker suggested a match with the daughter of the great Rabbi Akiva Eger, the rabbi of Poznan. Rabbi Moshe decided to write to Rabbi Akiva and ask him directly about his daughter.

Rabbi Akiva Eger's daughter was a righteous woman, and so her father sang her praises in his reply. But at the end of the letter he wrote, "I feel it incumbent upon myself to confess to the honorable rabbi that while my daughter is beautiful and pious, a pure soul like yours desires to marry the daughter of a great scholar. However, with all my many sins, I have not yet reached the level of a great scholar."

WHERE ARE YOU FROM AND WHERE ARE YOU GOING?

Rabbi Meir Shapiro, rosh yeshivah of Lublin, once visited the city of Bilitz. Thousands of Jews gathered to welcome him with regal honor, with large posters, torches, and honor guards. The purpose of his visit to the city was to give a speech in the great beit midrash.

As he ascended the first step that led to the holy ark, the crowd burst out in a spontaneous cheer, "Long live our master and teacher!"

One of the *gabbaim* who led the way up to the bimah with Rabbi Meir noticed that the rabbi covered himself with his *tallit* and whispered to himself over and over the sentence from the High Holiday prayers: "The origin of humans is dust, and their end is in dust."

NEW INTERPRETATIONS OF THE TORAH

Whenever Rabbi David Jungreis, head of the *beit din* of the Haredi community in Jerusalem, was scheduled to give a public lecture, he would review aloud to himself the entire lesson. He did this because his lectures would invariably contain novel interpretations of his, which he was loathe to publicize as his own. Once he rehearsed the lecture aloud to himself, however, he could truthfully tell his listeners "I heard this new idea," or "I heard this explanation."

WORDS OF WISDOM

AVRAHAM, MOSHE, AHARON, DAVID

Our father Avraham, a very modest person, said, "I am but dust and ashes" (Genesis 18:27). Moshe and Aharon said, "Who are we?" (Exodus 16:7). King David said, "I am a worm, less than human" (Psalms 22:7).

But there is an additional, even greater level of modesty – and that is to say nothing.

Rabbi Barukh of Medziboz

WHO IS A HASID?

Am I a Hasid? King David, of blessed memory, was a Hasid. He wrote: "Preserve my life, for I am *hasid* (steadfast)" (Psalms 86:2).

Rabbi Yaakov Shimshon of Shepetovka

FALSE MODESTY

There is a modest person who sees both himself and others as nothing. This is false modesty. A truly modest person has full awareness that others are better than he, and are superior to him in worth.

Rabbi Shalom Rokeach of Belz

WHAT IS HE PROUD OF?

It is difficult to see how some people are so proud of themselves.

If one thinks of oneself as great, then he does not fulfill the words of Scripture that warn us, "Every haughty person is an abomination before God" (Proverbs 16:5). We are also taught, "Be humble before all" (Pirkei Avot 4:12). If such a one does not observe the words of the tradition, what greatness has he, what is his merit, and what is he proud of?

Rabbi Pinhas of Koretz

PRIDE IS WORSE THAN SIN

Pride is worse than sin. Regarding all impurities and sins it is written, "He abides with them in the midst of their impurities" (Leviticus 16:16). But about one who is coarse in spirit, the rabbis wrote: "He and I (God) cannot live in the same world" (Talmud, Tractate Sotah 5a).

Rabbi Yisrael Baal Shem Tov

UNWORTHY

"I am unworthy of all the kindness that you have so steadfastly shown Your servant" (Genesis 32:11).

The fact that I feel myself small in my own eyes is also due to the kindness that the Creator has bestowed upon me.

The Seer of Lublin

NOTHING

"Human superiority over the beast is nothing" (Kohelet 3:19).

This is the superiority of a human over a beast – that a human in his own eyes realizes that he is nothing.

Rabbi Menahem Mendel of Kotzk

In the Presence of God

MAY MY SOUL BLESS GOD

Once when the Baal Shem Tov was speaking with Rabbi Yaakov Yosef of Polnoye, the Besht explained how he had come to his philosophy of life. "I am the child of honest and upright parents," the Besht related. "My father was outstanding in moral qualities, and especially in the mitzvah of *hakhnasat orhim* (hospitality). I was orphaned as a young child, but I recall that my late father, just prior to his death, took me on his knees and said to me, 'It is clear to me that you will someday bring great joy to the world. But the obstacles you will encounter on the path will be many and formidable. There are two things you must always remember: love of God and love of the Jewish people.

"'These two ideas must be planted and guarded in your heart and etched in your memory, at every moment and in every place. And if so, Hashem will be with you in every place where you turn, and you need not fear any hindrance.' My father's words filled, and continue to fill even now, all the crevices of my heart.

"After my father's death, the people of his town remembered his kindnesses and in turn bestowed kindness on me. They placed me in heder, and I began to study Humash. Nevertheless, my every thought remained rooted in those two principles that I had received from my father's house. My soul yearned for God, and my heart was filled with love for every Jew whom I saw or met.

"I loved my teacher, even though he did not show me any special affection. I loved the other children in my class, my peers, even though they would look down on me.

"As far back as my early childhood I yearned for Divinity, and I would leave the heder and wander in the fields. I would gaze at the miracles of nature, the handiwork of the Blessed Holy One, the grass of the field, the glory of the heavens. I would listen to the song of the birds praising the Creator of the world, and the lowing of the sheep and of the cattle grazing at the ends of the fields. I would turn my ear to hear the conversation of the palm trees, the melodies of song that the beasts and the birds were chanting. And my soul was filled with love of God, and of every living creature.

"The people of my town, including my teacher, considered me a wild-eyed child and a dreamer, and stopped taking care of me. My good teacher ceased teaching me, and I started to spend time alone among the mountain ranges, between the towns of Kitov and Kosov. There I would wander and be alone, day and night, with my Maker, my Creator.

"I studied Torah under the wide, blue heavens, and I prayed beside a spring of water. In the course of time I began to study about nature, about the plants and the shrubs, and how helpful they were for curing and healing. My research and knowledge stood me in good stead later, in my adolescence, making a living among the masses as a healer.

"But my research into nature was only a secondary pleasure relative to all my affection and longing for the beauty and purity, and the visions of God that I saw surrounding me. I loved the sun when it shone on the face of the universe, making no distinction between good and evil, between a tzaddik and a *rasha* (evil person), between one who worshipped God and one who didn't. I loved the moon in its modesty and humility; it quietly fulfilled the will of the Creator as it waxed and waned. I loved the shining stars, the mountains and the valleys; I loved the beasts and the wild animals, and everything that the Blessed Holy One created in His world.

"And above all I loved my God, the God of the heavens, Who created the entire splendor and the glory around me. From time to time my heart was filled with joy and song, praise and tribute to the Living God, just as the birds and the streams of water sang to Him. At such moments I would lie on the ground, on the soft grass, and I would bow before the greatness of the Creator, just as the branches and the bushes would bow before Him as the wind blew them.

"I confess that at those moments I would occasionally pause in my studies and in my prayers, and would pay attention to the simple talk or the sweet singing of the shepherds, who were spread out together with their sheep and cattle. Even though these shepherds were conversing about mundane matters, nevertheless their words would enter my heart, because they pure and without sham. The shepherds' hearts were full of love, mercy, and compassion for every lamb, goat, and sheep; they did not gloomily dwell on their worries, but instead were content with their lot. Their song was humble, simple, honest, filled with faith and trust, and overflowing soul."

"I AM WITH HIM IN TROUBLE"

When Rabbi Yisrael of Rizhin was imprisoned, he accepted his sorry lot with equanimity; his spirit did not waver, nor did he complain. He would interpret the verse in Psalms, "Yea, though I walk in the valley of deep darkness, I fear no evil, for You are with me" (Psalms 23:4) in light of his own predicament: "Master of the Universe, 'even though I walk in the valley of deep darkness,' imprisoned by the government, 'I shall not fear.'"

YOU, ONLY YOU, O GOD

Reb Levi Yitzhak of Berditchev would sing:

"I shall sing to *You*, *Ribbono shel olam* (Master of the Universe) – the song of *Du* (You).

"Everywhere I go – there are *You*; everywhere I stand, there are *You*.

"Only *You*, and again *You*, forever *You* – just *You*, only *You*!

"If things are good for me, it's *You*. And if things are bad for me, God forbid, it's *You*.

"Only *You*, again *You*, forever *You*!

"In the heavens, *You*, on the earth, *You*. Above, it's *You*, below, it's *You*. Wherever I look and whatever I see, it's *You*.

"Only *You*, and again *You*, forever *You*!"

WHENCE YOUR ECSTASY?

The Holy Jew, Rabbi Yaakov Yitzhak of Peshischa, asked his student Rabbi Simhah Bunim:

"Bunim, please tell me, from whence comes your ecstasy for worshipping God?"

The pupil answered, "From the ecstasy in the Book of Isaiah: 'Lift your eyes to the heavens, and see, Who created these?' (40:26)"

ARISE AND CALL UNTO YOUR GOD

A certain scholar boasted that there was no dilemma in the Talmud that he could not solve.

When Rabbi Menahem Mendel of Kotzk heard of this he approached the scholar. "And what about the question of the captain?" he demanded. Before the scholar had a chance to understand the rabbi's question, the rabbi turned and left the room.

Later, one of the rabbi's students explained what had happened. The rabbi had not referred to a section in the Talmud, but rather to the question asked by the captain of the ship on which Jonah the prophet was sailing. When the ship was rocking in the stormy sea, the captain asked Jonah: "Why are you sleeping? Get up and call unto your God!"

The arrogant scholar thought he knew it all, but he did not know how to call to God.

WORDS OF WISDOM

THE NEED FOR DIRECT EXPERIENCE

It is impossible to explain the love of the Creator, since it is a matter of the heart.

In the same way it is impossible to describe the taste of food to one who has never in his life tasted it.

Rabbi Yisrael Baal Shem Tov

WHAT IS A MIRACLE?

Everyone thinks that an event that occurs outside the rules of nature is a new thing, a miracle.

But I say that when God "renews in His goodness every day the work of creation" – that is much greater.

Rabbi Dov of Liava

THERE *IS* A CREATOR

"In the beginning God created the heavens and the earth" (Genesis 1:1).

In the beginning, the first thing one has to know is that "God created the heavens and the earth."

One has to know, first and foremost, that there is a person in charge in the palace, and that things do not just happen, Heaven forbid, by accident.

Rabbi Moshe Leib of Sassov

TWO THINGS TO ALWAYS REMEMBER

"Two offerings every day" (Numbers 28:3).

Every person must take care that one has two things in mind every day: "I have placed God before me every day" (Psalms 16:8), and "I am conscious of my sins every day" (Psalms 51:5).

Rabbi Yisrael of Rizhin

DON'T DISTURB GOD

"...Harden your necks no more" (Deuteronomy 10:16).

Don't throw hard questions at the Master of the World.

Rabbi David of Lalov

THIRSTING FOR GOD

"My soul thirsts for You.... I shall behold You in the Sanctuary" (Psalms 63:2–3).

To the extent that I have thirst in my soul for You, God, "I shall behold You in the Sanctuary," – so will I merit reaching You and gazing at You.

Rabbi Simhah Bunim of Peshischa

Interpersonal Relationships

UNCONDITIONAL LOVE

Rabbi Yisrael Baal Shem Tov taught: "There is no Jew who does not have some good quality, some spark of holiness." Furthermore, he pointed out that twice in the Torah we find the command to love: "Love the Lord, your God" (Deuteronomy 6:5), and "Love your neighbor as yourself" (Leviticus 19:18). This linkage comes to teach us that our love for Jews must equal our love for God.

We must love God, despite the fact that at times He seems to act against us; a Jew must bless the evil as he blesses the good. And so must we love every Jew – even when we decry his actions, and even when those actions hurt us.

OUR TORAH TEACHES US ABOUT ALL MATTERS

Rabbi Yosef Zundel of Salant taught: "Our Torah teaches about God's ways: 'God did not see wickedness in Yaakov [the Jewish people], nor did God view affliction in Israel' (Numbers 23:21). On this verse Rashi comments: 'The Blessed Holy One does not see wickedness in Yaakov, and even as they transgress God's commands, God does not pursue them [for punishment].' And if the Blessed Holy One, Who knows our secrets and discerns the thoughts of every one of us, nevertheless ignores those who disobey and does not see the wickedness of Yaakov, how much more so should humans, lacking God's omniscience, be slow to accuse each other of wrongdoing."

Rabbi Yosef Zundel of Salant not only loved peace, but actively pursued peace, and tried with all the strength of his influence to bring peace between people.

It happened once in the Old City of Jerusalem that a certain Jew opened a grocery store. Not many months passed, and another Jew opened a similar store nearby. Naturally the first grocer became angry, and his abhorrence toward the neighboring grocer grew from day to day.

The matter came to the attention of Rabbi Yosef Zundel, who paid a visit to the first store owner and bought some groceries. During his visit he began to speak to the owner about the quality of *ahavat Yisrael* (love of the Jewish people), that it is not only forbidden to hate any Jew, but it is required to love all Jews.

The grocer deduced from the words of preaching that Rabbi Yosef Zundel was indirectly referring to his relationship with the other grocer. The owner turned to Rabbi Yosef Zundel and asked him, "Honored Rabbi, is it possible to love a Jew such as him, who comes and violates the Torah law of *masig gvul* [trespassing on the rights of another] by opening a grocery store like mine?"

In a gentle voice, Rabbi Yosef Zundel replied, "The Torah commands us to love our neighbor with this kind of love, even when he is competing against us, since it teaches explicitly in the Torah (Leviticus 19:18) 'You shall love your neighbor as yourself' – namely a storekeeper as yourself, a shoemaker as yourself, a tailor as yourself – and in this way one must demonstrate true love."

TO RISE AND LIFT OTHERS

On the Shabbat of Parashat Kedoshim, one of the senior Hasidim of Rabbi Menahem Mendel of Kotzk got an urge to hide himself behind the door of his rabbi's room in order to hear the rabbi reviewing the weekly Torah portion.

He sat and listened, and soon heard the rabbi muttering to himself, "'Love your neighbor as yourself…' How?? Like yourself?"

After a long silence, the Hasid heard the continuation in the form of a pause: "Aha, like yourself!"

The elderly Hasid did not comprehend the meaning of the rabbi's words. He turned to Rabbi Hersh of Tomashov, a confidant of the rabbi, and inquired as to the meaning of the rabbi's words. Rabbi Hersh explained, "The rabbi was asking: How can the Torah tie the obligation of loving a neighbor to loving oneself? Is it permission for one to love himself? Does this not fly in the face of everything we learned in Kotzk? That the root of evil in man is hidden in self-love. Does not the love of a person for himself bring self-deceit and sham? Is this not the 'thief' who is hidden inside each person, which we are obligated to uproot?

"Then the rabbi answered his own question. 'Like yourself!' Just as your role in this world is to perfect yourself, again and again and again – so are you required to love your neighbor, to perfect him, to raise him up higher and higher."

LOVE YOUR NEIGHBOR AS YOURSELF

Rabbi Shmelke of Nikolsberg taught: "How is it possible to fulfill the mitzvah of 'Love your neighbor as yourself' if your neighbor wrongs you? It is possible to explain this logically. Every soul is included in the soul of the first man, Adam. Each person contains one soul, yet all the souls together comprise one entire body.

"Sometimes a person accidentally hits himself with his own hand. Would he take a stick to punish the hand that struck him? That would be foolish. That would be requiting evil for evil, and cause double harm to himself. Rather one should consider that everything comes from the Blessed One, Who has many messengers at His disposal. One does not get angry at messengers, nor hate them."

HONORING YOURSELF AT THE EXPENSE OF ANOTHER

When the Gaon of Vilna, Rabbi Eliyahu, was a little boy, he went out to play with his friends. He saw them on the seesaw, as one went up and the other went down. He left them and went in the house.

"Eliyahu, my dear son," asked his father, "why are you not playing with your friends?"

"Abba," answered the child, "it says in the Torah, 'You shall love your friend as yourself.' How can I raise myself up and lower my friend through my ascent?"

LET YOUR NEIGHBOR'S MONEY BE AS VALUABLE TO YOU AS YOUR OWN

Rabbi Yaakov Ornshtein of Lvov was known as a liberal interpreter in matters of ritual. One Yom Kippur eve he met the head of the town's *beit din*, who was widely known as a strict interpreter of halakhah. When they parted the judge extended his hand and blessed Rabbi Yaakov, "May God bless us with a *gemar hatimah tovah*, a favorable new year."

"You," remarked Rabbi Yaakov with a smile, "will have to pray more intensely than I."

"And why is that?" asked the judge in astonishment.

"Because I," Rabbi Yaakov answered, "only have to fear lest I declared something permissible that was really forbidden – and that is merely a sin between man and God, and for that Yom Kippur atones. But you, as a strict interpreter, often you are liable to forbid what might be permitted, and thus cause Jews to lose money. That, of course, is a sin between one person and another, and for that Yom Kippur does not atone until pardon is asked of one's fellow Jew."

ETERNAL PROOF

Rabbi Barukh Epstein (author of *Torah Temimah*) tells this story:

One day a large group of distinguished scholars sat with Rabbi Naftali Tzvi Yehudah Berlin (the Netziv) of Volozhin, when the door opened and a portly butcher entered the room with a question for the rabbi. "A number of years ago," said the butcher, "I had a partner in my business, also a butcher, and a quarrel broke out between us. In the course of the argument I became very angry and swore that I would never again lay eyes on the former partner. From then on we were implacable enemies. I kept my oath fastidiously: I refused to meet my former partner, stopped praying near him in the synagogue, and if I passed him in the street, I would quickly turn the other way in order not to see his face. This situation continued for a number of years.

"I have just received word that my former partner has died. The news made a deep impression on me, and instead of the hatred that filled me until now, I feel a profound sense of regret. I want to request from the deceased forgiveness at the time of the funeral. If I am not able to do this, I fear that I will never find rest. On the other hand, I made a solemn oath that I would never look upon him again. Please, Rabbi, what can I do?"

The question aroused serious debate among the scholars. Some said yes, others said no. They debated with expert and learned arguments. Each one quoted in his remarks the wisdom of many authorities from the Talmud and legal authorities, and seasoned their proofs with authoritative opinions, as can be expected.

"My students," said the Netziv as he turned to the other scholars, "we find a clear and simple answer in Parashat Beshallah, this week's Torah portion." Those gathered around raised their eyes in astonishment. The Netziv opened the Humash and explained, "It is written: 'The Egyptians you see today you will never see again…' (Exodus 14:13). The promise of the Blessed Holy One is certainly as important as the oath of a person of flesh and blood. Yet, immediately after that the Torah says, 'The Israelites saw the Egyptians dead on the shore of the sea' (Exodus 14:30). The midrash elaborates: 'Each Israelite recognized the faces of the dead, those who were their brutal taskmasters in Egypt.'

"Is this not an obvious contradiction to the previous verse, 'you will never see [them] again'? This is proof, therefore, that the expression 'see them' refers only to the living, and not to the dead."

CONNECTED IDEAS

Rabbi Yitzhak of Vorka taught: "Everything in the world can be tested to see if it is worthwhile or not. How can you test whether the path that a Jew is taking to worship God is a worthy one or not? The test is this: whether or not he has a love for other Jews. If we see that his path to worshipping God raises the level of love of humanity in his heart, this is a clear sign that his path is the right path. And if it does not, then it is not the right path.

"From this we learn that if a person were to fulfill all the mitzvot in the Torah relating to his service of God, even to the point of clinging to God, but remain detached from his brothers and sisters and their burdens – then it is clear that even his worship of God is faulty."

LIGHT YEARS

When man landed on the moon for the first time in human history, a journalist asked Rabbi Yosef Kahaneman, rosh yeshivah of Ponevitch, "What is the attitude of Judaism toward this unprecedented event? In the prayer for the sanctification of the moon we recite these words: 'Just as I dance toward you, but cannot touch you....' Here we say that we cannot touch it, and yet now we are stepping on its soil!"

Rabbi Kahaneman replied, "When I heard about this great event, I approached the windowsill, looked at the people in the street coming and going, and I said to myself, 'You wretched world, what a foolish world you are! We reach up and connect with the moon, but we cannot connect with our fellow man.'"

WORDS OF WISDOM

KISSING THE TORAH

I wish I could kiss the *Sefer Torah* with the same love with which the Baal Shem Tov would kiss a Jewish child when he tested him and found that he knew the letters of the *Alef-Bet*.

Rabbi Dov Ber of Mezritch

L'HAYYIM!

The true meaning of "*L'hayyim*," the frequent blessing recited when sipping wine, is like shaking hands. This shaking of hands is a pledge to love one another.

Rabbi Yitzhak Meir of Gur

REJOICING WITH OTHERS

When a Jew rejoices in the celebration of another, and offers him a blessing, the joy and blessing is received in Heaven the same as the prayer of Rabbi Yishmael, the high priest in the Holy of Holies.

Rabbi Yisrael Baal Shem Tov

The Jewish People

LOVE OF JEWS

Rabbi Yisrael Baal Shem Tov taught: "The mitzvah of *ahavat Yisrael* (love of the Jewish people) is divided between two kinds of Jews – simple Jews and learned Jews. It is a mitzvah to love simple Jews because they are simple. They have not read much, nor studied much, and nevertheless they believe in the Blessed Holy One, and keep God's commands with a full heart.

"It is a mitzvah to love learned Jews because they have learned much, and the holy Talmud teaches that "whoever is greater than his neighbor, his evil inclination is also greater" (Talmud, Tractate Sukkah 52a). It stands to reason therefore that those who are learned have a great *yetzer hara* (evil inclination), tantamount to a burning flame, and nevertheless they are good Jews. As such they are cerainly worthy of love."

A TRUE LOVE

The Komarno Rebbe, Rabbi Yitzhak Isaac Yehudah Yehiel Safrin ben Alexander Sender, related the depth of love that the Baal Shem Tov felt for the Jewish people. The Komarno Rebbe recounted that the students of the Besht, who knew that their beloved teacher was a superb instructor on love of the Jewish people, sat up once after midnight, recalling how often their rabbi spoke about loving one's fellow Jew.

The Besht, with his holy spirit, saw that these words were not flowing from the depths of their hearts, but were said in order to bring satisfaction to God.

The Besht said to them, "Did you hear the story about a woman who spoke to her husband, and praised the children born to him from another woman? These words of praise were uttered only to bring satisfaction to her husband, and not because she loved the children with sincere love.

"I, Yisrael ben Eliezer, say that Israel is in truth a holy people. And I say it not only to bring satisfaction to the Blessed Holy One. Even a Jew who sins is essentially a good person."

LOVE OF OTHERS IS A FOOTSTOOL OF GOD

The rabbi who is most known for his love of the people of Israel is Rabbi Levi Yitzhak of Berditchev. He explained that since one God created us all, and the people of Israel is called *knesset Yisrael* (the family of the Jewish people), it stands to reason that we are all hewn from the same quarry. When one person is in trouble, his friend feels the pain. It is like a person who has a pain in one limb – the whole body feels the pain. So when one Jew celebrates a joyous occasion, his friend feels the joy.

Thus it is written: "You shall love your neighbor as yourself, I am God" (Leviticus 19:18). Since God created all human beings, we must love everyone.

IT'S A FEELING

Rabbi Shneur Zalman of Liadi taught: "It is necessary to feel a heightened sense of connection with regard to the Jewish people. When someone meets a friend, he asks him, 'Brother, how are you?' It's a customary Hasidic phrase. One kisses the other and asks, 'Brother, how are you?' But just this by itself is pure habit.

"Such was the custom of my father, his father, and his father. But this is dry love, without vitality. There must be tears. One must see the good qualities of one's friends. And if one sees a fault, it is really your own fault that you see. And if you fix the fault, your friend will feel it in his heart."

THE TRICKLE-DOWN EFFECT

Rabbi Hayyim Leib Shmulevitz, rosh yeshivah in Mir, Poland, was sitting and chatting with the students of the yeshivah. He remarked, "Do you know, my children, that the diligent student in our yeshivah who studies night and day, twenty hours a day, prevents Mr. Rothschild in Vienna from removing himself from the household of Israel."

The students look at Rabbi Hayyim Leib in surprise. "Honored Rabbi, what is the connection between this and that?"

"Think about it," answered Rabbi Hayyim Leib. "The *matmid*, the diligent student, spends twenty-two hours a day in study. He sets the bar for the regular students in the yeshivah, who spend about fourteen hours a day in study. Because of this the people in town spend three hours a day in study. For this reason the merchant in Minsk spends an hour a day in Torah study. Because of the devotion of the merchant in Minsk, the merchant in Warsaw prays three times a day. Because of the merchant in Warsaw, the merchant in Moscow keeps Shabbat religiously. Because of the merchant in Moscow, the merchant in London keeps a strictly kosher diet. Because of the merchant in London, Rothschild in Vienna keeps himself bound with the rest of the Jewish people.

"But – if the *matmid* reduces his study of Torah to less than twenty hours, then he lowers the bar for everyone else. The other students of the yeshivah will study less than fourteen hours. And then the rest of the people in town will not keep to a daily routine of an hour a day of Torah study. Then the merchant in Warsaw will not keep to a regular routine of daily prayer. The merchant in Moscow will violate the laws of Shabbat. The merchant in London will partake of forbidden foods, and Rothschild in Vienna will remove himself from the household of Israel."

WORDS OF WISDOM

THE UNITY OF THE PEOPLE

"When the leaders of the people assembled, the tribes of Israel [were] together" (Deuteronomy 33:5).

First of all, the leaders of the people, the heads of the generation, must be united. Only then is it possible to hope that "the tribes of Israel [will be] together." And only then will the people themselves have unity.

Rabbi Yaakov Yosef of Polnoye

GOD'S LOVE IS FOREVER

"With everlasting love have You loved Your people, the House of Israel" (daily prayers).

"With everlasting love": even though Your people are absorbed with the love of this world and with the pleasures that emanate from this world, and not the World to Come, nevertheless, You, Master of the Universe, "You loved Your people Israel."

Rabbi Aharon of Karlin

Joy and Sadness

A GREAT MITZVAH TO BE JOYFUL

Rabbi Yisrael Salanter, father of the *musar* movement, was standing in the market one day engaging in small talk with one of the passersby. Rabbi Yisrael continued the conversation with words of humor and wit, causing the listener to laugh at his jokes.

People standing nearby were astonished. Rabbi Yisrael, who was constantly studying Torah, and whose heart was always concerned with issues of import, was just standing and joking around in the marketplace?

One of those nearby turned to Rabbi Yisrael and inquired about the reason for this behavior.

"What you see is what it is," responded Rabbi Yisrael. "This gentleman is filled with sadness, and a dark bitterness fills his soul. Whoever can make him laugh is doing a great act of kindness."

THE EVER-FLOWING FOUNTAIN

Rabbi Levi Yitzhak of Berditchev taught: "There are two kinds of pain, and two kinds of joy.

"What are the two kinds of pain? There is the pain of a person in trouble, who worries about loss or about some other difficulty that happened to him, and he walks around bent over and gloomy, and fallen in spirit to the point of depression. This is the kind of person about whom it is said that 'the *Shekhinah* cannot abide sadness.'

"But there is another kind of pain. This is that of a person who feels that his days are being wasted, and he examines his deeds and persists in the improvement of his soul. This kind of pain is a source of blessing and strength which moves a person to improve his way of life.

"And there are two kinds of joy. There is joy that has neither taste nor fragrance. This is the joy of a food, which does not stem from any lack in oneself, and which is not concerned with self-improvement.

"But one who is enmeshed in a joy that is positive resembles a person whose house is burning: not only is his world not darkened, but he has hope in God, Who will replace what he lacks. When he reaches the strength of being able to hope that he will be able to rebuild his home, he is able to access joy and gladness."

KEYS TO THE HEART

After Rabbi Elimelekh departed from Lizhensk, his students started to search for a tzaddik to replace him. They came to Lublin to Rabbi Yaakov Yitzhak, the Seer of Lublin. When they realized that the Seer's method of seeking God was not the same as they were accustomed to with their rabbi in Lizhensk, they planned to move on from Lublin and search for another tzaddik.

But when they entered the private room of the Seer to receive a parting blessing, he said to them, "The Torah has seventy faces, but in the matter of worshipping God there are four hundred methods. What kind of value would there be in God, as it were, if there were only one way to worship God? Our master, the holy Baal Shem Tov taught us: God wants to be worshipped in all ways. But the way itself, each person must choose wholeheartedly.

"There is a long corridor which leads to the inner room in which the Creator resides, and there are many gates with which to enter it. Each has its own key according to the nature of the person who crosses the threshold.

"There is a gate that is opened with joy, and another that is opened with tears. There is a gate that is opened with the power of praise and acclaim, and there is a gate that is opened with prayers of confession. There is a gate that is opened with love, and a gate that is opened with awe."

Then the Seer impressed upon the students the importance of undertaking an individual search for one's life path.

COMPLETE JOY

The Netziv of Volozhin used to say, "Do you know where Rabbi Yosef Ber Soloveitchik [the Beis Halevi] and I differ? When Pesah arrives, I bless Sheheheyanu out of joy and gladness. Thank God that I have so many mitzvot to perform: I burned the leaven in my house; now I can prepare to fulfill the mitzvot of eating matzah, drinking the traditional four cups of wine, and just rejoicing in the joy of the festival.

"On the other hand, when Rabbi Yosef Ber recites the Sheheheyanu blessing he is filled with worry lest he did not fulfill every mitzvah in exactly the right way and in the right measure. Perhaps he did not burn the leaven in his house in all its details. Perhaps the little piece of matzah that he eats has not been supervised properly. And the wine for the four cups, perhaps it is not kosher in the complete sense. And with all these doubts gnawing at his heart, how can he fulfill the mitzvot of rejoicing in the holiday according to Jewish law?"

WE MUST REJOICE!

In the gloomy ghetto of Warsaw lived Rabbi Kalonymus Kalmish Shapira of Piaseczno, surrounded by Jews who were crushed and dejected in spirit. In 1941, when Purim arrived, no one was in the mood to rejoice.

The scholarly rabbi said to them, "In the book of the Zohar it is written that Yom Kippurim is like Purim. Namely, just as on Yom Kippur we must fast according to the decree of the Sovereign, the Ruler of all Rulers, the Blessed Holy One, whether we want to or not – so must we rejoice on Purim. Even if Ashmedai, King of the Demons, is running wild in the streets, so must we rejoice."

Judging on the Side of Merit

THE SIDE OF MERIT

The Holy Jew of Peshischa taught: "It is fitting and worthy to judge every person on the side of merit. If he is truly innocent of any sin, and committed no evil, then a decision of innocence is appropriate and upholds the truth.

"On the other hand, if he is indeed guilty, then this too is not a tragedy. Either way one has fulfilled the mitzvah of 'Give everyone the benefit of the doubt' (Pirkei Avot 1:6).

"Against this is the instance of speaking evil about another person, which in all cases is a bad thing. If one is innocent of sin, then people are slandering someone – a serious sin. And even if one has sinned and is guilty, then we are violating the words of the Mishnah, which requires that we give everyone the benefit of the doubt."

A GOOD EYE

Rabbi Yaakov Yitzhak, the Seer of Lublin, used to say: "If a person saw someone commit an offense against another, and does not give him the benefit of the doubt, it is because of one of two reasons. Either because he does not see his own faults, and thus he sees the faults of others more clearly, as we are taught that 'whoever sees his own faults, it is in his nature not to see the faults of others.' The second possible reason is that since he does not love our Father in Heaven, he finds faults with His child. As we are taught, 'If one loves the Blessed Holy One, it is natural that one who loves the Father loves His son, and overlooks all his failings.'"

Thus the Seer once said to his student the Holy Jew: "Before I came out of my mother's womb the Blessed Holy One bestowed on me a gift – to see far in the future, and to perceive the depths. I knew how to examine the inclinations of all people. I saw what was engraved on the foreheads of all who passed over my threshold, both the good deeds and the evil deeds.

"But I realized that my vision into the future caused a defect in my love for the Jewish people, and I decided that it was better not to see things that weakened my love for my fellow Jew. So I prayed to the Creator that He take His gift back from me.

"The Blessed Holy One answered my prayer, and from then on I stopped being able to see into the future."

A GREAT LOSS

Rabbi Yitzhak Blazer, one of the founders of the *musar* movement, lectured on the value of good deeds. He emphasized that there are times when even a very small act has a strong impact on the fate of a person. He gave the following example:

"A man went on a train ride to reach a certain metropolis. But he had only enough money, and not a *perutah* more, for a ticket to the station which was before the place he wanted to reach. If he had had just a few more *perutot*, he would have been able to buy a ticket to reach the desired station. But because he lacked those few *perutot*, he never reached his destination.

"We learn from this," continued Rabbi Yitzhak, "that sometimes, due to a small detail in action that is neglected, a person's good deeds will not be sufficient to give him the benefit of the doubt, and on the Day of Judgment he will be found wanting."

PRICELESS

A certain preacher visited Medziboz, the city in which the Baal Shem Tov lived. He was one of those preachers who were accustomed to speak harshly to people about their sins. On Shabbat before the afternoon prayers the preacher ascended the bimah and slandered the Jews there, condemning them for their sins.

A group of the audience, who knew that the Besht did not approve of such scolding preachers, got up and left the beit midrash in the middle of the speaker's talk. The preacher became furious at those who had left and the next day came to the Besht to complain.

The Besht, who normally spoke very gently and calmly, reacted this time with anger. "You speak such slander regarding the conduct of the Jewish people? You blemish the reputation of your fellow Jews? Consider a simple Jewish merchant: He runs around in the market during the day, and at evening is shaken up when he realizes that the time for Minhah (the afternoon prayers) has already passed, and he has not recited the prayers. So he hurries to one of the nearby homes and prays an abbreviated form of the prayers, and he does not even understand any of the words he is reciting – even so the seraphim and the heavenly angelic choir shake with joy from the sincere prayer of this wonderful Jew."

SPLIT THE DIFFERENCE

Rabbi Zusha of Anapol amassed a large sum of money. He took the cash and placed it inside a Humash, on the page that reads "You shall not steal" (Exodus 20:13), as a warning to potential thieves.

A certain thief came and removed the bills. Half the money he kept for himself, and the other half he replaced inside the Humash, next to the verse that read "Love your neighbor as yourself" (Leviticus 19:18).

After some time Rabbi Zusha looked for his money in the Humash and discovered what the thief had done.

Rabbi Zusha sighed. "Go and see, Master of the Universe, what the difference is between Zusha and a kosher Jew. When Zusha had the money in his possession he declared: "It's all mine." But this Jew went beyond the letter of the law, and took only half for himself, in order to fulfill the mitzvah of 'You shall love your neighbor as yourself.'"

On another occasion Rabbi Zusha saw someone steal a loaf of bread and gobble it down in a few bites, without first reciting the requisite blessings.

Said Rabbi Zusha, "Thank you, Master of the Universe, for giving this Jew such a strong appetite that he did not have time to wash his hands or recite the blessings."

EVERY HOUR, EVERY MINUTE

Once Rabbi Levi Yitzhak of Berditchev saw a wagon driver standing in a pit, greasing the wheels of his wagon, wearing a *tallit* and *tefillin*.

Rabbi Levi Yitzhak reacted in this way: "Master of the Universe, look to what extent this man's love of the Creator reaches. Even when he is greasing his wagon he does not forget, Heaven forbid, to recite his prayers to You."

THE SPAN OF OUR LIFE IS SEVENTY YEARS

Rabbi Levi Yitzhak of Berditchev was once told about an elderly gentleman, seventy years old, who had converted from Judaism to another faith.

"Israel is a holy people," said Rabbi Levi Yitzhak. "For seventy years this man wrestled with his evil inclination, and all that time he did not deny the God of Israel."

JUDGE NOT THE SINS OF YAAKOV

The Netziv, Rabbi Naftali Tzvi Yehudah Berlin, once visited Odessa, where one of the city's wealthy leaders, who kept Shabbat and the mitzvot religiously, invited him to spend Shabbat in his home. In the midst of the elaborate Shabbat meal, the Netziv looked out the window and saw that right next door builders were raising a new home. The building was being carried out by Jews, in flagrant desecration of Shabbat.

Naturally this public violation of Shabbat upset the Netziv. Noticing the Netziv's reaction, the host commented, "See, good rabbi, what kind of Jewish community we have here in Odessa. Jews violate the laws of Shabbat publicly."

The Netziv replied, "I am certainly pained by this. But have you considered that perhaps these Jews would rather be sitting now together with their families around the table, and eating a hearty meal, rather than working with the sweat of their brow and breaking Shabbat? Who knows what might be the financial situation of these Jews? It is forbidden to condemn them."

A PURE PRAYER

Rabbi Zusha of Anapol once entered the beit midrash for Kol Nidre and saw with what warmth and enthusiasm the congregation was reciting this pure prayer. The eyes of the congregants were full of sincere tears. Rabbi Zusha approached the holy ark, lifted his eyes toward Heaven, and declared, "If for this alone, Master of the Universe, it would be worth it for the Jews to commit sins. If for this alone, that they would pray so sincerely before You as they are doing now. Because were it not for their sins, when would You hear such heartfelt prayers?"

WORDS OF WISDOM

SEE THE GOOD IN PEOPLE

"Go and inquire about the *shalom* [welfare; lit.: peace, wholeness] of your brothers" (Genesis 37:14).

Go and inquire about the *shalom* of your brothers. See their better sides, their positive qualities, not their faults.

Rabbi Simhah Bunim of Peshischa

THE BENEFIT OF THE DOUBT

"Give every person the benefit of the doubt" (Pirkei Avot 1:6).

If our sages were concerned about giving the benefit of the doubt to a single individual, how much more so about groups of people. For sure – for sure – is it forbidden to say anything at all unpleasant about the people of Israel. For sure must one give them the benefit of the doubt.

Rabbi Levi Yitzhak of Berditchev

PROJECTION

"All the faults one sees, outside of one's own faults..." (Mishnah, Tractate Nega'im 2:5).

All the faults one "sees outside" – sees in others outside of oneself, all come from "one's own faults." As the sages taught in the Talmud (Tractate Kiddushin 70b), "Whoever stigmatizes others as unfit stigmatizes his own blemish."

Rabbi Yisrael Baal Shem Tov

Kindness and Compassion

"TRAIN A CHILD IN THE WAY HE SHOULD GO" (PROVERBS 22:6)

There were three partners involved in the education of Rabbi Yosef Zundel of Salant: his father, Rabbi Binyamin Beinish, and two great rabbis: Rabbi Hayyim of Volozhin and Rabbi Akiva Eger. From his father he inherited a greatness of spirit, and a generosity for every charitable cause and act of kindness. Joined with these were other positive qualities and attributes, such as ethics, integrity, justice and compassion.

This last quality was recognized from his early childhood. The story is told that when he was only five years old he returned from heder (religious school) without shoes on his feet. It was fall, and his mother was appalled when she saw her beloved child walking barefoot. With motherly affection she asked him, "Yossele, where are your shoes?"

"*Mamme*," answered the child innocently, "I saw one of the children in heder going barefoot, and he was freezing cold. I felt terribly for him, so I gave him my shoes."

"And where will you get shoes for yourself?" asked his mother.

"*Tatte* will surely buy me a new pair of shoes," answered the child, with a face brightened with joy.

KINDNESS TO THE LIVING AND TO THE DEAD

On the day of his father's yahrzeit (anniversary of his death) Rabbi Yisrael Salanter attended synagogue to lead the prayers, as is the custom for those in mourning. Among the worshippers was one man who had yahrzeit for his daughter on the same day, and had come to say Kaddish. Even though, as a Torah scholar, Rabbi Yisrael had first priority according to halakhah (Jewish law), when he saw that this other man was deeply grieved by not being able to lead the services for the ascent of his daughter's soul, he deferred his right and granted it to the other gentleman.

The worshippers were astonished. Why would Rabbi Yisrael defer to another person to lead the prayers and Kaddish on the day of his father's yahrzeit? One of them asked that question to Rabbi Yisrael.

"Excuse me, Rabbi Yisrael," said the man, "what prompted you to give up your privilege and transfer it to a stranger? Is not the act of leading prayer and reciting kadddish an important sign of honoring one's father, to aid in the ascent of his soul?"

"I declare to you, sir," answered Rabbi Yisrael, "that it is an even greater honor to the memory of my father, of blessed memory, to perform an act of kindness to a Jew. This is worth more than a hundred recitations of Kaddish."

"CLEAR THE WAY, MAKE A PATH FOR OUR GOD" (ISAIAH 40:3)

Rabbi Hayyim of Volozhin loved the students in his yeshivah, and honored them more than himself. At first he accepted in the yeshivah only some twenty elite students from Volozhin families. He studied together with them, fed them, and clothed them, all from his private funds. Little by little the reputation of the yeshivah grew in the wider Jewish community, and students from the area deluged his yeshivah to study Torah from the mouth of the rabbi of Volozhin. Rabbi Hayyim supported them generously, supervised their health, rejoiced in their celebrations and participated in their sorrows.

Once, before the Days of Awe, Rabbi Hayyim went himself to one of the shoemakers and bought a large number of shoes for his students. While he was there he asked the shoemaker to craft for him a pair of large boots, like the ones worn by wagon drivers. When the shoemaker brought him the boots, his family and friends wondered what the rabbi needed them for, but Rabbi Hayyim offered no explanation.

On one cold winter morning shortly thereafter, the mystery was solved. After a night of heavy snow, the Jews of Volozhin went to pray Shaharit (morning prayers) – and found Rabbi Hayyim treading a path in the deep snow.

"Our master," they inquired, "why are you walking up and back, treading in the deep snow?"

"I am cutting a path for the yeshivah students," answered Rabbi Hayyim, in all innocence.

KINDNESS WITH HIS FEET

Rabbi Akiva Eger was traveling from his city to a small village to be the *sandek* (godfather) at a *brit milah* (ritual circumcision). It was winter, and the heavy rains had filled the roads with mud and pools of water. In the darkness of midnight the wagon driver was forced to get down from the platform of the wagon, walking up to his knees in water and mud, in order to hold up the wagon to prevent it from turning upside down.

When they reached dry ground, the driver returned and sat on the platform, and took off his shoes which were soaked through.

After a few minutes Rabbi Akiva took out a pair of socks and said to the driver, "Change your wet socks, lest you catch cold." The driver thankfully did so, exclaiming, "You saved my life!"

When morning came and Rabbi Akiva got down from the wagon, the driver noticed that the rabbi had shoes without socks on his feet. He quickly understood where the rabbi had gotten the socks that he had given him the night before.

"Is it possible, Rabbi?! Had I known..."

"So what," replied the rabbi, interrupting the driver. "Is it fair that I should sit with shoes and socks, and you sit barefoot, with soaking wet socks?"

THE UNPAID GUARD

Rabbi Zev Wolf rode to a *brit milah* (ritual circumcision), and while he entered the house, the driver waited outside. It was a cold wintry day, with a heavy snowstorm raging outside. After a little while the rabbi went outside and suggested to the driver to go inside the house to warm up. The driver answered that he could not leave the horses alone. So Rabbi Zev Wolf promised to watch the horses in the meantime.

The driver entered the house and enjoyed himself with all kinds of delicious food and even several glasses of liquor, completely oblivious to his responsibilities.

Several hours passed. As the guests were leaving the *brit milah* they noticed Rabbi Zev Wolf standing guard, his teeth chattering from the cold, and his feet shivering.

"BOTH HUMANS AND ANIMALS, YOU DELIVER, O GOD" (PSALMS 36:7)

It is told of Rabbi Yosef Zundel of Salant that in his youth, when he was a merchant, he would travel to fairs, and become attached to every wagon driver, in order to help load and unload their wagons. He would even bring water, himself, to the horses whose masters had neglected them.

Once he was seen at a fair walking on a road with two buckets filled with water suspended on his shoulders. He was staring at the thirsty animals standing in the market. His friends and admirers were surprised and asked him, "Revered rabbi, to what extent will you go?"

"Our sages taught," answered Rabbi Yosef Zundel in innocence, "that just as God is kind and compassionate, so we too should be kind and compassionate" (Talmud, Tractate Shabbat 133b).

We are taught regarding the Blessed Holy One, "God is good to all, God's mercy is extended to all creatures" (Psalms 145:9). God does not distinguish, not only between one person and another, but also between a human and an animal.

CHASING AFTER CHARITY AND KINDNESS

One winter day the neighbors of Rabbi Yosef Zundel of Salant saw him standing outside his house hammering nails into his front door. Surprised, they asked him, "Rabbi, what kind of work are you doing?"

He replied that the lock on the door had become broken, and when the door was locked it was difficult to open. "I am thus concerned about the poor folks who go from house to house in the wintertime. It will be hard for us to open the door quickly to let them in."

They also told of Rabbi Yosef Zundel's unusual conduct one Yom Kippur. He was standing in prayer with the congregation, with their *tallitot* (prayer shawls) wrapped around them, praying with deep fervor. Rabbi Yosef Zundel happened to look out the window and saw the sheep of a Jewish farmer jumping into the garden of a gentile.

He paused in his prayers, went outside, and chased the sheep from the garden of the gentile. The worshippers noticed this and were astonished. Rabbi Yosef Zundel would interrupt his holy prayers, go out of the synagogue on this holy day, and chase goats that belong to someone else?

Rabbi Yosef Zundel replied, "The gentile would certainly ask to be paid for damages from the owner of the garden, and the Torah warns us to be extremely careful with funds of Jews."

"GATHER WATER IN JOY" (ISAIAH 12:3)

In the town of Rabbi Yisrael Meir Hakohen of Radin, author of the *Hafetz Hayyim*, was a simple water carrier, who knew neither Torah nor good manners. The children in the area would mock him and pester him in every possible way in order to anger him.

In the winter, on their way home from school, the youth would pass by the local well, fill the bucket with water, and leave. At night the water would freeze and become blocks of ice.

In the morning the water carrier would be the first to draw water, and he was forced to crack the ice and empty the bucket. Then this poor fellow would become angry and curse the boys.

When the matter became known to Rabbi Yisrael Meir he began to do the following. Each night, at midnight, as he returned home from the beit midrash, he would pass by the well, pour out the water and empty the bucket, so that the water carrier would not be bothered the next morning.

MISTAKEN IDENTITY

When Rabbi Yosef Zundel of Salant left the Diaspora and settled in Jerusalem, he made his home in the Old City, in the neighborhood of the Hurva

Synagogue. It happened that a certain woman came to draw water from the well in the courtyard. However the water carrier was nowhere to be found. The woman looked around for help, and noticed Rabbi Yosef Zundel strolling near the well. She thought to herself that this must be a poor person seeking a few *perutot* at the well. She asked him to draw two pails of water for her. She told him that she did not have any coins at the moment, but promised him that when she would return again to draw water, she would pay him his wage.

"No problem," answered Rabbi Yosef Zundel. "I will be happy to pour water from the well for you, and I trust that when the opportunity arises, you will pay me." He drew the water, and parted.

A few days later the woman returned to draw water, and to pay her debt. She searched for the old man who drew water for her a few days before, and she became aware that this man was Rabbi Yosef Zundel of Salant. She was embarrassed and went to apologize.

"I am so sorry, Rabbi, and beg your forgiveness," she said in a plaintive voice. "I did not recognize you – I did not realize who you were."

"There is nothing for which to ask forgiveness," interrupted Rabbi Yosef Zundel in a gentle voice. "On the contrary, I am obligated to thank you, since you enabled me to fulfill a great mitzvah such as this."

Life and Death

A SIGNIFICANT LIFE

Rabbi Leib ben Sarah taught: "I am astonished with human beings who constantly complain about how short life is. What are humans that they complain about the length of years which they are granted? Are seventy years just a pile of straw on the ground? Does an animal live longer? What about little creeping things that have such a short life? The flies that buzz for only a day? And yet humans still are full of complaints."

Rabbi Leib ben Sarah would further point out: "Is the quality of life dependent on the length of years? No, the longest life is one filled with good deeds. Whoever increases good deeds, directs his heart to the Creator of the world. He clings to the Blessed Holy One, and is connected to eternal life. Such a person never worries about death."

FOR YOUR SAKE, IF NOT FOR OURS

Rabbi Yehezkel of Kozmir once complained to the Master of the Universe: "It is true that we owe you many great debts, indeed, many. But the way of the world is such that when a merchant sees that the situation of his customer is down, and is near bankruptcy, he does not let him fall. He supports him so that he can get back on his feet, and then he can pay what he owes.

"So it is that we ask of you, Master of the Universe, 'Write us in the Book of Life,' give us a little extended credit for more life. We ask this of You also for Your sake, *'lema'ankha Elokim Hayyim'* – so that we will be able to repay You our former debts."

BLESSED BE THE ONE WHO REVIVES THE DEAD

Rabbi Menahem Mendel of Kotzk once said just before his morning prayers: "This morning, when I awakened, I thought I was not alive. Then I opened my eyes and saw light. I stretched out my hands and touched my body. I moved my legs and realized that I could walk. And then I looked at the other limbs of my body and said, 'It seems that I am alive.'

"I acknowledged this awareness to the Blessed God and recited, '*Barukh Mehayei hameitim* (Blessed be the One Who revives the dead)' (Shaharit service). I saw that I was a living being."

GOD GRANTS LIFE TO EVERY LIVING BEING

It happened once that a Hasid entered the home of Rabbi Pinhas of Kinsk, the grandson of the Holy Jew, and found him lying in bed, gazing at the broken parts of his pocket watch.

Since the hour was close to noon and the rabbi had not yet prayed the Shaharit (morning) prayers, the Hasid stared at the rabbi in amazement.

Rabbi Pinhas explained, "You are surprised at me. What is my absorption with this watch all about? I am learning from the broken parts of the watch the secret of brokenness. I am learning the process of death."

"IN RIGHTEOUSNESS I WILL SEE YOUR FACE" (PSALMS 17:15)

To Rabbi Eliyahu, the Gaon of Vilna, death was very painful. The Gaon was one of the pillars of halakhah (Jewish law), and deemed the goal of life to be the fulfillment of the mitzvot of the Torah in all its fine points and details.

Just prior to his last breath he took out his *tzitzit* (fringes on the *tallit*), gazed at them, and said in tears, "How difficult it is to part from this world, in which a righteous person can, after the fulfillment of the simple mitzvah of wearing *tzitzit*, see the face of the Divine Presence. In the next life it will be impossible to acquire a mitzvah even for all the fortune in the world."

As the tears flowed from his eyes, he kissed the *tzitzit*, and his eyes closed forever.

TO YOU, GOD, ONLY TO YOU

On the morning of the holiday of Shavuot, the Baal Shem Tov lay in bed, deep in thought and in severe pain. The master's students did not dare approach him.

When his pain diminished a bit, the Besht lifted his head from the pillow and asked for a copy of the siddur, and his lips whispered these words, "Master of the Universe, I desire to speak with you one more time."

Rabbi Nahman of Horodenka was leaning on the wall and stood up to plead for mercy for the life of his teacher. The Besht noticed this and said, "My student is praying in vain, since the decree has been announced."

A while later one of the Besht's leading students asked to approach his master's bed. The Besht began speaking about the fleeting paths of life in this world, and about the thin path which leads from the lower Gan Eden to the upper Gan Eden.

Tears filled the eyes of his students. When the Besht saw this he pleaded with them not to cry. Death is only a transition from a passing reality to a permanent reality.

"I don't worry at all," said the Besht. "I am confident that immediately after I pass through this door I will enter through another door, to a more beautiful place."

The Besht lay his head down on the pillow, closed his eyes, and his lips voiced these words: "Master of the Universe, I have only a short time left to enjoy this world, and I offer them to you as my gift."

Life Paths

THE SEARCH FOR THE "*PINTELE YID*"

Rabbi Pinhas of Koretz and Rabbi Leib ben Sarah loved each other as soul mates, though their paths to holiness differed. Rabbi Pinhas was fully involved in his own community, teaching Torah and providing spiritual guidance to the Hasidic congregation that he led.

On the other hand, Rabbi Leib ben Sarah was preoccupied with traveling from city to city, coming and going in marketplaces, and busying himself with various community matters – some of which were publicized and others which were kept confidential. Some said that he was occupied with redeeming captives, while others claimed that he was busy supporting hidden righteous scholars. Still others said that he traveled around the world perfecting souls.

On occasion he would make his way to Koretz to be near his beloved friend, Rabbi Pinhas, and enjoy pleasant discussions on Hasidism and other Divine matters.

Once Rabbi Pinhas asked him, "Rabbi Leib, my dear friend, why do you always keep traveling around from city to city? What are you searching for in your journeys?"

Rabbi Leib replied, "I am roaming around the world because this is my mission. What am I searching for? For the spark, Reb Pinhas, the hidden spark of Yiddishkeit (*Das Pintele Yid*)."

"But Reb Leib," countered Rabbi Pinhas, "the hidden spark of Jewishness, the quintessential Jew, is the secret of the holiness of our Creator, Whose glory fills the world. The whole world is the Blessed Holy One Himself."

"You speak the truth, Reb Pinhas, and the sanctity of the Holy One fills the entire universe completely. '*Leit atar panui minei* – There is no place devoid of God's presence.' But humans of flesh and blood in the entire world have only one spark in which is their vitality. Only with the help of God can one achieve it. Fortunate is the one whom the Blessed One merits to reach the place to find this spark. Perhaps Leib ben Sarah is a worm and not a person, and as a worm he has to crawl on the ground and lick the dust of the earth. Therefore, we must come and go, Reb Pinhas, to seek out the hidden spark to perfect one's soul."

"And it seems that we, Reb Leib, have come into the world for our special spark, and in every place where we perform God's mitzvot, there alone can we perfect our soul."

WITH THE EYES OF MY HEART

When Rabbi Menahem Mendel of Kotzk was still a very small child, his teacher, Rabbi Simhah Bunim of Peshischa, called him and taught him the custom of *hitbodedut* (isolation for the purpose of meditation).

"Mendel, it is true that there is nothing more effective in life than *hitbodedut*. But it is also true that there is no place more fitting to be alone than in the midst of a large crowd. When I look at the world through the eyes of my heart, the world appears to be filled with horror and desolation, and in this world there is one lonely tree – a single juniper. This is me. Just me, alone.

"The Almighty has no one in the world but me, and I have no one to whom to turn but God. And when the two of us are in the wilderness, it seems to me, that I peer at God, and God looks at me. Thus is created the unity between God and me."

WHO IS THE TRUE PERSON OF SPIRIT?

A young man, among the many seeking a mission in life, came to Rabbi Shlomo of Karlin in order to model himself after the teacher's path in Hasidism, and to examine whether it fit his own temperament.

The young man lingered in the sphere of the tzaddik for many days and weeks. As time went on and the young man made no indication of moving on from Karlin, Rabbi Shlomo explained to him, "Do you think that the mighty Samson did nothing but cut up lions, or beat Philistines with the jawbone of an ass? No! Samson would also lift stalks of straw from the ground, and tear paper, and do many simple things like every other normal person. But even then, when he would do all these simple acts, his bravery and heroism did not leave him.

"A truly spiritual person remains a spiritual person in all situations. Not only when he is deep in important thoughts, but also when he is occupied with the simple acts of every day."

THE HUMAN AND HIS IMAGE

When Rabbi Yisrael of Rizhin would speak to a large group, he had the unique ability of reaching each individual. Each student received a private message; each person felt as if the rebbe's words were aimed specifically at him. Thus, the teacher would not assign everyone the same path, and would not advise each one with the same counsel. He would consider each student's personal qualities, each one's particular spiritual tendencies, and with this in mind he would guide his students to select their own paths.

Rabbi Yisrael of Rizhin would say: "In the beautiful palace of a wealthy king there were many officials and leaders, and a troupe of the most talented and sweetest musicians would play beautiful songs in order to entertain the heart of the king and his retinue.

"In the king's palace there was also a canary that chirped in a sweet tone, and the king would enjoy the chirping of this little bird more than all the singers and musicians. Why? Because the voice of the canary was purer than all the mix of imitation. The trill of the canary was its own, and that of no one else."

KNOWING WHAT TO ASK FOR

A wealthy Hasid lost all his wealth, and went to pour out his heart to his teacher, Rabbi Shneur Zalman of Liadi. He needed money to pay debts, he had to pay his childrens' teachers for their instruction; he had to make a wedding for his daughter; he had to develop his business back to the level it had been, etc., etc.

Rabbi Shneur Zalman looked straight into the eyes of the Hasid. "You have enumerated in great detail what your needs are. But it is amazing to me that you did not ask yourself, even for a second, what is it that you need to find yourself, your mission in life!"

Suddenly the Hasid's eyes filled with tears. Never again did he have cause to ask for anything.

APPRECIATING THE BEAUTY OF THE WORLD

The Baal Shem Tov, founder of the Hasidic movement, asked: "Who, in truth, expelled Adam from the Garden of Eden?

"Did some angel drive him out? Did the Creator open a gate in Gan Eden, or did God break a hole in the garden's fence and throw him out? Common sense would not accept such a story.

"Rather," explained the Besht, "when the Torah says, 'And God drove Adam out' (Genesis 3:24), the Targum Yonatan translates, '*vetarid yat Adam*, Adam became troubled.' And of course a man who is troubled cannot live in the Garden of Eden."

The Besht further taught: "In the first days of the creation of the world, when everything was still new and vernal, man's heart was open to the spark of the world. And for everything that he saw, he would offer praise to the Creator, recognizing that all was '*tov me'od*, very good.'

"However, after man sinned, he was no longer satisfied with what was laid out for him and instead became aware of lacking. As a result he became overwhelmed with great anxiety which prevented him from appreciating the glory of the world.

Thus were the gates of Gan Eden shut before him."

THE PURPOSE OF CREATING HUMANS

Rabbi Menahem Mendel of Kotzk asked Rabbi Yaakov of Radzimin, "Yaakov, why was man created?"

Rabbi Yaakov replied, "Man was created to perfect his soul."

Rabbi Menahem Mendel retorted, "Is this what we learned from our teacher, Rabbi Simhah Bunim, of blessed memory?

"No, that's not what he taught. He taught that man was created in order to raise the heavens."

WHAT DID WE LEARN?

Rabbi Aharon of Karlin was one of the pupils of the Maggid of Mezritch, and would travel to him often.

Once some of Rabbi Aharon's friends asked him, "What new teachings did the Maggid of Mezritch add to your knowledge?"

Rabbi Aharon replied, "Nothing!"

His friends were astonished. "Then why do you travel to see him so often?"

Rabbi Aharon explained: "What I learned by visiting him was that I am nothing..."

A PHONY EXCUSE

Once Rabbi Simhah Bunim of Peshischa was traveling on the road in a wagon. The road was filled with mud and huge puddles of water. At length the wagon became trapped in the mud.

The driver pushed in exhaustion to free the horse and wagon.

"Please help me," said the driver to Rabbi Simhah Bunim.

"I can't," answered Rabbi Simhah Bunim.

"No," answered the driver. "You can but you don't want to."

From that moment on, Rabbi Simhah Bunim would reprove himself: "You can but you don't want to..."

WORDS OF WISDOM

BECOMING AN ANGEL

Some think it is difficult to reach the level of an angel. However, what is really difficult is to reach the level of a human being.

Rabbi Moshe of Kovrin

BRINGING HEAVEN TO EARTH

The Holy Arizal would stroll in the kingdom of Heaven, and the paths of paradise were as clear to him as the streets of the earth. He desired to raise people upward to show them the world above the firmament. But our master Rabbi Yisrael Baal Shem Tov revealed the divinity in the paths of the earth, and he would bring down, as it were, the upper worlds, and plant them in the hearts of people.

Rabbi Shlomo of Lotzk

CHANGE IS CONSTANT

Not only does each person not resemble his neighbor,

Not only does each day not resemble the next one,

But no single minute resembles the minute that follows it.

The four children of the Haggadah of Pesah are only four types of one person. Because at any minute a person is liable to change from being "wise" to "wicked," and from "wicked" to "simple."

Rabbi Nahman of Breslov

GROWING YOUR SOUL

"*Asher bara Elokim la'asot*, Which God had created, to make" (Genesis 2:3).

Why does the verse add the word "*la'asot* (to make)"? The Blessed Holy One created man in order that man should perfect himself, i.e., in order that man should "make" himself.

Rabbi Yehezkel Halbershtam

"*LEKH LEKHA*, GET THEE..." (GENESIS 12:1)

The call to "*lekh lekha* (lit., go to yourself)" was not directed only to the first Jew. Rather it was directed to everyone created in God's image. "Go" to yourself – i.e., "Be who you are!" Go on the path that fits your own essence.

Rabbi Shmuel of Sochochov

TRUE SATISFACTION

"Naftali is fully satisfied, and filled with the blessings of God" (Deuteronomy 33:23).

Only one who is "fully satisfied" and "happy with one's lot" can be "filled with the blessings of God." If one is not "fully satisfied," he is constantly lacking something – in which case whatever such a person possesses will never be enough.

Rabbi Shlomo Kluger

Mitzvot

THE REWARD OF A MITZVAH

Before Rabbi Levi Yitzhak of Berditchev was ordained as a rabbi, he lived with his father-in-law. It was his custom to serve all the many guests who came to stay with his father-in-law, who was a wealthy and respected member of the city. Rabbi Levi Yitzhak would trouble himself to bring sheaves of straw for the guests to lie on, and he would prepare their bedding.

Once his father-in-law asked him, "Why do you bother yourself so much? Can't you hire a local worker to carry the bundles of straw?"

Rabbi Levi Yitzhak replied, "Is it right to honor a worker with this mitzvah, and on top of that to pay him for it?"

AMASSING MITZVOT

Rabbi Elimelekh of Lizhensk went to the river one Rosh Hashanah to recite Tashlikh (a ceremony in which one empties one's pockets of bread and throws the crumbs into the water, symbolically detaching oneself from one's sins). When he reached the river, he found a place to shake out his pockets. A certain Hasid followed him, explaining, "I want to see where our master throws his sins so that I can gather them to myself."

What does this mean? Rabbi Yitzhak of Vorka explained, "Relative to other people, the sins of a tzaddik are considered mitzvot."

ROTE PERFORMANCE

The Maggid of Mezritch taught: "There are some people sit all day draped in their *tallit* and *tefillin*, studying and praying, but without excitement or passion. They do it as a mechanical act.

"They are not worshipping God, and in fact they are worse than sinners. Sinners are occasionally aroused to repent, and may come to genuinely regret their evil actions and return to the right path.

"Those who do all the mitzvot routinely and without feeling consider themselves tzaddikim. It seems to them that they are worshipping God in the best possible way, and as a result they never examine their deeds. Therefore, they will never be able to achieve a high level of Divine service. They think that their worship is perfect, yet, in fact, they are really as far from God as east is from west."

DON'T EXPECT REWARDS

A certain Hasid came to Rabbi Yissakhar Dov Ber Thornheim Hakohen of Wolborz and said to him, "Rebbe, I am fully ready to do *teshuvah*, but on condition that in return for this act I shall be rescued from the harsh punishments due me."

Rabbi Yissakhar Dov replied, "Were your sins also committed on condition?"

SPIRITUAL AGONY

The rabbi of Radzimin came to visit Rabbi Yitzhak Meir of Gur to celebrate the holiday of Shavuot. Rabbi Yitzhak Meir saw that the face of his guest was gaunt and sickly, so he asked him, "Is it that the hot sun in the summer is harmful to your health, or that you are being constantly criticized, which is affecting your well-being?"

"Neither," the rabbi answered. "In the summer we read in the Torah about the wanderings of the Israelites in the wilderness, and about the sins they committed in those days, like the sin of the spies, the golden calf, and Baal Peor. These sections of the Torah, which tell of the sins of our ancestors, cause me spiritual agony."

Rabbi Yitzhak Meir replied, "Listen! Out of the stories of the sins of our ancestors came many passages in the Torah. But from the mitzvot that we do will there be stories in the Torah? Though our people have indeed sinned, surely good has come out of their transgressions."

WORDS OF WISDOM

FROM A LOVING HEART

Every mitzvah that a Jew fulfills is fulfilled from a place of love. Even the mitzvah of "You shall love" is fulfilled from a place of love – including "You shall love the Lord your God," and "You shall love your neighbor as yourself."

Rabbi Yisrael Baal Shem Tov

CHASE AFTER MITZVOT

"Ben Azzai taught: Run to do even a minor mitzvah, and flee from sin..." (Pirkei Avot 4:2).

We learn from this that one must run after a minor mitzvah, and one must run away from a minor sin.

Rabbi Yisrael Salanter

JUDGMENT AND RECKONING

"Whether you like it or not you will in the future have to give an account and reckoning before the Supreme Ruler of Rulers, the Blessed Holy One" (Pirkei Avot 4:29).

What is meant by "account (*din*)" and "reckoning (*heshbon*)"?

Every person will be required to pass judgment (*din*) on the sin he committed, and the reckoning (*heshbon*) will be made for him on the time that he wasted on that sin. In that period of time he could have fulfilled a mitzvah.

The Vilna Gaon

HOW DO WE "CLING?"

"Let our hearts cling to Your mitzvot" (morning prayers).

The meaning of this prayer, which a Jew recites daily, is this: That the mitzvot that I fulfill will be etched on my heart. That they will be an integral part of my being. That I will be totally filled with them, and that I will not ever part from them. In this way the love that I have for You, my Creator, will no longer remain a transient phase.

Rabbi Uri of Strelisk

Money

WITH ALL YOUR MIGHT

It happened that one small town did not have a place for observant Jews to bathe and go to the mikveh for ritual immersion. When Rabbi Nahum of Chernobyl discovered this, he turned to a close friend and admirer, who was very wealthy, and the rabbi sold his friend his portion in the World to Come for the price of building a bathhouse and mikveh in the town.

When his Hasidim heard of this they were astonished. Rabbi Nahum answered them in all sincerity: "The Torah teaches 'You shall love the Lord your God with all your heart, with all your soul, and with all your might' (Deuteronomy 6:5). Rashi explains that 'with all your might' means 'with all your financial means.' I recite this verse every morning and evening, and I ask you: A Jew like me, who has not even a *perutah* to his name, how can I fulfill the command to love God with all one's wealth?

"But if I have a small piece of the World to Come, and there are people who value this piece in a monetary way, I am thus duty bound to sell my property, in order to fulfill the mitzvah of loving God with all my might, and not, Heaven forbid, to say my words in vain."

KNOW HOW TO ANSWER

Rabbi Tzvi Hersh Kalischer wrote a popular book explaining that Jews were obligated to rebuild Eretz Yisrael on their own and not wait for the coming of the Messiah. As a result, throughout Europe people started to organize groups for the resettlement of the Holy Land.

In response to Rabbi Kalischer's teachings, a group of wealthy merchants approached Rabbi Yehoshua Isaac Shapira, the spiritual leader of Slonim, and asked him his opinion. Were they truly obligated to take concrete action to rebuild the Land, or should they rather wait for the coming of the Messiah, as was the common practice at that time among Jews.

The rabbi answered them, "In the body of the prayer known as the Amidah three paragraphs follow each other in succession: 'Heal us and we shall be healed…,' 'Bless this year for us…' and 'Sound the great shofar for our freedom, raise high the banner to gather our exiles….' In other words, a prayer for healing, a prayer for sustenance, and a prayer for redemption.

"It is fascinating to me that the prosperous people of Slonim never sent for me when they were sick in bed to ask if it was acceptable to go to a doctor, or if they should wait for God to heal them. The merchants of Slonim, when their income was slacking, never came to me to ask if they should take action to increase their financial status or not. But when it comes to the matter of redemption they come to me to ask if it is permitted to take action to bring the redemption, or if perhaps they should wait.

"The answer is simple. Healing and income affect people individually, and therefore they do not rely on prayer alone. But when it comes to redemption, which is a matter not only for each individual but for the whole people of Israel, they come with complaints and questions, in order to find a way not to contribute."

WHOSE MITZVAH?

A wealthy person brought a large sum of money to Rabbi Pinhas of Ositla and asked him to use the funds for *tzedakah*.

"Why do you bring the money to me?" asked Rabbi Pinhas. "Give it out yourself."

"If it becomes known in the city that I distribute *tzedakah*," answered the wealthy person, "all the poor people and charity collectors in town will congregate at my home, and I will have no rest."

Rabbi Pinhas replied, "Take your money and give it out yourself. The ancient custom of *matan b'seter*, giving charity anonymously, was not initiated for the benefit of the rich, to alleviate their burdens, but for the poor, so they will not be embarrassed."

MUTUAL ASSISTANCE

A wealthy man entered the home of Rabbi Akiva Eger. During the conversation the visitor pulled out a cigarette from his silver case, lit it, and began to smoke. Rabbi Akiva naively asked why he smoked.

"My dear rabbi," answered the affluent visitor, "it is my custom to eat my dinner at a leisurely pace. I eat several kinds of dishes, and drink several kinds of beverages, until I am quite full. It gives me pleasure to smoke on a full stomach."

A few days later a poor man of a pious family visited Rabbi Akiva and began to pour out his heart, telling of his difficult financial straits. During the discussion he took out a cigarette from his pocket, lit it, and smoked. Rabbi Akiva asked this time too why the man was smoking.

"Honored rabbi," answered the guest, "sometimes I have not even a tiny piece of bread in my cupboard, and am extremely hungry, and it helps me overcome my hunger when I smoke."

"Look at that!" said Rabbi Akiva. "A wealthy man smokes because of satiety. A poor man smokes because of hunger. If they took the virtuous path, the rich man would give his surplus of food to the poor man, and they could both eat a normal meal, and neither would have to smoke."

ACCORDING TO LAW AND CUSTOM

When Rabbi Yisrael Salanter traveled to Frankfurt, Baron Rothschild, a God-fearing man, invited him to visit his mansion. When the rabbi was about to leave, after having marveled at the contents of the house and its appointments, he turned to the baron and said, "Forgive me, but I must tell you the truth. The appearance of your home is not completely consistent with the Torah."

"How so, Rabbi?" asked the God-fearing baron with trepidation.

"Very simply," smiled Rabbi Yisrael. "In the Torah it is written, 'And Yeshurun grew fat and kicked' (Deuteronomy 32:15). When a Jew rises to greatness and becomes wealthy, he tends to rebel, and the Master of the Universe disappears from his heart.

"But with you it's just the opposite. You are very prosperous, and yet your home is a kosher Jewish home in every way, and everything is according to the total spirit of Judaism. Nu, this is not the way the Torah expected!"

WHAT MONEY CANNOT BUY

The famous and prosperous Baron Maurice de Hirsch was once asked, "How does a wealthy person see life through the lens of affluence?"

The baron replied, "A poor person thinks that money will solve all his problems. A wealthy person knows that money cannot buy everything."

PRIORITIES

Rabbi Barukh of Medziboz traveled widely to earn money by preaching, so he lived comfortably. But his brother, Rabbi Ephraim of Sudylkov, lived simply with meager means.

It happened once that Rabbi Barukh spent Shabbat with Rabbi Ephraim, and noticed a pair of brass candlesticks in his brother's house. He sighed and asked, "My dear brother, are you not worthy of having a pair of silver candlesticks in your home?"

Rabbi Ephraim replied, "Better that I should have a pair of silver candlesticks in some faraway place, while I am at home, than having silver candlesticks in my home and I am wandering abroad."

DON'T TEST ME

Rabbi Hayyim of Zanz once entered the beit midrash, approached a group of young students, and asked one of them, "What would you do if on Shabbat day you found a wallet full of coins? Would you pick it up?"

"No, Rabbi, I have no doubt about that. It would not occur to me to touch money on Shabbat."

"You are quite sure of yourself," replied Rabbi Hayyim wryly. Then he turned to the next student and asked, "And you?"

"I think I would pick it up."

"*Oy!*" cried Rabbi Hayyim. "And desecrate Shabbat?!"

Then the rabbi turned to the third. "And you?"

"At this moment, Rabbi, it seems to me that I would be faced with a crucial test, and I would not pick up the wallet. However, who knows how powerful my yearning for money would be at such a time, and whether it might overpower me? How can I know right now if at such a moment I would be able to stand up to the test?"

"You are a wise young man," said the rabbi.

THE GIFT

As the wedding day approached for Rabbi Aryeh Levin and his bride, Tziporah Hannah, the tzaddik of Jerusalem said to his fiancée, "It is customary in Jerusalem that the groom presents a gift to his bride, and the bride also presents a gift to her groom. But what can we do since we are both poor orphans, and unable to buy each other gifts?

"So here is my idea. We can present each other a gift without it costing either one of us any money. Let's promise one another that in the course of the years of our marriage, we will be generous and forgiving to each other. This will be the real gift that we can give each other, and it will not cost either of us a penny."

GENEROSITY

Rabbi Issar Zalman Meltzer, rosh yeshivah of Etz Hayyim, was so engrossed in his Torah thought that while he was taking a walk he fell right into a pit of plaster, and the white paint got all over his clothes.

The owner of the pit ran right over to the rabbi, and Rabbi Meltzer asked forgiveness for the plaster that had stuck to his clothing.

HOW THE WORLD IS SUSTAINED

Rabbi Yehezkel Sarna, rosh yeshivah of Hevron, tells of an elderly woman who for many years collected money for the yeshivah. Each week she would give the yeshivah whatever she had collected; normally the sum came to less than ten liras.

Rabbi Sarna was asked, "How is it possible for the yeshivah to be maintained by such small contributions?"

He answered, "The yeshivah cannot sustain itself from such small amounts, but it is clear to me that due to the merit of righteous women like her, the world is sustained."

WORDS OF WISDOM

SILVER AND GOLD

What is the difference between the earlier generations and the later generations?

The generation of the wilderness, those who marched in the Sinai desert with Moshe, parted with their silver and gold in order to make themselves a god – the golden calf.

Later generations parted with their God, in order to make silver and gold.

Rabbi Aisel Harif

Parents and Children

BE YOUR OWN CHILD

The famous Holy Jew was reflecting on the ways of humans, and commented, "Woe to those who practice through self-deception." He then explained his remark with the following tale:

> A wise teacher once asked a certain Jew, "Why are you always busy with making a living and chasing after business, such that you don't have any time left to pray with sincerity or to glance at the page of a holy book?"
>
> The Jew answered him thus, "Do I pursue a living for my own personal needs? I have a yoke over my neck! Thank God I have children to raise and educate in Torah and in the performance of good deeds. My oldest son will soon be of age to marry, and I will have to pay for his wedding. Then I will want to support him for several years at my table so that he can sit and study in the beit midrash with the other young men who are studying Torah."
>
> Not long after, the son of this man married according to Jewish law and tradition. He studied Torah for several years, but not as long as his father had hoped. During his first year of marriage he took a stab at working in a business, to adjust to making a living. During that period he set aside only a very limited amount of time for Torah study, as his work responsibilities stole from him most of his free time. As time went on, his leisure for Torah study continually diminished, until it ceased completely.
>
> During that time the young man's wife gave birth to two boys and a girl, whom he had to support. It became increasingly difficult to live in his father's house, such that after the birth of his second child it was already extremely crowded. He thus had to rent his own place.
>
> The older man lived many years, and when he saw what was happening, he asked his son, "Is it possible for a man who is busy making

> a living and enveloped all his days in the vagaries of the world, that he will also have time for Torah study and prayer? And what about some free time to reflect about life and personal spiritual examination?"
>
> But his son gave him the same answer that the man himself had given years earlier: "Do I pursue a living for my own personal satisfaction and personal needs? All my labors are exerted only to engage excellent teachers for my children."

After recounting the story, the Holy Jew remarked, "Generations come and generations go, and the excuse is the same. 'Not for my own pleasure, but rather for the welfare of my children I pursue a living.' So when will some Jew speak up and declare: 'I am my own son, and I myself am obligated to study Torah!'"

KEEP FULFILLING YOUR MISSION IN THE WORLD WITH FAITHFULNESS

In a certain village there lived a simple and honest man. In that part of the world he was known as Mendel the Innkeeper, because he made a living from his small inn which stood at the crossroads.

As Mendel aged he began to contemplate life. "Most of my life has passed in this small village in superficiality and emptiness. I've mixed drinks for drunken gentiles and for inebriated lords. My eyes have seen horrible acts of low-class men addicted to filth, and my ears have heard screams of riots from farmers wild in disgrace. My prayers were not prayers, but rather rushed mumbling as I was on the go. The only words I can utter are *Shema Yisrael*. Once a year, on Yom Kippur, I prayed with the whole community, but even then I didn't know the meaning of the words in the mahzor. Now that I am getting older, it's time that I prepared my soul for my final journey.

"My son, Shiyke, who is now of age, can attend to those who come for a drink and provide the family income, so that I can attend to my spiritual needs. I'll travel to the city, buy myself a Humash, and I'll even buy myself a book of prayers. Like every Jew I'll pray three times a day with deep feeling, and I'll try to study some Torah."

Mendel called his son, Shiyke, and placed in his hands the responsibilities of the inn.

Shiyke served the visitors to the inn with alacrity, and the peasants were pleased with him.

But from the time Shiyke took over the responsibilities of the inn, the inn took on a new character. For many years the inn had served as a place of meeting for Jewish travelers. When their feet were tired and weary, the travelers knew that at the crossroads Mendel's inn would be waiting for them. There would always be a warm meal, and a ready bed on which they could stretch their weary limbs. Mendel would always welcome them with a cheerful smile. He would make certain to give them personal service. With bright eyes he would serve this one with warm tea, and that one with a glass of schnapps.

But now that Mendel had removed himself from his daily chores, the inn was not open to travelers. The little bit of service that Shiyke would offer to those who happened by his way, he would offer with an angry mien, with the result that trekkers began to pass by Mendel's inn.

When the matter came to the attention of Rabbi Levi Yitzhak of Berditchev, he invited Mendel to a meeting. When they met, Rabbi Levi asked Mendel why he had deserted his business and handed it to his son. Mendel presented his case before Rabbi Levi Yitzhak:

"My hair is gray, Rebbe, and I have aged. Who knows how many years Hashem will allow me to remain on earth? And with what good deeds can I come before the heavenly court? How can I face my Judge, as a poor, ashamed man, who has neither Torah nor prayer to his credit? Now that my son deals with the household needs, I have leisure, Rebbe. I awaken each morning, wrap myself in a *tallit*, pray every word with sincerity, and I even have time to glance at a Humash and some mishnayot. Now I feel that I can face the heavenly court with ample mitzvot, with having studied Torah and prayed with fervor."

Rabbi Levi Yitzhak placed his hands into the sleeves of his coat, deep in thought. Then he turned his cheerful face toward Mendel and said in a gentle tone, "Our sages taught: 'Who is wise? The one who knows his place.' Every Jew must know his place, which our Creator set for us in this world. We must each remain firmly in the place assigned to us and not try to seize the place of another.

"Our holy sages further taught the Kingdom above is just like the Kingdom here on earth. And the customs of the Kingdom here are similar to the customs above. Pity on the Kingdom that has only officers, and lacks simple soldiers. An ordinary soldier who runs from his post thinking he can become a general is considered a traitor to the Kingdom.

"Know, dear Mendel, that the Blessed Holy One has enough distinguished leaders and generals in His world. What God is lacking are ordinary, faithful soldiers who are loyal to the Ruler of the Universe. The Creator sets each individual in his special place. One person God places in the beit midrash, and another he locates in a distant village.

"You, dear Mendel, God has placed in an inn, so that you can serve a warm drink to tired, passing travelers. When you present yourself before the gates of the Garden of Eden and the court on high, you can do so without shame or reproach. The travelers will testify on your behalf because of the warm meals you served to passersby, and the soft beds you prepared for them.

"Go now, dear Mendel, and return to the inn and open its gates to the trekkers, weary from their long journeys."

Whereupon the famous inn at the crossroads reopened, spreading its doors wide to all those who were tired and in need of refreshment.

MAY THE ALMIGHTY PROVIDE FOR US WITH HONOR

A Jew from a Hasidic family came once to Rabbi Ben-Zion of Bobov and requested that the rabbi bestow upon him a blessing. The rabbi engaged him in conversation, and inquired about his physical and spiritual well-being. The rabbi especially asked about the education of his children, and their status in the realm of faith.

The man related that one of his children was exceptionally bright and talented, and that the father had decided to send him to university so that he could matriculate in science.

The rabbi asked, "Why do you think that it's more important for your son to study science, rather than specialize in the study of Torah?"

The man replied, "If my son succeeds in his studies and achieves the degree of Doctor, he will be able to acquire an honorable position and make a nice living. Then he'll be able to support me until I'm 120."

"And who will sustain you after 120?" asked the rabbi.

"PLEASE GOD, GRANT US SUCCESS" (PSALMS 118:25)

Rabbi Yehezkel of Kozmir taught: "A literal translation of '*Ana Hashem hatzliha na*' is not 'Please, God, grant us success,' but actually 'Please, God, succeed.' We pray to the Blessed Holy One that He have success, since He is our Father. What consists of success for a father? When he has *nachat ruah* (contentment) from his children."

Prayer

MINYAN

The Maggid of Koznitz taught: "If ten people meet together in a synagogue to pray with a minyan (quorum), and they all pray for their own needs, even if they are all in one building, under one roof, they are still considered separate, since each one focuses his thoughts on his own desires. One for his vineyard, one for his olives, one for his life and one for his children.

"The most important thing in prayer, however, is that all ten people are in one place, directing themselves toward the Unity of God's name – so that God shall be one and God's name one, and that God should reveal His Kingship to us in the near future."

YOM KIPPUR PRAYERS

As the congregation was preparing to begin the Yom Kippur prayers, Rabbi David of Mikolov, one of the veteran students of the Baal Shem Tov, mounted to the platform and addressed the congregation: "*Oy*! Our world is upside down. In olden times the streets and markets were filled with truth and in the synagogue they spoke lies. Now, in the streets and markets there are lies and deception, and in the synagogue is truth and justice.

"In olden times people dealt with their businesses in truth and faith. Their yes was yes, and their no was no. Then they came into the synagogue on the Days of Awe and confessed: 'We sinned, we rebelled, we stole' (Yom Kippur liturgy). None of this was true. They did not sin, nor rebel, nor steal.

"Nowadays, to our great sorrow, the matter is reversed. In the streets and marketplaces they lie, their mouths are full of deception, and here in the synagogue their confessions are accurate: 'We sinned, we rebelled, we stole....'"

With bitter tears Rabbi David began to recite the Confessional, and his Hasidim responded after him, with cries that could pierce the hearts of the angels and break through to the throne of glory.

FORGET NOT!

Rabbi Simhah Bunim of Peshischa recounted this tale:

> A prince rebelled against his father, the king, and it was decreed that he be sent into exile. After some time the king took pity on his son, and sent a representative to find him. After a long search the representative found him in a far-off city in a tavern, barefoot and dressed in rags. He was dancing there together with the drunken beggars.
>
> The representative prostrated himself before the prince. "I was sent by your father, my master the king, to ask you what request you might have." The prince broke out crying and answered, "If my father wishes, let him send me a good strong pair of boots, polished and shiny."

Rabbi Simhah Bunim remarked, "So it is with us. In our prayers before our Father in Heaven we bring before God minor requests, for food and sustenance. But we do not cry out that the *Shekhinah* is in exile, nor do we plead for the redemption. The greatest sin of a Jew is to forget that he is the child of the Sovereign."

MY PRAYERS ARE MY VITALITY

Rabbi Avraham Simhah of Nadvorna was accustomed to reciting his prayers at great length. The daily Shaharit (morning) prayers would take him the entire day. On Shabbat he would conclude his prayers at dark, and eat the second meal when the stars came out.

It happened once that he went to greet Rabbi Moshe Teitelbaum at Uhel on Shabbat. Rabbi Avraham Simhah prayed, as was his custom, until dark.

"Please tell me," asked Rabbi Moshe, "why do you pray at such great length? I am also a pious Jew, and I pray regularly, but even on Shabbat my prayers do not extend beyond the normal hour."

Rabbi Avraham Moshe replied with the following example: "Compare a piece of bread on the table of the rich and one on the table of the poor. One is not the same as the other. The wealthy man only nibbles on the bread, since he has many other foods to enjoy. But a poor person, who is hungry and has nothing else to eat, consumes the entire piece of bread.

"The same is true in my case. All Jews pray. One may be an average Jew, and another a tzaddik. The prayer of the average Jew does not compare to the prayer of the tzaddik. Besides prayer, the tzaddik has many other opportunities to obey God's will – Torah study, the performance of mitzvot – so his prayer is only part of his worship. But I – all I have is prayer. It is my only path to religious vitality."

GOD HEARS ALL PRAYERS

Rabbi Levi Yitzhak of Berditchev was traveling, and stopped for the night at an inn. At the same inn were merchants from the land of Israel, on their way to conduct business in the marketplace. They did not know Rabbi Levi Yitzhak and thought he was just one of the other travelers who stopped at the inn.

The next day the merchants arose early and immediately recited their prayers. Since they had only one pair of *tefillin*, they passed them from one to the other and recited their prayers in a hurry, in order to get to the market on time.

When they had finished their prayers Rabbi Levi Yitzhak approached two of the younger men in the group and said to them, "Please let me ask you a question." They came over to him and Rabbi Levi Yitzhak began to mumble, "Ma, ma, ma, na, na, na."

"What are you saying?" asked the merchants.

Rabbi Levi Yitzhak continued to mumble, "Ba, ba, ba, ta, ta, ta."

The merchants stared at him in surprise. The man must be out of his mind!

"Really?" asked Rabbi Levi Yitzhak. "You don't know what I am saying? But this is how you spoke to God!"

"That's ok," answered one of the merchants. "I'll give you an example. A baby lying in a crib mumbles, 'ba, ma, ta, ba…' If all the scholars of the world heard, they would not understand what the baby was saying. However, if the baby's mother and father were with him, they would immediately understand what he wanted – whether he was hungry, or thirsty, etc.

"So it is with us Jews. We are children to the Almighty, and God knows the requests of every heart, and understands the prayers of every soul."

"Beautifully said," replied Rabbi Levi Yitzhak. And he began to dance with joy, murmuring, "Our Father in Heaven listens to the prayers of all His children."

THEIR SYNAGOGUES AND OUR SYNAGOGUES

Once the Maggid of Dubnow, Rabbi Yaakov ben Wolf Kranz, visited a large Jewish community in Germany, and he stopped to see the synagogue. The *gabbai* (person in charge) recognized him, and welcomed him graciously. He showed him the great beauty of the synagogue – the Torah scrolls wrapped in silk, the holy ark made of silver and decorated with precious stones.

The *gabbai* said to Rabbi Yaakov, "Look at the difference between German Jews and Polish Jews. We create synagogues of extraordinary beauty, and dress the Torah scrolls with 'crimson and finery' (II Samuel 2:24), while you build small and unattractive study halls, with a Torah scroll covered with rags."

The Maggid replied, "Let me tell you a story. Once there were two sisters – one married to a wealthy man, the other to a poor man. One lived in a home in a faraway city; the other, with her poor husband in the city of her birth. One lived with wealth and worldly goods, the other lived all her days in poverty and hardship.

"Once the wealthy sister visited the city of her birth to see her family face-to-face. She sat down with her poor sister, and the two of them had a heart-to-heart talk.

"The wealthy sister began: 'I am extremely affluent, I have everything I need, delicious food, a spacious home, beautiful vessels, valuable jewels, and a great deal of money. But my life is miserable. What is my status there? Like a doormat on which my husband tramples. He never asks my advice; he doesn't even speak to me about anything. He is the boss and he makes all the decisions.'

"The poor sister confided, 'I have very little food to eat, and do not have a large house. I live from day to day, and needless to say I do not have gold or silver, or precious jewels – but I have no complaints. Thank God, I am never embarrassed, Heaven forbid, by my husband in my home. Just the opposite. He honors me more than himself, and does not lift a finger without asking my opinion. We have no wealth, but I am happy.'

"When the wealthy sister heard this, she said to her poor sister, "I only wish my lot were like yours."

"So, my friend the *gabbai*," the Maggid concluded, "you German Jews give the Master of the Universe everything good – gold and silver, precious jewels, and the Blessed One sees your life of abundance, but not of honor or satisfaction. You do not ask God's advice on any matter, and neither do you keep God's commandments. Just the opposite. You are the bosses and you make all the decisions. And when the Master of the Universe desires a bit of satisfaction, God attends morning and evening prayers in our study halls. They may not be spacious, but inside there are joyous hearts and honor for the Torah."

WHO ARE WE, COMPARED TO AVRAHAM AVINU?

The Maggid of Dubnow was lecturing on the High Holiday prayer that beseeches God to answer us today as He has answered our forefathers in the past: "May the One Who answered Avraham at Mt. Moriah, also answer us." As was his custom, the Maggid brought home his point with a story:

> There was a storekeeper in a town who had two customers who would buy all their needs from him. One was a wealthy person, and the other a poor individual.

One day the wealthy person held a wedding for his daughter, and as was the custom, the storekeeper sent him a valuable present worth fifty rubles. Sometime later the poor man also held a wedding for his daughter, and the storekeeper sent him a gift worth two or three rubles.

The poor man was insulted, so he went to the storekeeper with a complaint. "Is that fair? That wealthy man, who already possesses so much, you go and send him a gift worth fifty rubles, and to me you get away with a pittance. Am I not a regular customer, just as he is?"

The storekeeper replied to him: "There is a big difference between the wealthy man and you. I bought him a large gift, not because he is wealthy or that I have respect for wealth, but rather because he buys a great deal from me. Almost half of my income comes from him. But from you what do I get? Half of a herring, a quarter of a liter of gas, a set of matches – and even these I sometimes have to let you have on credit. It costs me money until I am able to extract from you a penny in cash. How can you compare yourself to the wealthy customer?"

"This is the case with us," continued the Maggid of Dubnow. "How do we dare stand before the Master of the Universe and request from him: 'May the One Who answered Avraham Avinu at Mt. Moriah also answer us?'

"From Avraham Avinu the Master of the Universe had much pleasure. Avraham brought God many mitzvot and good deeds. But what does God receive from us misers? The 'purchases' that we occasionally make are only a chapter of Psalms, Kedushah, Barekhu. And often we remain in debt even for this. So how do we have the hutzpah to stand on the same footing as Avraham Avinu?"

AWAKENING THE HEART

Rabbi Yisrael of Rizhin wanted to teach his students about the need to be meticulous in praying at the proper time, even when the heart was not yet aroused. To get his point across, he told a story:

> In a small village there lived only one watchmaker. After he died no other watchmaker came to live in the village. Since there was no one to fix watches the hands on the watches stopped showing the correct hour. Some were slow and others were fast.
>
> Some of the people in the village decided not to keep their watches in their pockets since anyway they did not keep the proper time. They left their watches in their homes, hid them in a drawer, and forgot about them. Others kept their watches in their pockets and wound them every day as they had done before.
>
> Several years passed and a wandering watchmaker passed through the village, and the residents rushed to bring him their watches to be fixed. As it turned out, the watches that had been hidden away had been eaten away by rust, to the point that they could not be fixed. But those watches whose owners had continued to wind them every day were able to be set once again to the correct hour, after the watchmaker made a few small adjustments to the mechanism.

The students understood the point of the story. No one should sit and wait until the heart is aroused and the will moves one to action. Without constant action, the mechanism of the soul is likely to produce rust.

ACKNOWLEDGING GOD'S JUSTICE

Rabbi Eliyahu David Rabinowitz-Teomim (known by his initials, the Aderet), was one of Europe's leading rabbinic figures. His daughter, who was extremely pious, passed away. The announcement was made that the funeral would be at one o'clock in the afternoon.

When the appointed hour arrived a very large crowd assembled near the house, and the only one not there was the father of the deceased. His family explained that the rabbi had shut himself up in his room and it was impossible to bring him out. Those present were amazed to hear this since the Aderet was known for his scrupulous punctuality.

Only after half an hour had passed did the rabbi come out of his room and explain to those present, "It is stated in our tradition that 'One must bless the evil that comes to the world just as one blesses the good in the world.' I examined my soul and realized that I still had not reached the point at which I am ready to recite the traditional words, 'Blessed be the Righteous Judge,' with the same feeling that I had recited the blessing of thanksgiving when she was born. Therefore, I needed the extra time in order to work on myself, to reach the point at which I could feel comfortable reciting the blessing over the good that came to me."

WORDS OF WISDOM

PRAYER AND FOOD

Food is a better preparation for prayer than prayer is a preparation for food.

Rabbi Menahem Mendel Schneerson

EACH BOOK HAS ITS PURPOSE

The Zohar uplifts the soul.
The midrash arouses the heart.
And a chapter of psalms, said with tears, purifies the body.

Rabbi Menahem Mendel Schneerson

Rabbi and Leader

FOR THIS I SIGH

One night Rabbi Simhah Bunim of Peshischa, the prime student of Rabbi Yaakov Yitzhak, the Holy Jew, slept in a room next to that of his teacher. Toward morning the student heard sounds of sighing coming from his teacher's room. Curious as to the cause, when he saw the Holy Jew in the morning he asked him for an explanation.

The Holy Jew answered, "While in bed I thought about the eternal fate of the Jewish people – up and down, up and down. I thought to myself: The first one to save the people from their descent, when the people were subject to forty-nine gates of impurity, was Moshe Rabbeinu. When the people again fell into sin, the judges came and saved them. When they fell into sin the next time, the prophets came to save them. Again they fell, and the Men of the Great Assembly lifted them up. After them came the Tannaim, then the Amoraim, the Saboraim, and the Geonim. After that came the Rambam. Each person performed his act of salvation according to his own ability and the approach of his generation.

"When they sinned in our days, the maggidim and preachers came. The Jewish people descended once more and the righteous Hasidim came, and brought the Jews closer to their Father in Heaven. But I see now that even these sages are not preventing them from falling once more. Who will come after them? Who will save us in the next period of descent?

"With thoughts such as these," the Holy Jew concluded, "is it possible to sleep in peace?"

THEIR VOICE IS HEARD

General Zuritz was placed in charge of the region of Sokolov by the empress Catherine the Second. Zuritz was faithful to her, but was an enemy and adversary of the Jews. He was a corrupt ruler, and occasionally brought false libels against the Jews of Sokolov. In order to protect the Jews, Rabbi Yehoshua Tzeitels, the rabbi of the area, would have to bribe Zuritz, often taking the sums from his own pocket.

Zuritz ruled over the Jews in Sokolov with anger and hate. At the advice of Rabbi Yehoshua Tzeitels the leaders of the Jewish community brought a complaint to Catherine regarding Zuritz's harsh and unfair treatment of them, and requested her help.

Empress Catherine sent the head of her army, her beloved prince Potemkin, to Sokolov to investigate the matter. Rabbi Yehoshua Tzeitels, who knew Russian perfectly, appeared before him and with eloquent pleas, spoken with great pride, laid out the entire picture of the punishment and difficulties that Zuritz had foisted upon the Jews of Sokolov.

Out of his sincere and pure heart he expressed his strong feelings with great passion, and out of the depth of pain and anguish from the oppression and violence caused by this wicked adversary of the Jews, Rabbi Yehoshua wailed, screamed and began to cry.

"Why are you screaming?" asked Potemkin. "Speak softly."

"It is not I who am screaming," answered Rabbi Yehoshua. "It is the thousands of pitiful families of the Jews of Sokolov who are screaming through my throat."

Rabbi Yehoshua Tzeitels spoke at length about the situation of the Jews, and how they were capable with their energy and talent to bring great blessings to the entire government of Russia.

The speech, both in its style and content, made a strong impression on Potemkin. On the basis of the report he presented to the empress Catherine the rights of the Jews in Russia were expanded, and the situation of the Jews of Sokolov found great relief.

BETTER THAN US

After the death of the Seer of Lublin, Rabbi Naftali of Ropschitz said to his friend Rabbi Meir of Apta, "I see that in the Hasidic community chaos reigns, and different sects are splitting off. Therefore, in my opinion each person should be on his own. Everyone should sit in his own home, studying and worshipping God according to his ability, and no longer travel to the leading righteous men of the generation."

Rabbi Meir replied, "But I say: 'Tell the people of Israel to go forward [to travel]' (Exodus 14:15). You, my honorable rabbi, need not worry about the Blessed Holy One. If we are not capable of leading the congregation, others who are better than we are will be the leaders."

DON'T PRETEND

After speaking with some of his students, Rabbi Dov Ber of Mezritch discovered that the community's leaders were guilty of arrogance. Distributors of the community's charity took pride in the fact that all the indigent people in the region were under their control. When the rabbi heard this he related the following parable:

"A child is riding on a stick, galloping along and having fun, as if it really were a horse. From outward appearances the horse leads the rider, and not the opposite. But the stick does not move and lead; rather the opposite is the case, the child directs it. Nevertheless the child makes haste and runs and urges the horse with loud noises and blasts of victory. His father, too, who has great satisfaction from his child's fun, helps him, and when he is asked by his child to give him his stick, he gives it to him gladly in order to fulfill the wishes of his heart.

"So it is with these leaders and charity collectors, who ride the horse of authority, and appear to themselves as community leaders. They are riding on a stick given to them by the Blessed Holy One to play with it. About them it is written: 'God in Heaven laughs' (Psalms 2:4). God laughs at their games, as if to say: 'Let the children play.'"

WHO IS TRULY GREAT?

Rabbi Yisrael Salanter had no desire for gain or honor, he had little by way of possessions and worldly goods, and he did not hesitate from ethical behavior, even at the cost of offending the distinguished and wealthy.

It is told that once a wealthy Hasid came to him. Rabbi Yisrael greeted him kindly and began to instruct him in the ways of *musar*, as was his custom. When the Hasid left, he gave Rabbi Salanter one hundred rubles, which was considered a great deal of money.

"What is the reason for this gift?" Rabbi Yisrael asked.

"This is our custom among the Hasidim," the Hasid replied. "One who learns Torah from a tzaddik gives him a gift, so that the teacher will pray for him."

Rabbi Yisrael was taken aback. "With you a tzaddik is one who puts out his hand and takes money. But I think a tzaddik is one who puts out his hand and gives money. I request, therefore, from you, that you pray for mercy for me in your prayers."

SACRED LABOR

Rabbi Yitzhak of Vorka felt the problems of each individual, even regarding mundane matters. He was together with them in their sorrow – the pain of each individual became his personal pain. A drop in income, a troublesome child, a daughter for whom a suitable match had not been found, a woman who was ill and the doctors could not cure her, a cow in the barn that stopped giving milk – all of these were brought before Rabbi Yitzhak. His ear captured the sigh of every Jew in distress. The echoes of their sighs plucked the strings of his heart just like the light winds sway the tops of the trees in the forest.

Rabbi Yitzhak was an outstanding scholar and a person of great substance. He became a leader of all the ordinary and simple Jews. Merchants, salespeople, and laborers all poured out their daily worries to him. Rabbi Yitzhak listened to everyone, comforting them and imparting wise advice. He came down from the heights of his elevated philosophy in order to be of assistance to the simple Jew in his hour of need.

There was one verse in the Torah that stood him in good stead and smoothed his path: In dealing with the service of the Kohen in the Beit Hamikdash it is written, "He removed his clothing, and put on different clothing" (Leviticus 6:4). Even when the chosen leader of the people entered the inner sanctum, it was his duty not to forget the physical needs of the people.

It was his duty to remove his spiritual, Kohen-like garb, and don his everyday attire, attending to the humdrum needs of his people and praying for their welfare.

A HOOK ON THE WALL

Rabbi Moshe of Kovrin taught: "Let no leader think that the Blessed Holy One chose him because of his greatness, or because he is more worthy than others. Thus, even when a king of flesh and blood hangs his crown on a simple wooden hook, does the hook take great pride in that? Every leader must know that he is no more than a simple hook on which the king hangs his crown."

WHAT I LEARNED FROM MY TEACHER

Rabbi Avraham Baharan, who established an outstanding school for girls in Israel, reminisced on what made him decide to devote his life to Jewish education:

> It happened in my earth youth, when I was a student in the Etz Hayyim Talmud Torah. The study days in the Talmud Torah were very long, lasting until early evening. To keep us from getting hungry the teachers, during the afternoon, would give each student a dish with some cakes. When the child would finish eating, it was permissible to receive an additional portion.
>
> One day I received my portion and began to eat it. I was very hungry, and I was afraid that by the time I finished eating, the cakes would be all gone, so I went to the baker and asked for my additional portion. She answered, "But you already received your portion." I was very young, and in my anger I upset the small plate of cakes and they spilled on the floor. Naturally a big commotion broke out, and I didn't know what to do or where to go.
>
> The next day they told me that the spiritual director of the Talmud Torah, the tzaddik Rabbi Aryeh Levin, wanted to see me. I was fearful

> of such a meeting, and I was certain that he would chastise me, as I deserved.
>
> When I entered his office – a small room under the staircase in the Talmud Torah – he sat me down next to him and said to me, "I heard what happened with you last evening, and it sounds to me that you love to eat cakes. Here is a plate of them. Sit and eat to your heart's content, as much as you want."

At that moment I said to myself, "I just received a lesson in education. When I grow up, if God permits me, I want to be a Jewish educator."

FIND YOURSELF A RABBI

Rabbi Hayyim Klein, the director of the chief rabbinate in Jerusalem, visited the Lubavitcher Rebbe, Rabbi Menahem Mendel Schneerson. The rabbi asked him, "Who is the rabbi of your synagogue?"

Rabbi Klein answered, "We have no regular rabbi in our synagogue."

The Rebbe replied, "Take my advice, and go on Shabbat evenings with your young son to any synagogue, wherever you wish, as long as the synagogue has a permanent rabbi. One should accustom a young child, at the conclusion of the worship, to approach the rabbi, and wish him 'Shabbat Shalom!' and in return to expect a blessing from the rabbi."

WORDS OF WISDOM

PROPHECY

The prophet sees the future, and the rabbi sees the present. Sometimes it is more difficult to see the present than it is to see the future.

Rabbi Naftali of Ropschitz

HIDDEN FAULTS

Faults that are visible to the eye – in those I have no interest. Anybody can recognize these. You don't need to be a rabbi for that.

I try to uncover the imperfections that are hidden from human eyes – the blemishes that are not easily seen.

Rabbi Simhah Bunim of Peshischa

LEADERSHIP QUALITIES

Even a wagon driver can be considered a "leader." But *oy vay* to the driver if the horses run wild and take charge of the wagon.

Rabbi Menahem Mendel of Kotzk

Repentance and Regret

I WAS YOUNG, AND I HAVE AGED

Rabbi Yitzhak Blazer, among the earliest members of the *musar* movement, was invited by a group of young scholars to teach them about ethics and spirituality.

Rabbi Blazer ascended the platform, draped himself in his *tallit*, as was his custom, and began his speech with a story passed down by Rabbi Hayyim of Zanz.

> A man was lost in the forest for several days, and could not determine which was the correct path. Suddenly he saw another person walking toward him. He rejoiced greatly, thinking, "Now surely I will find the right path."
>
> When the two men met, the first asked, "My brother, please tell me which is the right path; I have been lost for several days." The other man said to him, "My brother, I do not know, since I too have been lost for several days. But one thing I will tell you: the way that I went you should not go, because that way you will get lost again. Now come let us search together for a new way."

Then Rabbi Blazer continued in an animated tone. "My students! You are young men, lost in the ways of life only a short while. But I am old and getting on in years, and my whole life I have been lost, searching for a path to get out of the confusions of life. How can I resist chasing after my urges? How can I improve my character?

"So before I rise to the correct path, how can I show you the path?" With this he broke out in tears, and the young men joined him in his sadness and tears.

"TAKE WORDS WITH YOU" (HOSEA 14:3)

A certain Hasid came to Rabbi Hayyim of Zanz with this problem: he was unable to repent, since he saw himself as inept and hopeless due to his past failures. Then he started to cry bitterly.

Rabbi Hayyim comforted him: "Don't take it to heart. The anguish of being unable to repent is also repentance."

MY PERSONAL GROWTH EXPERIENCE

Rabbi Levi Yitzhak of Berditchev taught: "When I realized that my community was not paying attention to me, I began to examine my deeds. I sat and realized that even my own household did not honor me. I examined my actions once more, and the Blessed Holy One opened my eyes and I understood that the fault was mine, since I was not acting appropriately.

"I attempted to improve myself. When my family saw what I was doing they began to obey me, and, of course, even the members of my community stopped disobeying me, and no longer refused to accept my opinion."

PEACE OF MIND

Rabbi Zusha of Anapol was wont to quote a verse from the Book of Psalms: "You return us to dust; You decreed, 'Return you mortals!'" (Psalms 90:3). He would interpret the verse as follows: "King David lamented before the Master of the Universe, 'You return us to dust.' You bring people down to the dust, You crush them, the poor souls, to dust. But at the same time, 'You decreed, "Return you mortals!"' – You require from us that we repent.

"How can one repent in such a situation? First of all, Master of the Universe, furnish the people of Israel with their needs, and then their minds will be tranquil and prepared to consider thoughts of repentance."

I AM CHASTISING MYSELF

The well-known preacher Rabbi Yehudah of Satmar tended to rebuke his audience harshly. One day he delivered a sermon that burned with fire. In the middle, he suddenly stopped, thought to himself for a moment, and turned to the congregation. "Do not think, my friends, that everything I am saying is to you. To tell you the truth, I am directing my words to myself, but since it's likely that you may benefit, I speak to myself in a loud voice, so that you too should listen to what I say to myself."

YOUR WORDS ARE NOT IN VAIN

A certain maggid complained to the Hafetz Hayyim, Rabbi Yisrael Meir Hakohen Kagan, "I teach *musar* to large crowds, but I do not sense that anyone is aroused to repent. If that is the case, then my words are in vain."

The Hafetz Hayyim answered him, "Even if only one of the listeners is stimulated to repent as a result of your words, and even if that person is you yourself, your words are not wasted."

GOD KEEPS FORGIVING

A certain baal teshuvah cried before Rabbi Yisrael of Rizhin: "There is no hope for me. I have been focusing on repentance for a long time, and yet I have just sinned again."

"Do not despair," answered Rabbi Yisrael. "Just as it is the custom of people to keep on sinning, so it is the custom of the Blessed Holy One to keep on forgiving."

GOD, GRANT ME A NEW HEART

Rabbi David of Lalov studied and prayed for many years. He fasted and undertook difficult ascetic practices. After that he fasted from Sunday to Friday for six more years, and despite all this he was still troubled that he had not attained perfection of the soul.

During this period of time Rabbi Elimelekh of Lizhensk became well known as a great tzaddik and healer of souls, so Rabbi David traveled to Lizhensk to see him.

On Friday afternoon, Rabbi David went with other Hasidim to the home of Rabbi Elimelekh to bring greetings. When Rabbi Elimelekh glanced at Rabbi David, he refused to welcome him, and even turned his face toward the wall away from him.

Rabbi David left the house with a broken heart, and returned to the inn where he was lodging. He walked to and fro, buried in thought. He was deeply disturbed, wondering what sin he might have committed to make Rabbi Elimelekh push him away and embarrass him.

The innkeeper noticed that he was blanketed in great pain and asked him what was troubling him. Rabbi David told him all about it. The innkeeper comforted him, suggesting that perhaps it was all due to a misunderstanding. He advised him to go to the beit midrash and stand praying in the corner, and after the prayers, before Kiddush, he should approach Rabbi Elimelekh, extend his hand to him and greet him with "*Shalom Aleikhem*!" Then perhaps Rabbi Elimelekh would reply in kind.

Rabbi David followed his advice. He stood in the corner praying. Because of the extreme enthusiasm in his prayers, he began to roam around the room, hither and thither, praying loudly with deep devotion. After the prayers he approached Rabbi Elimelekh to extend his hand in greeting. Rabbi Elimelekh rebuffed him again. "What is this frightened man doing here near me? I don't like frightened people."

Rabbi David returned to the inn with a broken heart, and cried bitterly. All night long he could not fall asleep. He concluded that Rabbi Elimelekh would not agree to see him, and he therefore decided to leave Lizhensk at the end of Shabbat. However as the time of the third meal of Shabbat approached, he decided to go to the beit midrash and try once more. During the meal Rabbi Elimelekh spoke some words of Torah with great enthusiasm, and then turned to the following subject: "There are some young men who come to me from long distances, who involve themselves in study of Torah, prayer, fasting, and harsh methods of asceticism for long periods of time. After all this difficult labor they see themselves as worthy of having the *Shekhinah* surround them. Then they come to me to ask me to help them overcome their small failures, and extend a hand to bring them closer to the holy spirit.

"But they deceive themselves. They have still not reached even the beginning of the service of the Creator, and of true fear of Heaven. And because they fooled themselves in believing that they have already done a great deal of Torah study and prayer, they have come to a high level of arrogance. It is a sign that they have selfish designs. All such designs have a rotten odor."

When Rabbi David heard this his heart was much shaken, and a great fear smothered him, lest perhaps he had plummeted to a very low level of disgrace and dishonor to which there was no way of repairing his soul. He went to be alone in a dark corner of the beit midrash, where he broke down in tears.

At that moment he decided to go to Rabbi Elimelekh's after Havdalah, and plead with him not to rebuff him again, but rather to show him the path to repentance.

After Havdalah Rabbi David approached the door of Rabbi Elimelekh, and opened it very slowly. When Rabbi Elimelekh saw him he got up from his chair and went to greet him, smiling warmly. "Welcome, Rabbi David, light of my eyes and joy of my heart!" Rabbi Elimelekh offered him a seat, treated him with great affection, and spoke to him with great love.

Rabbi David asked Rabbi Elimelekh, "Am I not the man whom you chased away twice?"

Rabbi Elimelekh replied, "You are not the same person. You are a completely different person. You are David, the light of my eyes."

WORDS OF WISDOM

GOOD TIMES AND BAD TIMES

Many people scrutinize their deeds, and want to know why they suffer. However, I never saw anyone scrutinize his deeds to find out why his profits and wealth increased.

Rabbi Eliyahu of Viskit

The Rewards of Dancing

DEVEIKUT – CLINGING TO GOD

The followers of the Baal Shem Tov once came into his home and began dancing joyously.

One of the group would from time to time go down into the basement of the house and bring up several pitchers of wine. The wife of the Besht came into her husband's room and said to him, "There will not be any wine left for Kiddush or Havdalah. You had better tell them to stop."

The Besht stood without moving, a smile spreading over his face. "You are right – you have spoken the truth. But why don't you go and tell them that it's enough dancing for today, and that they should all go home."

His wife girded her strength and approached the room where the Hasidim were dancing. But when she opened the door and saw them in a frenzy of dance, it was as if they were hovering between Heaven and earth. She instinctively went down into the basement and brought up another pitcher of wine to heighten the joy. All night long the dancing in the house did not stop and the singing did not cease.

The next day the Besht asked his wife, "The Hasidim danced all night long – why didn't you tell them to stop?"

"I couldn't," she said. "Dancing in a group in this way enabled their hearts to commune with each other. Open hearts lead to open doors, and the clinging of friends to each other leads to the clinging to the Creator."

LOSS OF FEELING

Rabbi Hayyim of Kosov's custom was to dance every Shabbat eve with his congregation of Hasidim. He danced with enormous enthusiasm.

Once his foot was hurt and for a while he did not dance on Shabbat evenings. Not many weeks passed and Rabbi Hayyim started again to dance with great enthusiasm.

Rabbi Hayyim explained, "It was not because I felt my feet that I stopped dancing, it was because I stopped dancing that I felt my feet."

THE MERIT OF DANCING WILL STAND US IN GOOD STEAD

One Friday afternoon a villager came to the home of Rabbi Elimelekh of Lizhensk, and poured out his heart, telling him that he had a daughter who was now grown, but he had no dowry with which to marry her off. Rabbi Elimelekh ordered the young woman to come to him immediately. He arranged a marriage for her with the son of a water carrier in the city, gave her a dowry, and organized the wedding.

The Maggid of Koznitz played the violin, the rabbi of Lublin was the comedian, and many family members and guests came to dance with the young couple.

Rabbi Elimelekh remarked to his guest Rabbi Shmuel ben Avraham Yeshaya of Karov, "Look how there is a fire blazing all around." Even Rabbi Elimelekh himself danced with them, and explained that the two Hebrew words "*hesed ve'emet* (kindness and truth)" are numerically equivalent to "*hatan ve-khalah* (bride and groom)."

Then Rabbi Elimelekh turned to God and said, "Master of the Universe, as a reward for the mitzvah of dancing that we have fulfilled, may we merit extinguishing at least one hot coal waiting for us in Gehinnom?"

CELEBRATING TOGETHER

Rabbi Avraham Grodzhinski, the spiritual director of the Yeshivah of Slobodka in Lithuania, was traveling, and he stopped one night at an inn. In the middle of the night the gentile innkeeper heard noises of dancing from the room of the Jew. He assumed that his guest had been drinking wine and had become drunk.

The next morning the innkeeper called Rabbi Avraham Grodzhinski over and asked him, "What is its name?"

"What name are you interested in knowing?" asked the rabbi.

"The name and brand of the wine that you were drinking last evening, when you became drunk and started to dance."

The rabbi replied, "I am a teacher of Torah and ethics in the academy of Slobodka. Last night one of the important students in the academy got married, and because it was not possible for me to participate in the joy of the wedding, I started to dance alone, in my room, in order to participate in this happy occasion."

Shabbat and Festivals

HAPPY IS THE ONE WHO HAS NEW LEARNING

The holy Zohar states, "Come and see, when Shabbat arrives all souls rise before the Holy Sovereign, and the Blessed Holy One asks them, 'What new interpretation in the Torah did you construct in the lower world?'

"Happy is the soul that recites before the Holy One new interpretations in the Torah. So much joy is given to God. God gathers the celestial family and says, 'Listen to these new ideas that this soul brought!'" (Parashat Tzav 29a).

NO MOURNING ON SHABBAT

In the year 1798 the father of the Holy Jew of Peshischa passed away. The funeral took place Friday afternoon close to Shabbat. Naturally the entire city came in honor of the Holy Jew.

On Shabbat the synagogue was packed. To the great surprise of all the congregants, the Holy Jew behaved on that Shabbat, the first day after the death of his father, just like every other Shabbat in the year. His face glowed with the true joy of Shabbat. He delivered words of Torah before all the Hasidim, and acted as if nothing had happened. The matter upset the leaders of the city, who thought that the Holy Jew was paying no attention to the fact that his father had just died. At the third Shabbat meal, the hour of great desire, again all the city's Hasidim gathered, and even then the Holy Jew's joy did not cease.

On Saturday night, at the end of the Shabbat, immediately after they had recited Havdalah, the Holy Jew fell from his chair to the ground and began to mourn the death of his father with heartwrenching sobs, even pulling the hair from his head. All the words of comfort of the city's rabbinic leaders did not help. He lay on the ground for many hours and cried bitter tears.

Then the people recognized the strength of spirit that the Holy Jew had shown. All Shabbat long he had restrained his terrible grief, and only after they recited Havdalah did he permit his grief to burst out.

WAIT JUST A BIT

Rabbi Shalom Rokeach of Belz would preach to each person according to his ability and his attitude. Once a villager came to him to receive a blessing. Rabbi Shalom began to talk with him, and asked him if he kept all the laws of Shabbat. The villager started to stutter, and finally admitted that to his great sorrow he did not keep Shabbat strictly. He did his labor in the field and in the vineyard on Shabbat. Rabbi Shalom began to chastise him, explaining the seriousness of his sin and the punishment for violating Shabbat. The words of the master of Belz entered the heart of the villager, who then began to cry.

"I promise you, holy rabbi, that from now on I will be very careful to observe Shabbat with all its rules, but in the season of the harvest, when the work in the field is extremely heavy, I will be forced to work even on Shabbat, and I hope that the honorable rabbi will forgive me for this."

A light smile crossed over the face of the Belzer Rebbe. "First of all, you should know that I am not in charge of Shabbat. Only the Blessed Holy One, in all His glory and honor, is such. And I do not believe that God is prepared to forgive you for the sin of desecrating Shabbat during the season of the harvest. Let me tell you a story:

> One nobleman made a great feast for all the noblemen of the area. After they had drunk quite a bit, each one began to tell the praises of his special "Jew." The host told about his Jewish tax collector who was the very, very best. "I tested him in several ways and he passed all the tests, and I am certain that he would never do anything against my will."
>
> "Even," interrupted one of the noblemen, "to convert from his religion?"
>
> "Yes," answered the host. "I am certain that even in this matter he would accommodate me."

He immediately sent for the Jewish tax collector and asked him, "Are you faithful to me?"

"Yes, my lord," answered the Jewish tax collector, "with all my heart and soul. I am fully prepared to go through fire and water for you."

"In that case," said the nobleman, "I want you to convert to my religion." The tax collector shook with anguish, but after the nobleman repeated his request several times, the Jew agreed to his request, and the nobleman ushered him into his faith.

After a while, the nobleman invited him to come to him, and said, "Now that you have fulfilled my will to change your religion, surely your conscience is bothering you a great deal, so I hereby permit you to return to the religion of your ancestors, the Jewish religion."

"My lord," answered the tax collector, "let me go consult with my wife about this." When his wife heard the suggestion of the nobleman, she was upset and called out in anguish, "*Oy*! In a few days it will be Pesah, and the expenses of the holiday are so great – matzot, wine, special dishes... Run to the nobleman and ask him if he will let you keep this religion and let us remain gentiles until after Pesah."

The master of Belz concluded, "Desecrating Shabbat in public is like converting from your religion, and you apparently want to follow in the path of that woman and permit yourself to violate Shabbat during the period of the harvest."

The words entered the heart of the villager. After a brief struggle within himself he promised Rabbi Shalom to observe Shabbat all year long, including during harvest time.

HONORING SHABBAT

Every Thursday Rabbi Yehudah Leib of Premislan prepared all his needs for Shabbat himself. Not his messenger, not even his wife, but he himself took his basket and went from store to store in the market, choosing the very best for the Shabbat table.

The mitzvah of Shabbat was so precious and dear to Rabbi Yehudah Leib that even when Yom Kippur fell on Shabbat it is told of him that he prepared all the needs of Shabbat – missing nothing – he set the table just so, with meat, fish, and wine, and after the chanting of Kol Nidre, when he returned home from synagogue, he sat down to a full table with all the special foods, and said, "It is well known before you, Master of the Universe, that I love Shabbat, and value Shabbat, and I am fully prepared to honor Shabbat with food and drink, just as we are commanded by you from olden days; but what can I do, my dear Father, if you commanded upon us on the day of this Shabbaton to fast? If it is acceptable to you, my Father, even Yehudah Leib, against his will, will accede and deny himself all the normal foods in honor of the holy Yom Kippur."

WHAT COMES FROM THE HEART ENTERS THE HEART

Rabbi Yisrael Meir Hakohen, author of the *Hafetz Hayyim*, once heard that the son of one of his friends opened a brickmaking factory in the city that remained open on Shabbat. Apparently it was not realistic to turn off the furnace, since if one puts out the fire for Shabbat, the heat dissipates and it is impossible to work there even on Sunday and Monday, until the furnace heats up sufficiently.

The first opportunity that the Hafetz Hayyim had to visit that city he visited the factory and asked to meet with the owner. The Hafetz Hayyim said to him, "I knew your father, of blessed memory. I was at his wedding, and I was also at your brit milah (circumcision ceremony). I am a very old man, and when I come to the World of Truth, your father will surely ask me about your welfare. What can I say to him? You tell me," asked the Hafetz Hayyim, as he cried bitterly. "Shall I tell him that you are working on Shabbat? Can I cause such terrible pain to your father?"

This man was not accustomed to stand before the tears of the Hafetz Hayyim, and immediately promised to get rid of the business.

Rabbi Aharon Baksht, who was present at the meeting, said, "To this day every bone in my body shakes when I recall how the Hafetz Hayyim cried."

When Rabbi Yehezkel Levenshtein, the spiritual director of the Yeshivah of Ponevitch, heard the story of this event, he said, "Very likely I too would have broken out in tears, but this kind of crying, that enters the heart of another and influences him to such an extent, would only result from the tears of the pure and broken heart of the Hafetz Hayyim."

THE KADDISH OF RABBI LEVI YITZHAK OF BERDITCHEV

Every day of the year Rabbi Levi Yitzhak of Berditchev presented his arguments for the household of Israel before the Creator. But more than any other time he did so during the Days of Awe, when every Jew is commanded to ask forgiveness of the Creator for the sins he committed. Especially on those days of judgment Rabbi Levi Yitzhak chose to bring the complaints of the people of Israel to the heavens, to argue with all his might for the welfare of his people.

Rabbi Levi Yitzhak was blessed with a sweet voice, and he himself led the congregation in prayer during the Days of Awe. Once, before Musaf on Yom Kippur, Rabbi Levi Yitzhak stood with bent knee before the rostrum next to the holy ark, when his whole body shook with fear before the awesome Creator, the Glory of Israel.

Rabbi Levi Yitzhak stood there for a full hour, as the congregation stood tense, wrapped in their *tallitot*, waiting with bated breath for their rabbi to begin the recitation of the Kaddish. But the rabbi was silent. With a torn heart and trembling knees, he stood with thoughts of regret for the sins that he had committed before his Maker all year long.

The silence was broken as Rabbi Levi Yitzhak whispered the traditional words of prayer: "I have come to stand and plead before You for Your people Israel who have sent me."

Suddenly the rabbi stood up and began to recite his Kaddish, whose words and melody the tzaddik composed at that very moment.

> Good morning to You, Master of the Universe. I, Levi Yitzhak son of Sarah of Berditchev, have come to stand before You in prayer, in supplication, and in protest.

Tell me, Master of the Universe, what is Your complaint with the people of Israel? Why have You imposed Yourself especially on Your people Israel?

In Your Torah You wrote "Speak." To whom are You speaking? To the people of Israel!

In Your Torah You wrote, "Say." To whom are You saying? Only to the people of Israel!

In Your Torah you wrote, "Command." To whom are You commanding? Again to the people of Israel.

Merciful and gracious Father, what do You want from the people of Israel? There are so many nations in the world: Babylonians, Persians, Ishmaelites, and Midianites – so what do you want especially from the people of Israel?

Because the people of Israel are precious to You, they are called "Children of the Almighty." So I ask you, Master of the Universe, is this how You treat Your children?

Master of the Universe, look: the English, what do they say? Their King is the greatest and strongest of all kings.

The French, what do they say? That their leader rules the world.

The Russians, what do they say? Their Czar is the greatest of all Czars.

And the Turks? Their Sultan is the ruler of all.

But I, Levi Yitzhak son of Sarah, I say: "*Yitgadal veyitkadash shmei rabba!* (Magnified and sanctified is God's great name!)"

I will not leave here. I will not move from my place. From my place I shall not move until there will be an end to the exile. Until the final days come, when Messiah arrives. Until all peoples know this truth: *Yitgadal veyitkadash shmei rabba!*

EXPLORATIONS OF THE HEART

A certain Jew stayed with Rabbi Yitzhak of Nadvorna. Just before Rosh Hashanah he came to his host to ask permission to part. The tzaddik asked him, "What is your hurry?"

He answered, "I have been appointed to lead the congregation in prayer, and I must look over the Mahzor (high-holiday prayer book) and put my prayers in order."

The rabbi said to him, "The Mahzor is the same as it was last year. Better that you should look over your deeds and put them in order."

"THE WHOLE ISRAELITE COMMUNITY SHALL BE FORGIVEN" (NUMBERS 15:26)

When Yom Kippur arrived, Rabbi Yisrael Haupstein, the Maggid of Koznitz, would get out of bed despite his ill health, muster all his strength, and stand at the rostrum to lead the congregation in prayer – not once, but for all five of the Yom Kippur services.

The story is told that one Yom Kippur eve he was particularly weak, and when he reached the verse "And God said, I pardon, as you have asked" (Numbers 14:20), he had to pause in his prayers because of his weakness. He lifted his eyes to Heaven and said, "Master of the Universe! You alone know my weakness and my frailty, and only You know Your strength and might. Now please listen: I, Yisrael, the son of Shabtai, am ill and weakened. I have mustered all my strength, I have prayed, I have recited all the prayers and entreaties for the welfare of Your people, Your beloved children. Is it so difficult for You, O mighty One of Power and Champion of Strength, to pronounce for their sake only these few words: 'I pardon, as you have asked'?"

BLESS GOD, MY SOUL

Rabbi Menahem Mendel of Kotzk was enjoying the fruits of Eretz Yisrael at a celebration in honor of Tu biShvat, the festival of the trees. He asked his student Rabbi Yitzhak Meir to present some ideas about the holiday. Rabbi Yitzhak Meir delivered some remarks from the Talmud about the new year of the trees, and there was intensive discussion back and forth.

Rabbi Menahem Mendel then commented, "Were we in Eretz Yisrael, it would be sufficient for us to go outside in the field and gaze at the trees in order to understand what the New Year of the Trees is all about."

COUNTING IT UP

During the first year that Rabbi Avraham Yehoshua Heschel of Apt became rabbi in Iasi, Romania, the people of the city sent him *mishloah manot* (a Purim gift) of golden dinarim on Purim day. The tzaddik took the dinarim and counted them one by one, with much joy. His son, Rabbi Yitzhak Meir, was greatly surprised, because he knew that his father abhorred greed and always rejected gifts of money. He turned to his father and asked, "Father, have you changed your attitude toward money?"

The tzaddik replied, "All year long I scorn money, and it is deemed in my eyes to be worthless. But since on Purim day it is a mitzvah to give money to the poor, and it turns out that I can give them only what I consider to be worthless, I have thus redirected my heart to appreciate money, and when my love of money rises sufficiently, only then can I distribute it to the poor."

TAKE CARE TO BE RESPECTFUL

Rabbi Yisrael Salanter was very careful in guarding the wheat and flour for the baking of matzah for Pesah, from the time it was harvested until it was baked. So much so that sometimes it cost him a great deal of money, depending on the circumstances. He explained, "The mitzvah of *matzah shmurah* (matzah that is carefully watched through all steps of its preparation) is no less important than having a very beautiful etrog for Sukkot, for which we are prepared to spend quite a lot of money."

Rabbi Salanter would himself stand near those who were engaged in the baking of his matzah, supervising with a careful eye the kneading, the rolling of the dough and its baking, so that everything would be exactly according to Jewish law in all its details.

After the completion of the baking of the matzot, when he would pay the baker his wage for the difficult work of baking, he would also give a generous sum to each person involved in the work. He did all this quietly and secretly.

It happened once, before Pesah, that Rabbi Yisrael was ill, and could not go to personally supervise the baking of his matzah. He requested that several of his prime students go in his stead. Before they went they asked him, "Tell us, Rabbi, is there any matter about which we should be particularly careful?"

"Yes," he said. "Be especially careful with the honor of the woman who kneads the dough – not to shout at her, and not to trouble or embarrass her, since the poor woman is a widow."

SPIRITUAL READINESS

During a conversation between Rabbi Avraham Yitzhak Kook and Rabbi Yosef Hayyim Sonnenfeld, the latter commented, "I don't understand what merit these young pioneers have. They have thrown off the yoke of the Torah and mitzvot – how do they deserve true redemption?"

Rabbi Kook replied, "When the people of Israel left Egypt, the Blessed Holy One commanded them to offer the Paschal sacrifice, and due to the merit of this mitzvah they would deserve redemption. Later, when they stood at the shore of the Red Sea they showed their real readiness for commitment. One person declared, 'I will be the first to go into the sea,' and another person declared, 'No, I will be the first to go into the sea.'

"The answer came from Moses: 'God will battle for you; you hold your peace!' (Exodus 14:14). Their commitment alone was enough merit to be redeemed."

SHALOM BAYIT (DOMESTIC HARMONY)

Rabbi Raphael of Bershad always made great efforts to bring peace among people. It happened once that during Tishah b'Av he passed through a community where there was a bitter quarrel.

The leaders of the community requested of him that he make peace between the warring parties. "But," they added, "it is not fitting for the rabbi to get involved in such matters on a fast day."

"Just the opposite," answered the tzaddik. "What better day is there to be involved in bringing domestic harmony than the day on which the holy city of God was destroyed due to causeless hatred?"

WHO CAN BE COMPARED TO YOUR PEOPLE ISRAEL?

Once Rabbi Levi Yitzhak of Berditchev was walking through the streets of the city on Tishah b'Av. He noticed a Jewish man openly eating and drinking on this public fast day. He approached him and asked, "My son, surely you have forgotten that today is Tishah b'Av?"

"No, Rabbi," he answered. "I know that today is Tishah b'Av."

"Therefore," continued Rabbi Levi Yitzhak, "you must not be aware that on Tishah b'Av it is forbidden to eat and drink."

"No, Rabbi," insisted the man. "I know that today is a public fast day."

Rabbi Levi Yitzhak continued to find a way to help the man find an excuse. "Surely, then, you are not well, and fasting today would be harmful to your health."

"No, Rabbi, smiled the man. "I am healthy and strong – and may everyone be as healthy as I am."

Rabbi Levi Yitzhak lifted his eyes to Heaven and said, "Master of the Universe, look down from Heaven and see your wonderful people, Israel – such a holy people! Three times I gave him an opportunity to lie, and still he tells the truth!"

AN ETERNAL SIGN

One Shabbat morning, Rabbi Barukh Ber Levovitz, rosh yeshivah of Kamenetz in America, passed by a store owned by a Jew and noticed that it was locked and bolted. In America at that time this was no small achievement, as much of a store's income came from purchases by gentiles on Shabbat.

Rabbi Barukh Ber approached the lock, kissed it affectionately, and said to himself, "This lock announces: All must know that the Lord is God, and we the people of Israel are God's servants."

WORDS OF WISDOM

SHOFAR

There are some exceptional Jews who hear the sound of the shofar of Rosh Hashanah every day of the year.

Rabbi Levi Yitzhak of Berditchev

"ON THIS DAY ATONEMENT SHALL BE MADE FOR YOU.... OF ALL YOUR SINS BEFORE GOD SHALL YOU BE PURIFIED" (LEVITICUS 16:30)

It is true that the essence of Yom Kippur brings atonement. But to become purified, that one must do oneself.

Rabbi Yitzhak of Vorka

Sincerity

"GOD'S TORAH IS PERFECT [*TEMIMAH*]" (PSALMS 19:18)

A Hasid came to the Baal Shem Tov and asked him to pray for him to be successful. The Besht took a piece of parchment and wrote on it a few words. He folded up the parchment inside an amulet and handed it to the Hasid.

After many years the amulet was opened and inside was found the words of the biblical commentator Rashi on the verse in Deuteronomy, "You must be wholehearted [*tamim*] with the Lord your God" (Deuteronomy 18:13). On this Rashi commented: "Walk with God wholeheartedly, and trust God, and do not search after the future, but everything that comes upon you accept wholeheartedly, and then you will be with God."

WRITING A *SEFER TORAH*

The Baal Shem Tov told Rabbi Yaakov Yosef Hakohen of Polnoye: "I love the simplest person among my people with the deepest and most faithful love. Often the simplicity of an ordinary Jew draws me with mystical bonds, more so than the connection I feel to a scholar who is proud of his scholarship.

"I will give you an example that illustrates what I mean. Before I invited Rabbi Tzvi Sofer, who is a humble tzaddik and a Kabbalist, to my home, my soul longed to fulfill the mitzvah of writing a *Sefer Torah*. I informed my friends of this, and they began to send me a number of different scribes. I began to check them out, and every one boasted that he was an expert in the Kabbalah of the Holy Ari (Rabbi Yitzhak Luria), in the writing of the combinations and permutations of Divine names, etc. This boasting, even though it was not in vain, was not pleasing to me.

"One of these scribes was a modest person, humble in spirit, who behaved with integrity and uprightness. I asked him if he were an expert in the books of the Kabbalah, and if he knew how to have the proper intentionality in the writing of God's name, according to Jewish law. He answered in full honesty, 'I am an expert in the laws of the writing of a *Sefer Torah*, as they are laid out in the *Shulhan Arukh* (*Code of Jewish Law*). But I have never delved into the secrets of Kabbalah, or into the mysteries of the Divine names. When I write a *Sefer Torah* I have only one intention: I accept the fee for writing in order to provide for my wife and children.'

"A noble intention, pure and honest, and it pleased me greatly. So I invited this scribe to write a *Sefer Torah* for me."

AN INNOCENT MISTAKE

A Jew who lived in a village near Austria came to see Rabbi Pinhas of Koretz, and began to cry. The man was a simple fellow, but had deep religious fervor. When Rabbi Pinhas asked him why he was crying, the man told him this story:

"Every Yom Kippur I recite the litany of Al Het, listing before God all my sins with deep conviction, and I ask God's mercy to be forgiven for all my sins and failures during the past year. This year something happened to me in my village. A lion escaped from the forest near my village, and came into town. Naturally there was a great outcry and terrible confusion among the people of the village. We all closeted ourselves in our homes; we shut tight our windows and doors out of our terrible fear.

"I looked out of my window and saw several youths starting a huge fire, in order to frighten away the lion. And since I saw these youngsters endangering their lives for the sake of the people of the village, I too went out to help them make the fire cover as wide an area as possible, until it covered a large section of the village. Finally, the lion was frightened and fled, returning to the forest."

"So," said Rabbi Pinhas, "you should rejoice for taking upon yourself this great mitzvah of saving many lives from the jaws of the lion. Why are you crying?"

"But I remembered," replied the villager in his naiveté, "that in the list of sins in the Al Het prayer is one that says I am sorry for the sin of *gilui arayot*." [The meaning of *gilui arayot* in the liturgy is "the sin of sexual immorality." The villager was confusing *arayot*, spelled with an *ayin*, with its homonym meaning *lions*, spelled with an *alef*. He thus thought the prayer was a confession for exposure of lions, instead of its true meaning, "sexual immorality," or "exposure of nakedness."]

Continued the villager, "So how can I confess on next Yom Kippur that I regret exposing lions?"

The Hasidim near Rabbi Pinhas were on the verge of breaking out in laughter over the villager's ignorant interpretation of the liturgy. But when they noticed the seriousness on the face of their teacher, they restrained themselves. Rabbi Pinhas turned to the man, gave him moral encouragement and made him feel better.

The villager left the rabbi with inner joy. Once he was out of earshot the rabbi's students expressed their great surprise that he had not explained to the man what the words in the liturgy of Yom Kippur really mean.

"I will tell you a story," Rabbi Pinhas replied. "A simple Jew was reciting his prayers, including the central prayer, the Shema, out of deep conviction. He also made a naïve mistake in mixing up some letters of the Hebrew alphabet. Instead of ending the Shema sentence with the words "*Adonai ehad* (God is one)," he said instead "*Adonai aher* (God is other)," – confusing the Hebrew letter *dalet* for a *resh*, which closely resembles the *dalet*. He recited the prayer with intensity and enthusiasm.

"The matter came to the attention of the community's rabbi, who then chastised the man, declaring that it is forbidden in Jewish law to make this mistake because its meaning totally distorts the declaration of the unity of the Divine name.

"That night in a dream the rabbi was rebuked by God for confusing the mind of this simple Jew, since from that point on he would not recite the Shema with the same feeling with which he had become accustomed to say it until then."

GOD DESIRES THE HEART (TALMUD, TRACTATE SANHEDRIN 106B)

One time the Baal Shem Tov instructed his students to go to a certain village near Medziboz, and find there a simple village Jew. He told them that this Jew was one of the righteous of their generation.

They went there and found the man. He did not know a word of Torah, except the Hebrew alphabet. He would sit all day in the field, among the grass, and call out the letters – *alef*, *bet*, *gimmel*.... When he finished reciting the letters of the Hebrew alphabet he would say, "Dear God, Master of the Universe, You created the *Alef-Bet* and from it You put together all the words, all the prayers, all the words of praise and entreaty. I do not know how to praise You or to recite the proper prayers. My Father in Heaven, would You please join together all the letters of the *Alef-Bet* from these letters and form them into prayers and beautiful songs of praise, so much better than I possibly could."

When the students returned to the rabbi and related to him what happened, he told them, "Sometimes simple childish sincerity of an untutored Jew is more prized than the deep Torah knowledge and lengthy prayers of the leaders of the generation and the tzaddikim of the people, for often it is the simple words that are able to reach Heaven and close the mouths of those who malign us."

FAITHFUL SHEPHERD

Rabbi Moshe Leib of Sassov would tour throughout many Jewish communities. Once he was standing on a high mountaintop and heard in the distance a sweet melody of someone chanting the psalms. He followed the sound and found a Jewish shepherd reciting the Book of Psalms. At the end of his recitation the shepherd added his own private prayer: "May it be Your will, Master of the Universe, that just as I am a faithful shepherd to my sheep, will You please be the faithful Shepherd to Your flock, the people of Israel?"

Rabbi Moshe Leib said to him, "You should know, my dear friend, that there is a similar prayer in the siddur, which you should recite at the conclusion of your recitation of the psalms."

The shepherd promised that from then on he would follow Rabbi Moshe Leib's advice.

The rabbi went on his way, but after he had traveled a few miles he heard a heavenly voice calling out to him: "Go back to the shepherd and tell him to conclude his recitation of the psalms with his own personal prayer, which is as important in the eyes of God as the songs of King David."

Rabbi Moshe Leib returned and persuaded the shepherd to return to the recitation of his own personal prayer.

SONG AND PRAISE TO GOD

In Okup, Podolia, lived a wealthy Jew named Rabbi Yoel. This Rabbi Yoel was an excellent scholar and fastidious in performing the mitzvot. For a long time he wanted to fulfill the law in the *Shulhan Arukh* (*Code of Jewish Law*), which states that 'it is a Torah command for each Jew to write for oneself a *Sefer Torah*' (*Shulhan Arukh*, Yoreh Deah, paragraph 270, section 1).

What did he do? He bought a cow, distributed the meat among the poor, and gave instructions for the skin to be prepared for parchment in order to have a beautiful *Sefer Torah* written. He brought a scribe, who was a reverent person, to the city, and hosted him in his home for several months. Every day the scribe entered the mikveh to purify himself, until he concluded his holy work.

Once the writing of the *Sefer Torah* was completed, the wealthy man prepared a fancy *seudat mitzvah* (meal in honor of a mitzvah), as Jewish law requires – "one makes a meal at the conclusion of writing a new *Sefer Torah*."

He invited to the feast all the leaders of the city – the rabbis and judges, the ritual slaughterers, the *hazzanim* (leaders of prayer), the wealthy people and leaders of the community, and he himself, the affluent Rabbi Yoel, being an advanced scholar, isolated himself for several days in his library and prepared a sermon that he intended to deliver at the feast, before the scholars of the city.

A certain water carrier in the city named Berl was not among those invited. His lot was not among the group of spiritual leaders, and certainly not among the wealthy. He was a simple person, among all the laborers and wagon drivers who would rise early and go to the house of prayer of the Hevre Tehillim (those who daily recite psalms), and before sunrise would chant aloud several chapters of the psalms of David, verse after verse, and only afterwards would they go to work to earn a living for their household.

When Berl heard that there was a *seudat mitzvah* at the home of the wealthy Rabbi Yoel in honor of a new *Sefer Torah*, he assumed in his naiveté that every Jew who loved Torah could participate in this Torah celebration. He dressed in his faded and tattered Shabbat clothing, combed his beard, and went to the home of the prosperous gentleman, where he found a seat among the invited guests.

When Rabbi Yoel saw Berl the water carrier in a seat set aside for scholars, he became angry and called out, "Just because he recites many psalms he considers himself a special and important person?" Berl took the hint, got up, and found himself a different seat elsewhere.

The feast was as one would expect. Silver candelabras and wine cups, bright candles shining, braided hallot, wine and liquor, and musicians with violins and drums. Those at the party rejoiced at the celebration of a newly dedicated Torah, and people danced all around the *Sefer Torah*, while Rabbi Yoel himself sang and danced in honor of the Torah.

When the party was over and the last guests had returned to their homes, Rabbi Yoel lay down on his bed with joy and satisfaction. Thank God his talk had gone over well. His Talmudic discourse had been delivered flawlessly, and the city's scholars had been quite pleased with his new interpretations. With a feeling of pleasure and contentment Rabbi Yoel closed his eyes and fell asleep.

However, the angel of dreams visited his bed that night. And in his dream a powerful storm arose with large waves, uprooted him from his bed and carried him to faraway places. He found himself alone in a barren desert. Suddenly he saw a house all lit up. He entered the house and saw before him a table, around which were people dressed as judges. He heard the chief judge call out his name and inform him that he had been called to a *din Torah* (a court hearing). The complainant was King David, the faithful shepherd himself.

King David stood up and said, "I accuse you, Rabbi Yoel, of discrediting my Book of Psalms, and of embarrassing Berl the water carrier." Next, the chief prosecutor arose and demanded from the court a harsh punishment: not to return Rabbi Yoel's soul to his body.

Next arose the defense attorney – the Baal Shem Tov himself – and requested that Rabbi Yoel's soul be returned to the world below, with the argument that if he did not return to his former place, no one would know the benefits of the recitation of the psalms.

Thus, the heavenly court accepted the argument of the Baal Shem Tov. Again came a strong wind and brought Rabbi Yoel back to his bed.

When he awakened he was full of fear. That very day, between the Minhah and Maariv prayers, he entered the small synagogue of the Hevre Tehillim, ascended the platform, and spoke words of appeasement to Berl. And from then on Rabbi Yoel ceased creating new interpretations of the Torah. Instead, every morning Rabbi Yoel would stand among the laborers of the Hevre Tehillim and recite psalms together with them.

"I PARDON, AS YOU HAVE ASKED" (NUMBERS 14:20)

It was in the beit midrash of the Baal Shem Tov on the eve of Yom Kippur. The Besht stood at the rostrum and led the Kol Nidre prayer. Suddenly he became silent. He pulled up his large *tallit* over his head, approached the holy ark, and hid his face inside the *parokhet* (ark curtain). In this fashion he leaned on the holy ark, standing for a long while without moving a bone in his body. The congregation in the beit midrash stood waiting in anticipation, all eyes turned to the rabbi.

But the rabbi was silent, his eyes closed, misty in sadness. Finally, the Besht raised his head, stood up straight, and approached the rostrum with an eager face, joyfully calling out, "And God said: 'I pardon, as you have asked!'"

The next day, after Yom Kippur had concluded, the Besht recounted to his students what had transpired.

"In a far-off village," related the Besht, "there lived a Jewish tax collector who was very beloved by the local nobleman. It happened that his wife died in childbirth, and out of deep grief he too died, whereupon the tiny baby was taken to the home of the nobleman. There he grew up together with the other children in the house. When the child grew up and became a young man, the nobleman revealed to him that he was not his real father, and that his parents were Jews who had died when he was a baby. He told him that in the attic were hidden different possessions left from his parents, which now belonged to him.

"The young man went up into the attic and found some books, in which there was an alphabet that he did not recognize. While he was perusing the volumes, the boy found one book whose pages were stained. He felt the pages, and his fingers sensed the moisture of the tears that were absorbed in them. He took the book with him, hid it under his coat, and went to the village.

"In one of the alleys the boy saw a wagon filled with Jews. They were traveling to the nearby city for the High Holy Days in order to pray together with their people. The boy ran after the wagon and asked that they take him with them.

"The night before," continued the Besht, "on the eve of Kol Nidre, the boy came into the beit midrash, and for the first time in his life his eyes saw men draped in white, standing and crying. He saw that each one held a book in his hand and was praying. He too took out from under his coat the book that he had brought, opened it and began to mumble something, though he did not know what he was saying. He wanted to cry like the others, but did not know why. The boy was distraught that he did not know how to pray. And because of his sorrow I also became sad. Because I was sad I could not pray, because one may not pray except out of joy.

"But after some hesitation the boy lifted his eyes heavenward and said, 'Master of the Universe, You took from me my father and mother when I was a baby in the crib, and no one taught me anything about my heritage. I know not what to say before You, and I know not what is written here, but You know all thoughts. Here before You is a book of prayer, and everything written in it is here as if I recited it before You.' He opened the siddur, put his head down on it, and tears began to flow from his eyes on the pages that had absorbed the tears of his parents.

"From these tears joy came into the heart of the young man, and I too rejoiced with him, and in this joy I continued my prayers and recited God's fateful words to Moshe: 'I pardon, as you have asked!'"

PRAYER FROM THE HEART

When Rabbi Simhah Bunim of Peshischa became ill, the people of the city decreed upon themselves a public fast and a cessation of all work. The stores were closed, and young and old were summoned to the beit midrash to pray for the rabbi's speedy recovery.

That day a Jewish wagon driver from another town was passing through the city. The wagon driver craved a glass of liquor, so he directed his horse toward an inn. However, the doors were shut tight. Passersby informed him that the whole city were involved in a fast and that they were in the beit midrash praying for the welfare of their sick rabbi. The wagon driver put down his reins, hurried to the beit midrash, and joined those standing in prayer.

Since he was not familiar with the Psalms, he created a prayer of his own: "Master of the Universe, it is well known before You how strong is my desire for a drink. Please, please God, send complete and speedy healing to the rabbi of Peshischa. Then the people of the city will end their fast, the bartender will open the inn, and then I will be able to make the blessing over a drink of liquor, '...Who creates all things.'"

When Rabbi Simhah Bunim arose from the sick bed the people told him about the public fast, and about the prayer of the wagon driver. He smiled and said, "It is possible that this man's prayer was heard in the heavens above, since it was said out of integrity and sincerity, with no falsehood, and out of a full heart."

YOU ARE WORTHY

The well-known scholar Rabbi Moshe Yehudah Leib Zilberberg, rabbi of Kutna, was very strict in the choice of the inspector of kashrut, and always made sure that he was a person of truth – one who did not show favoritism to the butcher, the *shohet* (ritual slaughterer), or the judge.

The day came when a new inspector was needed. Among the different candidates who were recommended to him, and who had made a good impression on Rabbi Moshe Yehudah Leib, was one very simple Jew.

The rabbi sat with him and tested him with several questions.

"Why do you want to be an inspector?"

"Because," answered the man, " – it shouldn't happen to you – I need the salary."

"Then why don't you become a teacher?"

"Because I am not knowledgeable enough to be a teacher."

"So why don't you become a merchant?"

"Because merchants who know me tell me that I do not have the skill to be a merchant."

"Well," smiled Rabbi Moshe Leib, "if you know enough about telling so much truth, you are indeed worthy to be appointed a faithful inspector!"

Songs and Melodies

WHAT A BEAUTIFUL WORLD

Rabbi Yisrael Baal Shem Tov taught: "When I was young, I was an assistant to a teacher of little children. In the morning I would wake them up very gently, wash and dress them, pray with them the traditional morning prayer, Modeh Ani, thanking God for restoring our souls to us every morning. I thanked the Blessed Holy One from the depths of my heart that I was given the opportunity to supervise these holy toddlers, the children of the Jewish people, to love them and bring them to school to educate them in Torah and mitzvot. With every part of my soul I loved these children, and if one of them disobeyed and refused to go to school, I would plead with him and persuade him, even giving him a copper penny so that he could buy some sweets.

"The children loved me too. They went to school with a happy heart, and on their way they would sing with me in their sweet voices, "*Hamalakh hagoel oti…*, The angel who has redeemed me from all harm – bless these lads" (Genesis 48:16).

"At times the children were so excited that they would join hands in the street and start to dance around me, and it seemed to me that the sweet melody penetrated every heart, and cheered the entire universe. It seemed as if the heavens and the earth and all their hosts – the trees and the grass, the birds, the animals and the beasts, and even the stones in the walls of the houses – were singing the blessing together with the children."

The Besht continued: "There are scholars who close themselves off within the four ells of the halakhah and the Talmud; they punish their body and soul with fasts, with self-mortification and separation, and they are constantly sad, troubled, and worried, forever crying lest they haven't fulfilled God's wishes. But this sadness comes from bitter depression and despair, and because of this they cannot feel the real joy of doing a mitzvah.

"But I am different. My father taught me from my earliest days, 'You shall have nothing but joy' (Deuteronomy 16:15). It is forbidden for a Jew to despair, even if, Heaven forbid, he reaches the very lowest level. Sadness and despair are signs of spiritual decay, and of lack of trust and faith in the living God, and in God's mercy. I despise such sadness, which is entirely filled with misery. But I love the joy that comes from the longing for God. This kind of joy is important and precious to the Almighty, because the sadness has been purged by spiritual longing and love; it is a longing for secrets that humans will not see with their minds or in visions, but only with the soul's Divine thirst.

"I don't disparage tears, Heaven forbid, since our sages taught that "the gates of tears are not closed" (Talmud, Tractate Bava Metzia 59a), but there is an extra measure in joy. If tears open gates, then joy can knock down walls.

"After singing with the young children, I would always feel special spiritual joy. I would then go out to the field to unite with my Maker and become purified in my longing for my Creator, and there in the open field the strength of God Almighty was revealed to me. When I go out to the fields, I stand silently and gaze in wonder at God's world, and my ear listens to the joyous singing of the chirping birds, and the buzzing of the bees, and it seems to me as if the spirit of God is teeming in all living things. In that moment I feel all my worthlessness compared to the light of the Infinite. And from my soul's arousal my heart warms, my soul opens up, and my mouth bursts out in song:

> Majestic, Beautiful, Radiance of the universe,
> my soul pines for your love.
> Please, God, heal her now
> by showing her the pleasantness of Your radiance;
> then she will gain strength and be healed
> and eternal gladness will be hers."
>
> (second stanza of the famous Shabbath hymn, Yedid Nefesh)

THERE IS A MASTER IN THE CASTLE

Rabbi Yisrael Baal Shem Tov taught: "Our sages stated, 'There was a harp hanging over the bed of King David, and at midnight a north wind (*ruah tzfonit*) blew on it, and it played by itself' (Talmud, Tractate Berakhot 3b).

In me too there is a hidden spirit (*ruah tzfunah*) and when I would roam among the hills and mountains, fields and vineyards, and see the expanse of creation, a northern wind would blow through my limbs, and I would make music by myself, singing and chanting to the supernal God, Whose world it is. Naturally a special feeling is required that not everyone merits. This parable will explain:

"A person who was deaf from birth came into a hall and found a crowd of people celebrating and dancing. As he looked he saw that even on the stage there was a group of people holding instruments in their hands, and one of them was standing in front of them waving a stick that was in his hand. Even more surprising was that he saw that the dancers were paying attention, from time to time, to the man shaking his stick to direct their dancing. Each time he saw the shaking of the stick, the people would increase their jumping and their excitement kept growing.

"The deaf person stood and wondered to himself, 'What is the connection between the shaking of the stick and the dancing and jumping of the people in the hall?' At that moment he entertained a suspicion that some crazy people were dancing and jumping in sync with the stick in the leader's hand. The deaf man had no idea that it was not the stick that aroused the crowd of dancers, but rather the musicians who were playing songs.

"The meaning of the parable is this: The world is filled with sounds and sights which are the strong voice of God, triumphant visions of God. All the sights of creation, the signs and wonders in Heaven and earth – they are the work of Divine Providence. But those who are deaf and blind cannot understand. They think there is no master in the castle, and the world rolls around on its own."

A SOUL CARVED FROM THE TEMPLE OF SONG

Rabbi Leib ben Sarah heard that in a certain city in Hungary there lived a Jewish boy who had a special soul, a boy who was destined to be a great Hasidic leader. He went to that city and searched for the boy in the classrooms of every school, but did not find him.

He left the city, went into the field, and tried to discover how to find the boy about whom a glorious future was predicted. He had spread the word far and wide, but had not succeeded in finding him. On his way through the fields he came to a hill and saw a flock of sheep and a young boy in rags, training to become a village shepherd, leading them.

Rabbi Leib ben Sarah thought to himself, "What connection do I have with a farm boy?" But he was drawn to the boy, and he therefore approached him and asked him in the dialect of a gentile, "Who are you, young man?"

"I am a Jew. Yitzhak Isaac is my name."

Rabbi Leib ben Sarah asked him, "Who is your father?"

"My father died," answered the boy, "and my widowed mother hired me out to a shepherd. I support my poor mother."

Rabbi Leib sought to sound him out and asked him, "Perhaps you know, young man, what the time is?"

"It is between the rising of the sun and its setting," answered the boy in fun.

Rabbi Leib continued the conversation. "What do you do, young fellow, between sunrise and sunset?"

"I follow the sheep and play tunes to them," answered the boy.

"Tunes? What are the words?"

"Some tunes have words, and some do not."

Rabbi Leib continued. "Young man, sing for me a nice tune – either with or without words. I like both kinds. I love songs."

The boy sang some songs. Rabbi Leib took the boy, and kissed him, as his tears fell on the face of the young shepherd who sang so beautifully.

Rabbi Leib waited until the sun set, and then went with the young shepherd boy and his flock of sheep down the hill. When he had handed over the flock to his master, Rabbi Leib went with young Yitzhak Isaac to the home of his widowed mother, and asked her permission to let him look after her son, who had such a special soul, to raise him to Torah and Hasidism.

Rabbi Leib expressed his confidence that someday the boy would be a faithful shepherd to his community, and his sweet songs would be sung by Hasidim the world over. Rabbi Leib pledged to support the widow until Yitzhak Isaac grew up.

The mother agreed, and Rabbi Leib took the boy, dressed him in fine clothing, and traveled with him to the beit midrash of Rabbi Shmuel Horvitz of Nikolsberg, a leading student of the Maggid of Mezritch. "I have brought you a special, holy soul," said Rabbi Leib, "one that was carved out of the temple of song and music. Teach him in your yeshivah and make of him a precious vessel, full of Torah and wisdom."

Rabbi Shmulke registered him in the yeshivah, and young Yitzhak Isaac brought his shepherd's music to the holy community.

Years later the young shepherd named Yitzhak Isaac became well known as a tzaddik and master of songs. His story and his name are famous in the community of Hasidim to this very day – he is Rabbi Yitzhak Isaac Taub, who became the rabbi of Kaliv and one of the leaders of Hasidism in Hungary.

SONG AND PRAISE TO THE ETERNAL ONE

Rabbi Noah of Lechovitz taught: "How can a simple human being find comfort? He is compared to a bird in a cage in the king's palace. Even though a choir of singers presents beautiful music, sometimes the king receives more pleasure from a tiny winged creature that bursts forth in song, since it is a little creature without consciousness, and for whom all the rules of musical rhythm are unknown, and therefore his music comes naturally from his heart.

"The Blessed Holy One also has in Heaven large groups of angels and seraphim who praise and extol God with serene spirit, pure speech, and sweet melody, yet it is a great pleasure for God to receive songs of praise from humans, who are lowly creatures with little beauty."

FUGITIVES OF THE SWORD

Rabbi Avraham Yeshayahu Karelitz, author of the *Hazon Ish*, lived in Bnei Brak next door to an orphanage for girls. The girls were refugees of the sword, saved from the Shoah.

Many evenings the girls would cry bitterly for their deceased parents, who had been slaughtered before their very eyes. Try as they might, there was little the orphanage staff could do to comfort them.

Months passed, and on an occasional Shabbat eve the girls overcame their grief and sang some of the traditional Shabbat *zemirot* (hymns). In the summer, when the shutters were open and the sound of their singing was heard outside the walls of the orphanage, some neighbors came to complain to Rabbi Karelitz. In traditional Jewish law it is forbidden to listen to the voice of a woman singing.

Noted for his unfailing commitment to halakhah, Rabbi Karelitz's response surprised his neighbors: "Thank you so much for taking the trouble to let me know about the girls' singing. You have no idea how much happiness you bring me. I thank God that finally the girls are singing instead of crying!"

WORDS OF WISDOM

PRAYERS WITHOUT WORDS

What is the nature of your prayer? Is it possible to pray to God with words alone?

Come and I will show you a new path to God. Not with words or speech, but with song. We shall sing, and God in Heaven will appreciate our thoughts.

Rabbi Nahman of Breslov

Sustenance

THE VALUE OF POVERTY

Rabbi Yisrael Baal Shem Tov could not rest in his compassion for the simple Jew who was lost in poverty, burdened to try to bring bread to his young child, wandering in the alleys and markets every day of the week in order to bring the spirit of Shabbat into his home.

Rabbi Yisrael realized the special merit of the poor person, who has the privilege every day of speaking to the Sovereign of Sovereigns, the Blessed Holy One. A wealthy person, whose financial status allows him an abundant supply of food for a long period, does not naturally feel gratefulness to God on a daily basis. This is not true of the poor person who at most has enough for one meal prepared, and every day requires mercy.

"In truth," said the Besht, "the poor person is among those who eat manna, about whom it is written 'The people shall go out and gather each day's portion' (Exodus 16:4). The poor person needs God to be near every day, more so than the wealthy, as it is written, 'God is near to all who call Him' (Psalms 145:18). Because he seeks God every day, he turns to God. God is near to those who are close to Him.

"From this we learn an important lesson. Why was this soul sent to earth? To be aware of the Creator. We thus learn that Jews who are poor and underprivileged, simple and sincere, fill their mission in his world in greater measure than the wealthy who know that their financial support is given to them in abundance."

FOR THOSE WHO HAVE NO BREAD TO EAT

One day Rabbi Menahem Mendel of Kotzk unlocked the door of his private room and called to his assistant. The rabbi asked his assistant, "Tell me, please, what is the conventional interpretation of the statement in Midrash Mekhilta, 'The Torah was given only for the sake of those who eat manna'?"

The assistant answered, "The conventional interpretation is that it refers to those who sit at the table of others and have no worries about financial support."

"No, no," said Rabbi Mendele. "This is not the meaning of the midrash. It's just the opposite! It refers only to those people who have a difficult time obtaining their daily portion of bread, and nevertheless they are not afraid, and have no worry about where their food will come from the next day – just as in the days of the Bible the Israelites did not worry about food for the next day. These are the people for whom the Torah was given."

Thereupon Rabbi Mendele went back into his room and relocked the door.

WHEN ONE'S WORDS AND ONE'S HEART ARE THE SAME

Many Hasidim gathered at the door of Rabbi Menahem Mendel of Kotzk, but most of them were turned away. His assistant fended them off.

However, one simple Jew, a farmer in the area, approached the door and even waited a very long time. His calf was sick, and his living was dependent on the calf. He had come to ask the rabbi to pray for the calf to get well. Upon being apprised of the farmer's predicament, the rabbi consented to his request immediately.

A few days later one of the rabbi's Hasidim asked apprehensively, "The rabbi opened the door of his home for the needs of calves, while human beings have to wait outside?"

The rabbi retorted, "A Jew who speaks about calves and thinks about calves is better than a Jew who speaks to God and thinks about a calf."

BREAD TO EAT AND CLOTHES TO WEAR

Rabbi Yaakov Yosef of Polnoye instructed one of his congregation with words of *musar* (ethical teachings). The man came to pour out his heart in bitterness about the situation of his finances. Out of deep pain and a sorrowing heart he said to the rabbi, "My teacher and master, my situation is awful. I have become impoverished, and have lost most of my possessions. I am aware that surely my sins caused this situation, as we learn in the Mishnah, 'I committed evil and lost my possessions' (Kiddushin 4:12)."

Rabbi Yaakov Yosef interrupted him in the midst of his words, and said to him in laughter mixed with a bit of annoyance, "There is a great difference between the words of the Mishnah and your complaint. The Mishnah emphasizes the commission of sins, and you stress your financial loss."

A deep sigh emerged from the heart of this poor unfortunate man.

Rabbi Yisrael Baal Shem Tov was standing nearby and heard the conversation. He felt pity for the depressed man and turned to Rabbi Yaakov Yosef, saying, "Even our father Yaakov emphasized the importance of material stability when he said, 'If God will be with me…and grant me bread to eat and clothes to wear…then Hashem will be my God' (Genesis 28:20–21). Your people Israel need to make a living, and we must try first and foremost to ask the Blessed Holy One to grant every Jew bread to eat and clothing to wear – and then to request of the people of Israel to improve their deeds, so that Hashem will be their God."

EIGHTEEN PIECES OF GOLD

Rabbi Yisrael of Koznitz subsisted on a piece of dry bread and a bit of chicken soup every day. He lived a life of pain, poverty, and hardship, and he labored in study of Torah and in worship of God every day and night. It is told of him that before he became well known in the world as a giant in Torah and a righteous person, he earned his living as a preacher and teacher in Koznitz. Since his wages did not suffice, he would from time to time visit several nearby towns, giving paid lectures.

It happened once that he came to a small town near Koznitz, in which were two community leaders. They gave him permission to lecture on Shabbat in the synagogue, and one of them invited him to stay in his home and join him for meals. His sermon mesmerized his listeners, whereupon the community leaders decided to compensate him for his talk, to the amount of nine gilders.

On Sunday morning Rabbi Yisrael parted from the community leader with whom he had resided, and was given nine gilders for his sermon. Rabbi Yisrael thought it appropriate to say good-bye also to the other community leader, and when he went to see him, he was given another nine gilders. This rabbi thought that his colleague had not yet given Rabbi Yisrael the nine gilders. Rabbi Yisrael thought that the leaders had decided to give him eighteen gilders, each one half. He took the nine gilders from the rabbi, thanked him, and left.

After he had gone from the town the two leaders met and they realized that the preacher had received double what they had decided. They sent the *shamash* (synagogue assistant) to Koznitz, where he immediately began upbraiding Rabbi Yisrael.

"You are a disgrace!" the *shamash* shouted. "One who preaches about ethics to others, not to take advantage of anyone, and he himself deceives the leaders of the congregation!"

Rabbi Yisrael asked his wife to return the nine gilders and told her, "They are right, and I hereby accept in love the censure that the *shamash* has given me. I should have trusted the Blessed Holy One who provides for all living creatures, rather than travel around to the nearby towns and forsake my study and my worship. From now on I will not leave Koznitz to find funds."

MAY WE NOT NEED....

During the recitation of *Birkat Hamazon* (Grace after Meals), Rabbi Barukh of Medziboz chanted the following sentence with particular intensity: "Do not make us dependent on the gifts of other people, or on the loans of others, but only on Your full, open and generous hand...."

When he finished, his daughter asked him in surprise, "*Tatte*, all our livelihood comes from the gifts that your Hasidim provide for us, so why did you pray with such fervor that we not rely on gifts?"

Rabbi Barukh answered her, "People who bring gifts to a tzaddik have one of the following three motivations: Some say to themselves, 'Everyone is giving, so I also have to give. How can I not?' For such people I prayed, 'Do not make us dependent on the gifts of other people.'

"Others say to themselves, 'I will contribute to a tzaddik so that God will bless me generously.' Such a person contributes in order to receive. For such a person I prayed, 'Do not make us dependent on the loans of others....'

"Still others know that their money is not theirs, but was given to them as a loan from God and when they give it is not really theirs. For such people I prayed, 'but on Your full, open and generous hand.' These people know from whom their money comes."

LECTURES READY TO DELIVER

Rabbi Yisrael Salanter felt the burden and the pain of every member of the Jewish people, and he tried to help each person according to his or her ability.

Once a scholar approached Rabbi Yisrael and poured out his heart to him. "Rabbi, I am in very difficult straits. We don't have a scrap of food in the house, and I don't foresee any possibility of making a living."

Rabbi Yisrael asked him, "Have you not studied for many years? Why don't you become a maggid and a preacher?"

"But I have never been involved in that field," answered the scholar, "and I have no lectures prepared."

Rabbi Yisrael calmed him down. "Don't worry! Come to me tomorrow and I will show you that it is not as difficult as you think."

The next day the scholar came to Rabbi Yisrael's home. Rabbi Yisrael gave him two lectures, all written out and artfully arranged, and did not permit him to leave until he had mastered the material.

In this way the poor man began to travel the circuit, lecturing in public wherever he went, and his finances improved greatly.

WORDS OF WISDOM

NEITHER A BORROWER NOR A LENDER BE

Being dependent for a living on other people is like taking honey from a bee. When you remove a bit of honey, you expose yourself to its stings, and to pain and sorrow.

Rabbi Naftali of Ropschitz

DON'T MAKE A LIVING OFF OF GOD

"With me, therefore, you shall not make any gods of silver…" (Exodus 20:20).

Do not make any business out of religion, and do not make your living from fear of Heaven.

Rabbi Yaakov of Volozhin

Thought and Speech

FIRST FRUITS OF THOUGHT

Rabbi Simhah Bunim of Peshischa was once asked, "The Torah is for all times, eternal, so how is it possible to fulfill the mitzvot of *bikurim* [bringing the season's first fruits to the Temple in Jerusalem] in our time, now that the Temple has been destroyed?"

The rabbi replied, "Even in the bitter exile it is possible to fulfill the mitzvah of *bikurim*. We can bring the first fruits of the thought of a Jew, and the first fruits of his speech and action. Every morning upon awakening, one should not think secular thoughts, nor speak words that are not Torah; one should not do anything except pray to God. In this way one can fulfill the biblical command, 'The choice first fruits of your soil you shall bring to the house of the Lord your God' (Exodus 34:26), and 'Consecrate to Me every firstborn' (Exodus 13:2). All people according to their own modes of Torah study, their paths of connecting with God."

NOTHING MORE VALUABLE THAN SILENCE

Rabbi Hayyim of Brisk was once invited to speak at a gathering where another famous rabbi was also scheduled to lecture. This famous rabbi was by nature an eloquent and verbose speaker. The latter began to speak and continued for an entire hour without stop. Rabbi Hayyim sat quietly and listened.

When the famous rabbi left, those gathered asked the rabbi of Brisk, "Our master! Why did you sit so quietly and allow this man to speak endlessly?"

Rabbi Hayyim replied, "This is the situation. My colleague can think for one hour in order to prepare a talk of twenty-three hours. But for me, it takes me twenty-three hours to prepare in order to speak for one hour."

YOUR HEART AND YOUR MOUTH

Rabbi Hayyim Auerbach, the rabbi of Lunschitz, had many opponents, among whom were some people who were not particularly worthy.

It happened once that Rabbi Hayyim was standing in the marketplace, having a conversation with a woman. His opponents spoke ill of him, a worthy rabbi, speaking with a woman in the marketplace!

When word came to Rabbi Hayyim about the grumbling, he smiled, and said, "It is better for a man to speak with a woman, and direct his heart to his Father in Heaven, than to speak to his Father in Heaven, and direct his heart toward a woman."

SILENCE IS GOLDEN

Rabbi Meir Yehiel, the tzaddik of Ostrovtze, was one of the leading scholars of Poland in the generation before the Shoah. He was known as a man of few words; every word out of his mouth was carefully measured as one who was counting coins.

When one of his students asked him why he was so restrained in his speech, he gave this answer: "When I was a child, I used to love to sit next to the burning oven in my father's bakery and watch my father, of blessed memory, while he was baking. Once my father said to me, 'Come and let me teach you the art of baking while I stand on one foot. You must know, my son, that the tighter the oven is shut, the warmer it gets.' That lesson stands me in good stead whenever I open my mouth."

WORDS OF WISDOM

HOLY OF HOLIES

A person's mind is compared to the Holy of Holies in the Beit Hamikdash in Jerusalem, in which the two tablets of the Ten Commandments lie. When foreign thoughts and evil designs enter the mind, a person desecrates his Holy of Holies.

Rabbi Levi Yitzhak of Berditchev

KNOWING WHEN TO KEEP SILENT

Some people think I don't know how to speak. The truth is that I know how to keep silent.

Rabbi Raphael of Volozhin

WHEN TO LISTEN

The world is of the opinion that humans have a great virtue in that they are born with the ability to speak. But I think that an even greater virtue is that humans are endowed with the ability to listen.

Rabbi Naftali of Ropschitz

WHAT IS EXILE?

What is the definition of the "exile of the *Shekhinah* (the Divine Presence)"?

It is when foreign thoughts rule one's speech.

Rabbi Yisrael Baal Shem Tov

THOUGHTS AND FACTS

Thought is a high mountain. Facts are the pointers toward the mountain.

Rabbi Dov Ber of Mezritch

Torah Study

TORAH OF LIFE

When the Maggid of Mezritch, Rabbi Dov Ber, entered the room of the Baal Shem Tov for the first time, the Besht asked him, "Do you know the proper methods of Torah study?"

"Yes," answered the pupil.

"Do you also know the deep wisdom of Kabbalah?"

"Yes."

On the table was a copy of the *Etz Hayyim* of Rabbi Hayyim Vital, student of the Holy Ari (Rabbi Isaac Luria). The Besht leafed through the pages of the book and set it down in front of the Maggid.

"Take a look at this passage and explain it to me."

The Maggid glanced at the passage and gave his interpretation. The Besht was silent. Rabbi Dov Ber understood that his interpretation was not acceptable to the Besht. He summoned his strength and broke the silence. "If my honored master knows a different interpretation, may I please hear it?"

The Besht replied, "Stand up."

The Maggid stood up, and the Besht repeated the very same words that the Maggid had said a few minutes before. The Maggid gazed at him, puzzled.

Suddenly there flashed an aura of fire, and the house was filled with light. After a brief pause, the Besht explained, "Your explanation was accurate, as the day is bright, but it had no soul. In your learning a shining spark is lacking."

By dint of this experience Rabbi Dov Ber of Mezritch became the leading student of the Baal Shem Tov.

HIDDEN TORAH AND REVEALED TORAH

Rabbi Zusha of Anapol came to visit Rabbi Shmelke, the rabbi of Nikolsberg, and asked him to study with him some parts of the revealed Torah.

Rabbi Shmelke asked, "What shall we study?" Rabbi Zusha answered, "Zusha is not well educated, and he wants to study Mishnah, but one has to explain to him every single word."

The two of them began to study the first Mishnah of Tractate Berakhot, which begins: "From what hour does one recite the Shema in the evening." Rabbi Shmelke explained it according to its plain meaning: "What is the hour that it is permissible to recite the Shema."

Rabbi Zusha became sorely afraid. He asked, "Perhaps the interpretation is different. The first word, *mei'eimatai* – could mean 'from what hour,' or it could be from the Hebrew root *eimah* – awe. In other words, the Mishnah could mean this: One must recite the Shema out of awe and fear."

Rabbi Shmelke said to Rabbi Zusha, "If this is what you consider 'revealed Torah,' then what do you consider 'hidden Torah'?" They agreed to study together no longer.

YOU SHALL PONDER THESE WORDS DAY AND NIGHT

The Gaon of Vilna, Rabbi Eliyahu, was an extremely devoted student of Torah, and did not spend one minute away from his Torah study unnecessarily. And if he had to be away from the Torah, he would mark down in his notebook when and for how long he had been away from Torah study.

On the eve of Yom Kippur he would calculate all the minutes that he was away from Torah study the entire year, and would cry and repent of his failure to study Torah.

It was said of him that when all the missed minutes were added up for a whole year, it never added up to more than three hours.

AN UNBREAKABLE BOND

Rabbi Hayyim of Volozhin loved his yeshivah with all his heart and soul. After the death of the Vilna Gaon, Rabbi Hayyim was almost unique in his generation in his love and study of Torah. Out of pure faith and deep understanding, he wrote:

> If, Heaven forbid, the world turned away completely, for even a minute, from the business of the holy Torah of the Chosen People, immediately the whole universe would be destroyed and expunged from reality. Even only one Jew has it in his hands to uphold the universe through his study of the holy Torah for its own sake.... (*Nefesh Hahaim*, gate 4, chapter 25)

In accordance with his beliefs, he set up shifts every night in his yeshivah. As one shift would leave, another would enter. In this pattern they would continue in Volozhin, being occupied with the study of Torah every night, including Shabbat and the festivals. He himself would go in and out of the yeshivah on Shabbat evenings to make sure that Torah study was continuing without pause.

At the end of Yom Kippur, he would sit alone and occupy himself with Torah study until midnight. He thought to himself, "The people of Israel are holy, and they fasted from sundown to sundown. Now they are all tired and weary from fasting all day, and I am afraid, Heaven forbid, that the world will be deprived for a short time of Torah study."

INGREDIENTS OF THE INCENSE

Rabbi Shalom Rokeach, the rabbi of Belz, was born in Brody in 1779. The Hasidim of Belz relate that when he was five years old he went with his sister in the rainy season over a narrow bridge, built for those who had to walk through mud. Once Rabbi Moshe Leib of Sassov passed by, and went down into the mud to make a path for the young child. When doing so he said, "This little fellow will one day be a great man."

While still a youngster Rabbi Shalom lost his father, and he was sent to live with his uncle, his mother's brother, Rabbi Yissakhar Ber, rabbi of Skohl. In his uncle's house he studied with great diligence, both Talmud and later Jewish law. As was the custom of Hasidim in those days, his uncle smoked while studying.

Once he saw one of the Hasidim beginning to clean his pipe in the midst of his studies. Half an hour elapsed before the Hasid refilled the pipe and was ready to resume study. Little Shalom noticed this, and said to himself, "If smoking can bring one to missing Torah study, I hereby accept upon myself never to smoke." From that day on a pipe never entered his mouth.

THE ETERNAL STUDENT

Once at the end of Yom Kippur, Rabbi Eliezer Yitzhak of Volozhin entered the home of his father-in-law and asked, "Please tell me, my beloved teacher, what is my obligation at this moment after the fast of this holy day?"

Rabbi Yitzhak of Volozhin replied, "Come and I will show you what to do."

He brought him into one of the rooms of the yeshivah, and there they saw Rabbi Naftali Tzvi Yehudah Berlin (the Netziv), standing with his feet in cold water to keep himself awake, occupying himself with Torah study with great diligence and joy.

This rare sight touched the heart of Rabbi Eliezer Yitzhak, and he said to his father-in-law, "Surely God is present in this place, and I did not know it!" (Genesis 28:16).

THIS IS OUR LIFE

Rabbi Naftali Tzvi Yehudah Berlin, the Netziv of Volozhin, was one of a kind in many generations. His soul was bound up with his yeshivah, and in it he found his purpose in life. Not only his own study, but even more so the study of the hundreds of students in the academy gave him an extra lease on life.

After the fire that occurred in his home, he lived in the yeshivah until his own home was rebuilt. The upper floor was set aside for the yeshivah, and several hundred students were occupied there, day and night, with Torah study and prayer. Their voices were heard far and wide. The bottom floor served as an apartment for the Netziv and his family.

Once he was asked, "Rabbi, how can you tolerate the loud noise above your head? How can you rest or sleep?"

The Netziv looked into the faces of his questioners, and after some thought, replied, "I will tell you a parable. What can this be compared to?

To a miller, grinding flour. Someone passes by the mill and hears the wheels going round, blasting one's eardrums, and asks in amazement, 'How can this miller put up with all the noise of the mill? He must not know a moment's peace!'

"Upon hearing this, the miller replied, 'This noise is excellent for my rest and sleep. Thank God that the mill is making noise, and the more noise it makes the easier it is for me to sleep. And if, Heaven forbid, the mill is quiet, the wheels stop going round, and the millstones come to a halt, I will not be able to relax, since my whole life depends on the mill working and making noise.'

"It is the same with my yeshivah. From it I draw my strength and my spiritual vigor. The noise and commotion there add to my ability to rest and sleep."

Every student who entered the yeshivah brought a new breath of life to the Netziv's soul. It is told that in his last years, before the yeshivah was closed by the government, it was financially unstable. A number of young students and Torah devotees wanted to study at the yeshivah, but his family informed him that the situation was very grave, and it would be impossible to accept new students.

The Netziv heard this news and cried bitterly. When they asked him why he was crying, he replied, "Woe to me, that this is happening in my lifetime. There are young Jews whose souls long for Torah and we cannot bring them in – how can I not cry?"

HERE'S MY SECRET

The Gaon of Vilna said to Rabbi Yaakov Krantz, known as the Maggid of Dubnow, "I am amazed at how you always find beautiful illustrations to explain difficult passages in the Torah and midrash."

The Maggid of Dubnow replied with a parable:

> There was once a duke who had an only son, much beloved, whom he would teach much wisdom and many languages. When the son grew up, the duke sent him to far-off lands to see different cultures and to learn there about the experiences of the world.

The son traveled for a long time, and finally returned to his father's house, full of wisdom and experience. The duke made a great feast in honor of his son, and invited all his officers and acquaintances in order to demonstrate to them all the wonders of his son's wisdom.

After the feast the duke accompanied his guests out, as is the custom, to the forest, to shoot arrows. The wise son also demonstrated his ability to hit his targets. The officials saw this and could not stop praising the son and remarking on his dexterous hands.

As they returned from shooting they passed through a village and saw a fence made of tin, filled with holes and punctures. Around all the holes was drawn a circle, signaling the target. They were all amazed at the expertise of one who succeeded with every shot, never missing the circle even by a hair's breadth.

They proceeded to investigate among the residents of the village to see who had done this. Their search led them to a simple farmer. When the duke asked him about his extraordinary success, the farmer answered in complete sincerity. "The matter is very simple, my lord the duke. Your honor first makes a circle and then shoots, so sometimes you succeed and sometimes not. But I do the opposite. First I shoot and make a hole, and only afterwards I surround the holes with circles. Thus I never miss!"

Rabbi Yaakov of Dubnow concluded thus: "My teacher Rabbi Eliyahu, I too first find a good supportive illustration to explain the difficulty in the text, and afterwards I find a text that fits the illustration."

"TO OBSERVE, TO DO, AND TO FULFILL" (MORNING PRAYERS)

Rabbi Yisrael Meir Hakohen of Radin, the Hafetz Hayyim, told this story:

A wealthy man had to go on a trip to a faraway place for an extended period. Before he left he handed his servant a detailed list of tasks to do during his absence, and warned him especially not to forget to read the list every day, in order that nothing be forgotten of all the items on the list.

When the man returned from his trip he immediately called his servant and asked him, "Did you do everything that I asked you to?"

"Certainly, sir," answered the servant. "I read the list every single day."

The man got very angry. "Did I intend that you just read the list and no more?! I gave you the list so that you would remember the items that you were supposed to do! Reading the list was not meant to replace doing what was written on it!"

The Hafetz Hayyim explained the parable: "It is the same with the study of Torah. The Torah details for us the actions that we are obligated to fulfill. Their value is great only when we practice what we are taught."

GET YOURSELF TO A PLACE OF TORAH

The Hafetz Hayyim was very pleased with the fact that young men from America would come to study in his yeshivah. He would excitedly petition God: "Master of the Universe: Come see! Here are young men who leave their homes, their parents, and their families in America – a country that has everything a person would want, all the pleasures and comforts – and a country in which there are yeshivot, and still they come across the ocean to study here. They come to a far-off small town, and live a life of hardship. This is exile in exile. For what and for whom? For Your will and for Your Torah.

"For this alone You should have mercy on Your people Israel, and gather them from all their places of exile. The time has come! The time has come!"

Then he would break out crying.

THE SENSE OF BELONGING

In the beit midrash of Rabbi Simhah Bunim of Peshischa they would interpret the statement in the Talmud, "This world resembles a wedding feast" (Tractate Eruvin 54a), as follows:

There are many preparations performed for a wedding, and the commotion is great. Guests and honored individuals are invited, musicians and comedians are contracted, new clothing is sewn, special food and drink is ordered, and everything is focused on only one word – the Hebrew word *li* (to me). [When the groom places the ring on the finger of the bride, he recites the essential legal formula, without which the marriage is not sanctified – "Behold, you are consecrated *to me*, according to the laws of Moshe and the people of Israel."]

Even if the groom acquires a valuable ceremonial ring and places it on his bride's finger, and recites in the presence of proper witnesses the formula "Behold you are consecrated," – if he does not add the word *li* (to me), then his words are invalid. If the Hebrew word *li* (to me) is missing – everything is missing.

In the same way, it is not sufficient for a Jew to say to the Torah, "Behold you are consecrated," because the main thing is the sense of belonging. Only to the degree that one is consecrated and committed *lo* – to the Torah, to that extent he himself fulfills what is written in the Torah.

LET OUR EYES SEE AND OUR HEARTS REJOICE

Rabbi Simhah Bunim of Peshischa once said about a certain person, who was known as a Kabbalist, that he knew nothing about Kabbalah.

His students queried him, "Rabbi, how can that be? Everyone knows that this person is a great expert in the wisdom of the Kabbalah."

Rabbi Simhah Bunim replied, "He may be an expert, but he knows nothing on the subject. There is no knowledge without visual experience. It may be that the streets of a city are clear to one according to the map, even though he was never in the city in his life. Since he was not there in the city and did not see it with his eyes, he does not know it, and does not know the spirit of its life.

"This person who you referred to was never in the 'city' of the Kabbalah, and never saw it with his eyes, and he therefore knows nothing about it. To truly know Kabbalah one must perceive its lights. Therefore the holy Zohar always states, 'Come and see....'"

THE SOUND OF TEARS

Rabbi Issar Zalman Meltzer related: "I had a set hour in which I prepared the daily lesson together with my teacher, Rabbi Naftali Tzvi Yehudah Berlin, which he then delivered in the yeshivah.

"One day, however, after we had prepared the lesson, Rabbi Berlin decided not to deliver it. I could find no flaw in what we had prepared, so I went to his room and asked him why he had decided against teaching that day."

Rabbi Berlin explained, "Every morning when I recite my prayers and reach the Ahavah Rabbah prayer, tears run down my face as I beseech my Creator to bestow upon me knowledge, understanding, and wisdom, in order that I will be able to study and be engaged in the Torah as one must. Today, for whatever reason, I did not cry. Because of that I decided not to deliver my lesson to the students."

TEACH THEM DILIGENTLY TO YOUR CHILDREN

Rabbi Aharon Kotler recalls this experience of his youth:

"We grew up in Lithuania, where my father was a well-known merchant in furs. In a certain period, when the situation in this market was especially bad, our family suffered from terrible hunger. There was almost no food in the house to eat.

"My father had a set two-hour period of Torah study every morning after prayers, which he never violated his entire life.

"One day a wealthy merchant arrived who wanted to purchase a large quantity of furs. My father was in the midst of his fixed period of Torah study. My mother approached the door of his room and knocked firmly on the door – once, twice, three times. When my father asked what was the matter, she explained that an important merchant was waiting for a large purchase, and it was important for him to come out and conclude the matter.

"From inside the room we heard my father's voice, 'Tell him that if he is interested in waiting until I finish my two-hour study period, fine. If not, let him go on his way in peace. If it is decreed that I sell the merchandise, I will sell it even without him. A person's income is fixed on high from one Rosh Hashanah to the next.' He did not come out of his room."

Rabbi Aharon Kotler concluded, "The inspiration that my father bequeathed to all of his children through his behavior was enormous. From him I acquired my dedication to Torah study."

"WHO SHALL ASCEND THE MOUNTAIN OF GOD?" (PSALMS 24:3)

The poet Uri Tzvi Greenberg celebrated the occasion of his son's becoming a bar mitzvah in the synagogue on Mount Zion in Jerusalem. The well-known Jerusalem tzaddik Rabbi Aryeh Levin was among the guests.

One of the participants recalls, "I was a young child, and I saw the elderly tzaddik making his way with difficulty up the dust path that led to the top of the mountain. I approached him and greeted him. Rabbi Aryeh Levin took my hand and caressed it, as was his custom, and asked me where I was studying, and which chapter of the Talmud I was studying. In the course of conversation we arrived at the top of the mountain.

Rabbi Levin said to me, "Do you see, my son, when people are occupied with words of Torah, one does not feel any difficulty in climbing. One can go to the top of a mountain easily in spite of the difficulties."

WORDS OF WISDOM

EFFORT, NOT ACCOMPLISHMENT

The Blessed Holy One does not count the number of pages of the Talmud that one studies. God is more interested in the number of hours one studies.

Rabbi Aharon of Karlin

"DON'T ADD OR SUBTRACT...."

"Do not add anything to it...or detract from it" (Deuteronomy 4:2)

The Torah is an elixir of life. It is medicine whose power is to purify people from all the evil in them. Therefore, "Do not add to it…or detract from it," since one should take medicine in just the right dosage, as the doctor prescribes.

Too little does not help, and too much can harm.

Rabbi Yonatan Eibschitz

DON'T MAKE IT TOO EASY FOR YOURSELF

"If you studied much Torah, take no special credit [*tovah*] for yourself…." (Pirkei Avot 2:9)

If you are a scholar, a rabbi, a teacher of Jews, don't take the easy (*tovah*) path for yourself, while enforcing stringencies on others.

Rabbi Menahem Mendel of Kotzk

Truth and Falsehood

WHEN DO WE BELIEVE?

Rabbi Hayyim of Zanz taught: "Wonder of wonders! When a person says he is sick no one believes him. When a person says that he has no money, again no one believes him. But if he says, 'Behold I have sinned,' then everyone believes him."

"KEEP FAR FROM FALSEHOOD" (EXODUS 23:7)

Rabbi Simhah Zissel of Kelm was among the students of Rabbi Yisrael Salanter. He and his brother-in-law accepted upon themselves to be extremely careful about not speaking falsehoods. It happened that his brother-in-law became ill with a malady that caused him terrible pain, and as a result he was wont to groan with pain.

One day Rabbi Simhah Zissel came to visit him, and after his visit the brother-in-law stopped groaning. His family asked Rabbi Simhah Zissel, "What elixir or medicine did you give him that quieted his pains?"

Rabbi Simhah Zissel explained, "I don't distribute medicine, and surely not elixirs. All I did was remind him that we accepted upon ourselves a commitment to be entirely truthful, and groaning too much may be considered a falsehood, from which we must separate ourselves."

CAREFULLY GUARD WHAT COMES OUT OF YOUR MOUTH (DEUTERONOMY 23:24)

Rabbi Avraham Yeshayahu Karelitz (author of the *Hazon Ish*) was a strong proponent of always following the truth. It was his custom to daven Minhah Gedolah every day at noon, to fulfill the injunction to pray the afternoon prayers as soon as the opportunity arises. It happened once that it was difficult to gather a minyan to daven Minhah in the synagogue in his home, and only after waiting a half hour did they find a tenth man.

Rabbi Karelitz's brother-in-law, Rabbi Shmuel Greinman, asked him, "I invited someone to my home this afternoon, and because the Minhah service was a half hour late I will be late for the meeting. What should I do?"

The Hazon Ish replied, "One who is committed to the truth has no room for a shadow of a question. Let the minyan be cancelled rather than have truth and accuracy be violated." Therefore, the crowd dispersed and the minyan was cancelled.

TO DUST YOU SHALL RETURN

Two people came for adjudication in court before Rabbi Zelig of Constantine. The matter dealt with ownership of a piece of property, with each litigant claiming full ownership.

While the two litigants were presenting their cases and arguing with one another, Rabbi Zelig said to them, "Let's go to the field in question, and there we shall be able to settle the dispute."

When they arrived at the piece of disputed land, the rabbi bent over and put his ear to the earth to listen. The litigants were astonished at his bizarre behavior. Rabbi Zelig straightened up and said, "You say 'It's all mine.' And *you* say 'It's all mine.' I asked the land, and it said, 'They both belong to me, as it is written, "You are dust and to dust you shall return" (Genesis 3:19).'"

DECEIVING THE PUBLIC

When the beloved Rabbi Yitzhak Isaac Sher, head of the yeshivah of Slobodka, died in Eretz Yisrael, his family requested that the spiritual advisor of the yeshivah deliver the eulogy. When he refused, there was great confusion.

After the funeral, the spiritual advisor explained, "About a month ago, my beloved grandson died, whom I loved so that our souls were bound together. Since I was still upset over his death, I was concerned that in the midst of the eulogy that I would deliver for the rosh yeshivah, I would break out crying over my personal tragedy. In such a case, the listeners would all think that my tears were for the esteemed rosh yeshivah, while in truth I would be crying for my grandson. I would thus be deceiving the public.

"Because of these thoughts I hesitated, and decided it better to forego the opportunity to give the eulogy, rather than give a false impression."

Tzaddik

AN UPSIDE-DOWN GENERATION

Rabbi Zusha of Anapol taught: "In Midrash Rabbah it is written: 'In the future the Garden of Eden will cry out, "Give me tzaddikim, I will have no truck with sinners." And at the same time Gehinnom (hell) will cry out: "I will have no truck with tzaddikim."'

"This seems difficult to understand. Why these cries? Does it make sense that the tzaddikim will be brought to Gehinnom, and the sinners to the Garden of Eden?

"This is not the case. Rather, in the future there will come a day when it will be impossible to distinguish between a righteous person and a sinner. The angels will be confused, bringing the sinners to the Garden of Eden, and the righteous persons to Gehinnom. At that time both of them – the Garden of Eden and Gehinnom – will have to warn the angels not to mix up their inhabitants."

TAKING A SECOND LOOK

Rabbi Meir Horowitz of Dzikov taught: "Scripture states about the prophet Elisha that 'as the musician played, the hand of God came upon him' (II Kings 3:15). How can we understand this? Why would music bring down God's presence?

"If one listens to a melody the first time, one may think that it has no charm or beauty, and that its different sections do not harmonize properly. However, after one listens several times, one begins to penetrate to its essence. One discerns the song's different layers and sections and appreciates how beautifully the different components synchronize together.

"It is the same with a tzaddik. Sometimes when one experiences a tzaddik for the first time he may seem strange and unusual in his ways, as if there were no connection between his presentations. But only after one spends more time with him does one begin to arrive at an understanding of his character. Once his actions are appreciated within the context of his entire personality, admiration and inspiration follow.

"This is the meaning of the scriptural verse: 'As the musician played, the hand of God came upon him.'"

THE CROWN OF THE TZADDIK

The beit midrash of the Maggid of Mezritch emphasized the ethic of mutual responsibility – to be part of the people of Israel. In this beit midrash it was possible for a tzaddik to say: "It is better to be in Gehinnom with the wicked, than to sit on a throne of honor in a crystal palace in the Garden of Eden, with a crown on my head, basking in the glow of the *Shekhinah* – alone!"

Rabbi Shalom Shakhna, the grandson of the Maggid of Mezritch, told of one of his visions: "I was strolling in the paths of Heaven, and I saw a palace decorated beautifully. Inside the palace there was a golden table on which was lying a crown embedded with innumerable precious stones. Next to the table sat a tzaddik wearing imperial clothing. I then heard a voice announcing, 'The crown on the table belongs to the tzaddik sitting on the chair. The number of jewels in the crown is as many as the good deeds of the tzaddik.'

"I then asked, 'If the crown belongs to the tzaddik, why does it lie on the table and not on the head of the tzaddik?'

"The voice replied, 'This tzaddik lived with holiness and purity throughout his lifetime. However he behaved with strictness and irritability with people, and distanced himself from them. Because of this he does not deserve to wear the crown on his head, since his actions brought out his bad side. The crown is his crown, but his distancing himself from the masses places a barrier between him and his good deeds.'"

GOD IS A TZADDIK

A certain Hasid asked Rabbi Yisrael of Chortkov to promise him that he would have a complete recovery. He quoted the saying of the Talmud, "A tzaddik decrees, and the Blessed Holy One accedes."

Rabbi Yisrael replied, "Who said I am a tzaddik?"

The Hasid countered, "If you, my master, are not a tzaddik, then who is?"

"God is," replied Rabbi Yisrael in a pleasant voice. "Is it not written, 'God is righteous (*tzaddik*) in all His ways' (Psalms 145:17)?

WORDS OF WISDOM

THE INFLUENCE OF A TZADDIK

The true tzaddik is one who influences his generation.

One who has influence must be like a funnel. The top end has an opening that is large and wide. The bottom end is narrow, as a thin pipe, so that he may pour his ideas even onto small heads.

Rabbi Yosef Yitzhak Schneerson

HIDDEN TZADDIK

"How abundant is the good that you have hidden for those who fear You" (Psalms 31:20).

It is well for a tzaddik that his good deeds are hidden and unknown from the eyes of all.

Rabbi Yisrael Baal Shem Tov

Tzedakah

"ALL THAT YOU GIVE ME I WILL SET ASIDE A TITHE FOR YOU" (GENESIS 28:22)

Rabbi Shalom, grandfather of Rabbi Mordekhai Hakohen of Birzan, made his living as a goldsmith. The tzaddik Meir of Promislan considered him a "hidden tzaddik." While he was plying his trade he would be engrossed in meditation. At night he banished sleep from his eyes, devoting himself to Torah.

It was Rabbi Shalom's custom to give a tithe of his income to charitable causes. It happened once that he suffered a significant loss of income from his work, and yet he gave a tenth of the loss to *tzedakah*. He explained it in this way: "We learn in the Mishnah that 'a person is obligated to offer a blessing on the bad things that happen just as one offers a blessing on the good things that occur' (Tractate Berakhot 9:5). As such, just as it is my custom to give a tenth of my profits, so I feel obligated to give a tenth also of my losses."

PUNISHMENT IS GOOD

Rabbi Mendel of Viznitz was very generous in distributing his money to *tzedakah*. Everything he had he gave to the poor. One of his family members asked him, "Rabbi, is this a good idea? Is there not a very clear law in the Talmud 'Whoever gives money away should not give more than twenty percent' (Tractate Ketubot 50a)?"

Rabbi Mendel replied, "To transgress an edict of the ancient rabbis is a very serious sin, and one is obligated to receive punishment for such a thing. But when I give away twenty percent of my money in the morning, and then someone comes to me crying that he has not even a crumb of bread for his family, I cannot stop myself from violating this edict and distributing the rest of what I have.

"Whatever happens to me, let it happen. For a transgression such as this, it is good to be punished."

EVERY PENNY COUNTS

The midrash comments: "'He wears *tzedakah* as a breastplate' (Isaiah 59:17): Every scale on the breastplate joins with the others and makes a large breastplate. It is the same with *tzedakah*: every penny adds up to make a large sum."

On this teaching Rabbi Levi Yitzhak of Berditchev elaborated: "It would seem that this is simple logic. What does the midrash add by saying this? It seems obvious that every penny that one gives to *tzedakah* today joins with the *tzedakah* one gives the next day.

"The midrash makes the comparison with *tzedakah* because if the breastplate is missing some scales, it serves no purpose. This being the case, when a person adds one scale it is considered as if he made the whole breastplate. This is the same with *tzedakah*. When a poor person says that he is missing one penny to make a gilder, in order to buy a chicken in honor of Shabbat, whoever gives him the last penny, it is as if he gives a whole gilder, and gets credit for contributing an entire chicken. And if several people contribute to the poor person one penny so that he has a gilder, each person who gives has the reward of giving a whole chicken."

"YOU SHALL SURELY GIVE" (DEUTERONOMY 15:10)

Rabbi Simhah Bunim of Peshischa was traveling back home, and stayed in an inn. In that town there lived a Rabbi Zalman Hasid, a giant in Torah and good deeds, but very, very poor. When Rabbi Simhah Bunim entered the inn he immediately sent for Rabbi Zalman. He saw him dressed in rags and tattered clothes, despite the freezing cold temperature.

Rabbi Simhah Bunim told Rabbi Zalman Hasid to go and buy food for a very elegant meal, a meal fitting for a Hasid, and gave him a large sum of money.

Rabbi Zalman went to the market and bought a large amount of food – meat, fish, delicious drinks – and there was still ample money left.

After Rabbi Zalman left, Rabbi Simhah Bunim sent a worker to buy boots, cloth for coats, and other necessary clothing. Before eating, the rabbi told the inn worker to bring all the clothing into the house of Rabbi Zalman Hasid. Rabbi Simhah Bunim went with Rabbi Zalman, sent away all the other people in the house, and gave Rabbi Zalman clothing from head to toe. When Rabbi Simhah Bunim saw that the other members of the household were also dressed in rags and tatters, he sent to buy fabric for everyone. The house was filled with light and joy. They sat down to a wonderful meal, drank and rejoiced.

When Rabbi Simhah Bunim was getting ready to leave, Rabbi Zalman came to see him and to give him a blessing. Rabbi Simhah Bunim gave him a gold dinar, but Rabbi Zalman refused. "My master," he said, "I still have money left from the sumptuous meal that you gave me, besides the clothing that you bought for me and my household."

Rabbi Simhah Bunim replied, "One who gives *tzedakah* out of pity, because he has mercy on the poor and cannot stand to see him in his pain, has not fulfilled the mitzvah of *tzedakah*. You see in such a case one is not giving to the poor, but to oneself, so his heart will not ache. Even when I gave you *tzedakah*, it was out of mercy. I could not bear to see your pain and the pain of the members of your household dressed in rags and tatters. But now that you are dressed in beautiful clothing, I am ready to fulfill the mitzvah of *tzedakah*."

"SHARE YOUR BREAD WITH THE HUNGRY" (ISAIAH 58:7)

Rabbi Shmuel Eliezer Halevy Edels, the Maharsha, was famous not only for his great Torah knowledge, but also for his righteousness and his good heart. It is said of him that all the years that he was rabbi in Austria, there was not one Jew hungry for bread. His wealthy mother-in-law, the generous Miss Edel, who was privileged to have her son-in-law called by her name, supported all the students in his large yeshivah for twenty years, and also gave food to guests, bread to the hungry, and *tzedakah* to the poor.

It happened once that one of the bakers in the city came into the beit midrash to pray. Rabbi Shmuel Eliezer noticed the beggar and saw that his face was drawn, so he asked him, "Why do you look so sad?"

"Rabbi," said the baker sadly, "the fair was this week in our city, and I lost a lot of money. I prepared a large amount of bread for the market, and I sold almost none of it."

Rabbi Shmuel Eliezer said to him, "Go bring to my house all the bread that you baked." When he brought the bread, Rabbi Shmuel Eliezer paid the baker for all the bread, and then distributed it to the poor.

EAGER TO GIVE

Rabbi Mordekhai Banet of Nikolsberg was stingy with himself, but generous with others who needed help and support. He was fortunate, in his wisdom and goodness, to be appointed by the government as chief rabbi of all the Jews in the region of Moravia, but a large portion of his salary and most of his income he would give to *tzedakah* and to support the students of his large yeshivah, which he had founded in the city of Nikolsberg.

It was said of Rabbi Mordekhai Banet that he never ate any breakfast until he had given *tzedakah* or had done a kind deed for another Jew. He would say in jest, "Our sages taught, 'Before one eats or drinks one has two hearts, and after eating and drinking one has only one heart' (Talmud, Tractate Bava Batra 12b). In other words, before eating and drinking one's heart feels hunger and thirst, and therefore also feels the heart of the poor, who are hungry for bread. But after eating and drinking, once one has satisfied his hunger, he again has only one heart. His heart is full, and cannot feel the heart of the poor who have no food to eat."

It is told that once a whole day passed, and there was not even one opportunity to give *tzedakah*. Rabbi Mordekhai went through the whole day fasting. At dark he went to the market to see if perhaps the Blessed Holy One would grant him the opportunity to help a poor Jew.

As he was walking he found a gentile from the village near Nikolsberg who had come to the city with his wagon full of wood, hoping to sell it – but there were no buyers. Rabbi Mordekhai knocked on the door of a Jew who was a carpenter, and told him that there was a wagon of wood for sale in the market. The carpenter went to the market and began to bargain with the man about the price of his merchandise. When they came close to a deal, the carpenter whispered in the ears of the rabbi that, to his regret, he did not have enough money to pay for the wood.

"I will be happy to lend you the necessary sum so that you can close the deal," answered Rabbi Mordekhai with delight. On the spot he took out money from his pocket and handed it to the carpenter. The carpenter bought the wood, and Rabbi Mordekhai returned home, with a full heart.

FOLLOWING GOD'S WAYS

Rabbi Mordekhai Banet went to a wealthy man, about whom many were complaining that he secretly gave contributions to nonbelievers, and asked him for a large donation to *tzedakah*, to be announced publicly.

The wealthy man refused and explained, "Rabbi, it is my custom to give *tzedakah* privately, as is the tradition."

"How surprised I am," answered Rabbi Mordekhai with a smile, "that the gifts you give to nonbelievers are discussed throughout the city, but for *tzedakah*, which you say you are giving privately, how come we do not know anything about them?"

Rabbi Mordekhai Banet was known for his charity to all Jews, no matter what their beliefs. When the rabbi discovered that a family of Reform Jews was suffering from hunger, he immediately called his assistant and gave him a significant donation on condition that he take it to the family without their knowing where the help was coming from.

Rabbi Mordekhai Banet's friends were surprised that their rabbi, whom they knew to be very strict in his observance, was nevertheless sending money to a Reform family. The rabbi understood their feelings and explained, "We are obligated to cling to the ways of the Blessed Holy One. We are taught that God is merciful 'to all God's creatures' (Psalms 145:9), making no distinctions between one person or another, whether strictly observant or not, whether good or bad, so must we have mercy on each and every Jew. So it is that we praise God who 'gives food to all creatures' (Psalms 136:25). So too we learn in the Talmud that the central praise in the Ashrei psalm is that it says 'God opens His hand feeding every creature to its heart's content' (Tractate Berakhot 4b). Rashi comments on this verse that the emphasis is the key phrase 'to every creature.' And who am I to disagree?"

SECRET *TZEDAKAH*

The leading scholar, Rabbi Yomtov Lipman Heller, author of *Tosfot Yomtov*, who was the rabbi of Cracow, was buried near the fence of the cemetery. Therein lies the following story:

There lived in Cracow at that time a wealthy man named Shimon, whom everyone called "Shimon the Miser" since he never gave a penny to a poor person, and everyone in the city cursed him for it. At the same time there lived in the city two simple men, one a butcher and one a baker, who were well known for their generosity.

Time passed and Shimon the Miser died, and as a punishment for his miserliness he was buried near the cemetery fence. After Shimon's death suddenly the butcher and the baker stopped giving *tzedakah*. This caused great surprise, and the poor made loud complaints. There was such vociferous protesting that these two men were summoned to come before the rabbi.

In the presence of the rabbi, the two men admitted that the charity funds that they were accustomed to distribute were not from their own money. It was Shimon, "Shimon the Miser," who had made the two men swear not to tell anyone the source of the money, since Shimon disliked being honored. But now that Shimon had died, they had no money to give to *tzedakah*.

The matter made a very deep impression on Rabbi Yomtov Heller, and after he died it was discovered that he had written in his will that he requested to be buried near the fence of the cemetery, next to "Shimon the Miser."

"HAPPY IS THE ONE WHO IS CONSIDERATE OF THE POOR" (PSALMS 41:2)

Prof. Ben-Zion Rubin relates that once at the beginning of the Hebrew month of Adar he visited his relative, the tzaddik Rabbi Aryeh Levin, in his modest room, and saw him leaning over his desk, counting money, and arranging the bills in piles.

Prof. Rubin asked Rabbi Levin the reason for what he was doing, and he answered, "This money came to me to be distributed as *tzedakah* as I see fit. Meanwhile I am taking care of it."

"Why do you not distribute it now?" he asked.

"I am fearful that the needy will be embarrassed if they receive a gift from someone. However, in a few days the festival of Purim will be here, and then perhaps I can combine the two Purim mitzvot of *mishloah manot*, giving gifts to friends, and *matanot la'evyonim*, giving charity to the poor. If I give the *tzedakah* at that time, those who receive the gift will hopefully accept the *tzedakah* without, Heaven forbid, feeling embarrassed."

DOWERING THE BRIDE

Kaiser Maximilian of Prague had a great affection and esteem for Mordekhai Maisel, who was one of the highly respected merchants in his day. He did business with integrity, and was well thought of by many. As a sign of honor and affection the kaiser presented him with a gift of a large gold chain, which the kaiser himself placed on his neck.

Once when Mordekhai Maisel was strolling through the streets of Prague, a certain poor man, of a good family, approached him and presented to him his wish for assistance to marry off his daughter. The young woman was soon to stand under the huppah, but the man did not have a penny to pay for the wedding.

Mordekhai put his hand in his pocket and did not find a single coin to give the man. He then removed from his neck the gold chain given to him by the kaiser, gave it to the poor man, and said to him, "Take this golden chain given to me by the kaiser, sell it, and you will have the funds necessary to make a wedding for your daughter."

The poor man refused to accept the golden chain and said to Mordekhai, "My honored sir, far be it from me to take from you a gift presented to you by the kaiser. I am afraid that the matter will become known to the kaiser, and he will take it as an insult that you gave his gift to some poor fellow. Tomorrow let me come to your store and you can give me some money, if you wish."

Mordekhai smiled and replied to the man, "All my money, my possessions and my wealth, were given to me as a gift from the Sovereign of Sovereigns. If I have permission to give of my wealth as a gift to the poor from the money of the Highest Sovereign, how much more so can I give a gift from the sovereign of this country as a contribution to the poor.

"Further, I advise you to take this golden chain now, because my heart is moved to give you this large gift, and who knows if tomorrow at this time my heart will move me as it does now?"

STAND IN ANOTHER'S SHOES

Rabbi Eliyahu Hayyim Maisel, the rabbi of Lodz and son of Mordekhai Maisel, inherited his father's compassionate nature. One winter the weather was unseasonably difficult. Heavy snows fell, and there was a terrible chill and frost. Prices soared, the availability of firewood diminished, there was high unemployment, and the poor were freezing from the cold.

Rabbi Eliyahu Hayyim pleaded with the wealthy to assist their unfortunate brothers and sisters. Of course, the rabbi first visited the home of the wealthiest Jew in Lodz, Mr. Kalman Poznanski. When Rabbi Eliyahu Hayyim came to the doorway, the doorman hurried to inform his master that the rabbi had come to see him. Poznanski, who was very close to Rabbi Eliyahu Hayyim and had great respect and reverence for him, came immediately to meet him in the doorway, dressed in light clothing. He greeted the rabbi and invited him into the living room. Rabbi Eliyahu Hayyim returned the warm greeting but remained standing in the doorway, and began to discuss with Poznanski matters of the day and the needs of the community. Poznanski stood and listened respectfully, shivering from the cold. Rabbi Eliyahu Hayyim continued to discuss matters at great length, going from one subject to another, speaking slowly, as if he were sitting in the warm living room, while Poznanski became extremely uncomfortable from the cold. He turned to Rabbi Eliyahu Hayyim and said to him, "Rabbi, I am freezing from the cold, and I request that you come into my living room."

"Now," said Rabbi Eliyahu Hayyim, who did not move from his place, "I will tell you why I came to visit you. The winter is very harsh, the poor of our people are many and they are freezing from the cold. I have come now to visit your honor, to ask you to make a sizeable contribution for the welfare of the poor."

Poznanski did not refuse and promised the rabbi a large contribution for the welfare of the poor. Then the two of them went into the living room and continued to discuss the plight of the Jews in Russia. During the conversation Poznanski asked Rabbi Eliyahu Hayyim, "Tell me, dear Rabbi, why you stood with me all that time in the doorway, and would not come into the house to ask for my contribution."

"I will tell you the real reason," answered Rabbi Eliyahu Hayyim. "There is a popular aphorism: 'The satisfied do not feel the pain of the hungry.' I came to tell you about the trouble and pain of the poor people who are freezing from the harsh winter. Had we sat in a comfortable living room, filled with light and heat, would you have felt the pain of our poor brothers and sisters?

"Only when we stood in the doorway long enough for you to feel the bitter cold did you experience a small measure of the cold that prevails in the homes of the poor. Then you agreed to give me a very generous contribution."

LIVING BOOKS

Once Rabbi Hayyim Ozer Grodzinski, a rabbi from Eretz Yisrael, met with Rabbi Eliyahu Hayyim Maisel, the rabbi of Lodz, and gave him his book, *Ahiezer*, as a gift. Then Rabbi Hayyim Ozer asked Rabbi Eliyahu Hayyim, "When will we merit seeing your book?"

Rabbi Eliyahu Hayyim took out a large envelope filled with loan documents of great scholars who had lost their property, and he also took out promissory notes of widows and orphans, and more notes of pitiful people for whom he was their guarantor for their release. Then he turned to Rabbi Hayyim Ozer and exclaimed: "*This* is my book!"

When Rabbi Hayyim Ozer heard this he burst out crying.

IT'S MY MISSION

Toward the end of his life, Rabbi Nahumke of Horodne was very ill and in great pain. Nevertheless, he continued his custom of going from house to house every day, collecting *tzedakah* for the many poor people who needed help.

One night, as he was on his way to collect *tzedakah*, terrible pain gripped him and he fell down. It was late at night, and no one heard Rabbi Nahumke's cries for help. His shouts finally reached a wagon driver who was driving his coach in the city street. The wagon driver got down from his seat and followed the voice. He spotted Rabbi Nahumke lying limp on the ground. He picked him up, put him in the coach, and began to drive him to his home.

On the way Rabbi Nahumke felt better, and asked the driver to stop and wait. He wanted to get down.

"Where are you going, Rabbi?" asked the driver. "I will take you; I will bring you home."

"No," insisted Rabbi Nahumke. "I must go to do a mitzvah, to collect charity for the poor who are in need of me."

"Dear Rabbi," pressed the wagon driver," you are sick. It is midnight, and very, very dark."

"Tell me," asked Rabbi Nahumke, "would you be driving at this hour in the forest unless you would have profit from it?"

"What can I do?" answered the driver. "This is my living, and I have a wife and five little children who depend on me!"

"How much more so for me," answered Rabbi Nahumke, "upon whom hundreds of souls depend."

GIVING TO THE NEEDY

Rabbi Hayyim of Zanz was accustomed to distribute his money to *tzedakah*.

His son asked him, "My father and teacher, have we not learned, 'One who gives his money to *tzedakah* must not give more than a fifth of his possessions' (Talmud, Tractate Ketubot 77a)?"

Rabbi Hayyim replied, "What does that refer to? To one who perceives his gifts to *tzedakah* as dispersing the money. This does not apply to one who sees the contribution of his money to *tzedakah* as an investment. For such a one, the limit of one fifth does not apply."

WORDS OF WISDOM

THE HAND IS A CHARIOT

The hand, when it gives *tzedakah*, becomes a chariot to divinity.

Rabbi Shneur Zalman of Liadi

DO NOT ROB THE POOR

"Do not rob the poor because he is poor..." (Proverbs 22:22).

When you see a poor person in his misery, do not justify his lot by saying, "That's the way it should be, he deserves it!"

The Seer of Lublin

Uniqueness of the Jewish People

THE INSULTED ONE

Rabbi Yaakov Yitzhak, the Holy Jew of Peshischa, together with his friend Rabbi David of Lalov, traveled from city to city in order to call on wealthy Jews to collect charity for those in need.

Once they entered the home of a very wealthy person. The resident assumed that they were beggars. He glanced at them and saw that one of them – Reb David – was short and emaciated. The Holy Jew, on the other hand, was strong, broad shouldered, and muscular.

The wealthy man turned to Reb David and said, "To you I am ready to give charity, since you are weak, and cannot work. But to the other, no. He has strong hands, and people like him can earn their living by hard labor."

The two of them left and went their way. About an hour later it became known to the wealthy man that the person he had insulted was none other than the famous tzaddik of Peshischa, the Holy Jew. He immediately regretted his words, ran out of the house, and chased after the two men until he reached them.

The prosperous man turned to the Holy Jew, and with tears in his eyes asked forgiveness for insulting him. As a token of his sorrow and regret he stated that he was ready to contribute any sum that the rabbi designated. He explained that he had not realized that the holy rabbi of Peshischa was in his house. He had assumed that he was a simple poor Jew roaming around for handouts.

The Holy Jew answered him: "You are mistaken. I am not at all the Jew you are looking for."

The wealthy man persisted. "I am not mistaken, Rabbi. I want to honor your scholarship in Torah, and to mollify you."

The Holy Jew replied, "Me you want to mollify? Me you offended? Did you not say that you offended me because I looked in your eyes like a simple, poor man? If so, it's not me you insulted, but that simple Jew. Therefore, it is him that you must seek out, and from him that you must ask forgiveness. Because that simple Jew whom you offended did not give me permission to forgive in his name the insults that he received. If you mean what you say, you have no choice but to ask forgiveness from every simple Jew you meet on the road for insulting him."

THE GLORY OF THE AVERAGE PERSON

During his seven years of *hitbodedut*, meditative isolation, in the Carpathian mountains, the Baal Shem Tov thought deeply about the simple people. In his kind heart there grew an abundance of love for all the disheartened and despondent of the Jewish community.

The common expression *am ha'aretz*, literally "the people of the land," was used by the scholars to refer to the simple, untutored folk. The Besht, however, had his own interpretation of the phrase. He said that they were truly the people resembling the land. The land is the source of life for all creatures; in it are locked treasures of gold and silver. All living beings rely on the land's produce, and yet people tread on it and it does not get angry. The same is true, said the Besht, of the masses of simple people.

At another time the Besht contrasted the simple Jew, whose field is watered from heavenly rain, to the scholar, whose field is watered by humans. It may be that the produce from the field that is watered by humans is more abundant; nevertheless the field that is watered by the heavens has the glory of nature which was blessed by God. Such is the field that drinks from the rains of the heavens.

TOGETHER YET SEPARATE

One spring day Rabbi Simhah Bunim of Peshischa told his followers to hire a wagon. "Tonight," he said, "we shall visit Warsaw, the capital of Poland."

When the rabbi and his followers reached Warsaw, they asked him in which inn he wanted to stay. He replied that he had a longing to ramble during the evening hours in the streets of the city. They peered into the display windows of the various stores, glanced into the stores and looked at the merchants. Suddenly the rabbi stopped and announced: "This is the inn in which we will stay."

The rabbi went inside along with his students. On one side of a table sat two Jews whose mien suggested that they had been drinking heavily. The straps around their waists were redolent of the porters of the town.

The rabbi and his entourage approached the table where these men were sitting, and made a point of placing themselves opposite the two porters. The innkeeper placed some drinks on the table and while the rabbi and his followers drank, they listened carefully to the discussion of the two porters.

One porter said to the other, "Have you studied this week's Torah portion?" The other answered, "Yes, of course I studied it. But I must admit that I did not understand the entire parashah. The Torah says in regard to Avraham and Avimelekh that 'the two of them made a covenant' (Genesis 11:27). How could it be that the righteous Avraham, who believes in one God, made a covenant with a non-Jewish idolater, Avimelekh? A Jew dealing with a non-Jew? I confess that I also deal with non-Jews, but to make a covenant with them?"

The other responded, "I also had difficulty interpreting that verse, but for a different reason. I noticed that there was a superfluous word, the word *shneihem*, "the two of them." Would it not have been sufficient for the Torah to say 'they made a covenant'?"

The other man answered: "Now I understand the verse, because your question provides the answer to my question. The Torah teaches that while Avraham and Avimelekh made a covenant, nevertheless they remained *shneihem*. They were neighbors, and it is obvious that they had common interests, but to be close friends? Unlikely! Avraham remained Avraham, and Avimelekh remained Avimelekh!"

The rabbi signaled to his group that it was time to leave. They left the inn, ascended the wagon, and the same night returned to Peshischa. On the road the rabbi explained to his students that the trip to Warsaw was worth the effort just to hear the words of these two porters.

"When two people establish between themselves a covenant, there lingers some doubt that one will absorb the qualities of the other. It is important to remember, therefore, the key word, *shneihem*, 'the two of them.'"

The rabbi became lost in thought for a bit, and then continued: "Not everyone is able to be together with others and yet remain separate and independent at the same time. This requires a great measure of wisdom."

ANY SMALL LINK

Rabbi Yisrael of Rizhin used to say, "One must never despair of a Jew. Every Jew, even a wicked one, maintains some small link with Judaism. When a bucket falls into a deep well, it's possible to pull it up from the bottom, as long as it is connected to a rope. It could be a thick rope or a very thin rope, as long as there is a rope."

A JEW OF INTEGRITY

When Rabbi Tzvi Elimelekh Shapira of Dinov died, Rabbi Shalom of Belz said to his wife, "What a shame that a Jew of such integrity left our world."

The rabbi's wife replied, "Was he only a Jew of integrity? Was he not also a famous rabbi?"

Rabbi Shalom answered, "There are, thank God, many famous rabbis, but Jews of integrity are far less common."

WORDS OF WISDOM

CREATING MIRACLES

Is it a novelty to be a person who creates miracles? Any simple person can do wonders and create miracles. It is indeed a novelty to be a good Jew. It is not easy to be a good Jew.

The Holy Jew of Peshischa

GODLINESS

Just as one who searches for a valuable treasure buried deep within the earth does so with great effort and struggle, so must one expend great energy in searching for the treasure of godliness that is hidden deep within the soul.

Rabbi Yosef Yitzhak of Lubavitch

GOD DESIRES REBELS

"You have been defiant toward God" (Deuteronomy 9:24).

Should not the Torah have used the word *neged* (against) God, instead of the word *im* (*with*, or *toward*) God?

Rather, sometimes defiant behavior is actually God's will, such that being defiant is also "with" Him.

Rabbi Mordekhai Yosef Leiner of Izbitz

Ups and Downs

A TIME FOR EVERYTHING

Rabbi Yehudah Aryeh Leib of Gur, author of the *Sfat Emet*, gave a novel interpretation to the verse recited in the morning prayers, "As for me, may my prayer come to You, God, at a time of favor" (Psalms 69:14): "The phrase 'at a time of favor' does not refer to God," explained Rabbi Aryeh Leib, "since with regard to God all times are good to pray. The phrase refers to humans who can be worthy at certain specific times to bring oneself close to God.

"There are days that are desolate, and days that are uplifting. There are times when the heart is like a blossoming flower, and other times when it's like a withering blossom. Thus one prays that God will instill in one the spirit that will elicit one's finest inner senses so that one will be ready for the deepest faith in God."

WHERE IS THE PLACE OF GOD'S GLORY?

Rabbi Yisrael, the Maggid of Koznitz, taught: "Many are those who mistakenly believe that God's place is in the heavens, and when they want to get closer to God they must elevate themselves. But it is not so.

"The Blessed Holy One prefers to dwell in this world, with the contrite and lowly in spirit. Therefore, to the extent that one diminishes one's ego, one draws closer to the Blessed One."

TRAIN A CHILD...

A student asked the Baal Shem Tov, "Why is it that at times one suddenly feels a great distance from the Blessed Creator, as if one is being pushed away from the Almighty, Heaven forbid?"

The Besht replied: "When teaching a child to walk, the parent stands the child up in front of him, and then immediately steps back a bit so that the child will step forward toward him. To prevent him from falling the parent holds him with his hands, and the child moves toward the parent. As the child learns to walk a little, the parent moves a bit farther away but still holds his hands close to the child.

"Moving farther away, therefore, is done for the purpose of learning and education."

WITHOUT STOPPING

Once Rabbi Yisrael Salanter entered the beit midrash and told his students, "As I was walking here today I gazed at a small bird flying in the sky. I learned an important lesson from it. A bird can soar higher and higher, as long as it flaps its wings without a pause. If it halts briefly, it will fall right to the ground. So it is with humans."

WORDS OF WISDOM

SPARKS

Even if one finds oneself on a ladder going downward, one can still cling to God with a few small thoughts. With the strength of these small ideas one can come to larger thoughts.

The same with coals. If there is still a tiny spark, it can still flare up and turn into a giant bonfire. But if there is not even a tiny spark with which to cling to the Creator, the soul will be completely extinguished.

Rabbi Yisrael Baal Shem Tov

BEING THERE

"And God said to Moshe: Come up to me on the mountain, and be there" (Exodus 24:12).

It is clear that if Moshe goes up the mountain, then he will be there. So why does the end of the verse stress that?

This shows that a person can make a strong effort to arrive at the peak of a high mountain, and nevertheless not be there. He may be standing at the top of the mountain, but his head is somewhere else.

Rabbi Menahem Mendel of Kotzk

THE NEAR AND THE FAR

"Peace, peace, to the far and to the near" (Isaiah 57:19).

Being far from the Creator is sometimes good. When one feels distant, one may experience genuine longing to come near.

Rabbi Yehudah Aryeh Leib of Gur, the Sfat Emet

Urges

"SIN CROUCHES AT THE DOOR"

When Rabbi Eliezer Horowitz of Dzikov was a youngster he engaged in typical childish behavior. His father, the saintly Rabbi Naftali of Ropschitz, chastised him.

The child responded, "What can I do, since the evil urge enticed me, and I succumbed."

His father replied, "Just the opposite, learn a lesson from the evil urge. It is faithful to its mission to seduce people, and it does its job religiously as it is commanded."

The child answered, "The evil urge does not have its own evil urge to push it not to do its task. With regard to humans, however – 'sin crouches at the door' (Genesis 4:7)."

WHAT ARE YOU DISCUSSING?

Rabbi Hayyim of Volozhin entered the yeshivah and noticed that two students were sitting with a copy of the Talmud open before them, having a discussion. The rabbi asked them, "My sons, what is your discussion about?"

"Our master," they answered, "we are not, Heaven forbid, having a social conversation. We are planning strategies and approaches to overcome the *yetzer hara* (the evil inclination), which is getting stronger and more resourceful every day."

"You must know, my dear children," smiled Rabbi Hayyim, "what the *yetzer hara* says to himself: 'You folks can plan strategies and tactics, and while you're doing that, you are neglecting study of Torah. I have succeeded in all my goals, just as I planned.'"

THE EVIL INCLINATION'S MANY SELVES

Rabbi Menahem Mendel of Kotzk noticed a young boy walking around the beit midrash, back and forth. He walked over and spoke to him. "Young man, it is written in our holy books, 'If you meet the evil one (the *yetzer hara*), drag him to the beit midrash.' Do you think, young fellow, that this is the end of it? That in the beit midrash, all the annoyance of the *yetzer hara* is taken care of?

"Not at all! The *yetzer hara* has many domiciles. Instead of the *yetzer* that ambles in the market, another *yetzer* will approach you in the beit midrash, with an appearance of someone honorable, posing as a student, for whom you must be careful no less than the *yetzer hara* that strolls in the market."

ADVICE OF THE EVIL INCLINATION

Rabbi Menahem Mendel of Vitebsk related that once, when he was in the midst of his prayers, an idea came to him. "You, Menahem Mendel, who are so full of sin, how do you dare stand up and recite your prayers before the Master of the World?"

"At first," said Rabbi Menahem Mendel, "I thought that this must be a strong warning from my *yetzer hatov*, my good inclination that wanted me to improve my ways. Then I reconsidered, and it became clear to me that this was coming from my *yetzer hara*, my evil inclination. I thought to myself, why have I never even considered the possibility that I am full of sin while I was eating? Would I ever think to myself, 'What a lowlife you are, who dares to sit at the table and eat a meal?'"

SOMETIMES SINS COME BECAUSE OF MITZVOT

Rabbi Shlomo Hakohen Rabinowitz of Radomsk taught: "You might think that the *yetzer hara* only tempts people to commit sins. However, sometimes it tempts people to perform a certain mitzvah in order to divert attention from a greater mitzvah which is more timely."

Rabbi Shlomo gave an example with the following story: "It happened once that the cost of purchasing an etrog for Sukkot was extremely expensive.

The rabbis collected from the wealthy people in town a huge sum to buy an etrog for the community. One of the affluent leaders complained that there was an orphan in town who had reached the age of marriage several years ago, and collecting funds for her wedding should take priority over purchasing the etrog."

Rabbi Shlomo summed up as follows: "Think about it. This orphan had reached the age of marriage quite a while ago, and in all those years the wealthy of the city had paid no attention to the mitzvah of raising funds for her wedding. Now that they were being asked to contribute money to buy an etrog it suddenly occurred to them that the mitzvah of *hakhnasat kallah*, arranging a wedding for a bride, is more important. The *yetzer hara*, for his part, tried to convince the community to buy an etrog, which is used for the one week of Sukkot, rather than perform the great mitzvah of *hakhnasat kallah*."

THE POSITIVE QUALITY OF THE EVIL INCLINATION

On the last day of creation the Torah states, "And behold it was very good" (Genesis 1:31). One of the wisest of all spiritual masters of the Aggadah (Jewish lore) commented on this: "'Very good' refers to the evil inclination" (Midrash Bereshit Rabbah 9:9). Our inclinations – both of good and of evil – are what create the essence of our humanness. The Hebrew word *yetzer* in fact comes from the root meaning *to form*; both inclinations enable us to express our inborn creative faculties. Thus, humans are blessed with the faculty of choice and the ability to make decisions.

"The idea that 'It is not good for man to be by himself' (Genesis 2:18) is written about the first man, Adam. Rabbi Simhah Bunim of Peshischa went so far as to say that 'by himself' means without the two *yetzarim*. In other words, it is not good for man to be without the good inclination or the evil inclination. Were it not for the clash of the two, the human soul would resemble a desert wasteland, and a human being would descend from the high level of one who can speak and think to the lowest level of a silent, lifeless being."

WORDS OF WISDOM

FOCUS ON YOURSELF

"Who is mighty? One who conquers his urges" (Pirkei Avot 4:1).

The Mishnah states that one should conquer one's own urges and instincts, not those of another. The common pattern on the part of most people is the desire and longing to control the urges of the other – that the next person should be kind and compassionate, that the other should be a God-fearing and pious person.

Rabbi Naftali of Ropschitz

TURN IT TO GOOD

The Mishnah does not adjure us to destroy our urges, but rather to "conquer our urges" (Pirkei Avot 4:1). After all, the Mishnah considers the person who conquers his urges to be mighty, but it does not take might to *destroy* urges. That only requires simple intelligence. It does, however, take might to *conquer* one's urges – in other words, to take charge of them in a way that leaves them healthy and whole.

One should use one's inner urges with all one's might and fervor for the purpose of performing mitzvot and good deeds.

Rabbi Yisrael Baal Shem Tov

Wisdom

GIVE US A WISE HEART (PSALMS 90:12)

One day two people with a dispute between them approached Rabbi Yehezkel Landau, the rabbi of Prague, for a rabbinic ruling. One of them was dressed in shabby clothing, the attire of a wagon driver. The other had the appearance of a successful merchant. The first one arose and tearfully related his plight.

"I am a grain merchant from a distant city who engaged this man, a wagon driver, to bring me to Prague. On the way, when we were passing through a thick forest, the wagon driver attacked me and forced me to give him all my money. Not only that, but he forced me to exchange our clothing and assume the role of wagon driver. In this fashion we arrived in Prague, and for the past few days this crooked driver has been presenting himself as an important merchant who has been robbed and was walking around the city without a penny in his pocket. I've been running around with the whip in my hands, telling everyone about the terrible tragedy that happened to me, but no one believes me – instead they laugh at me! Only after much pleading and bitter crying did I finally think of persuading several local people to convince this thief to come with me to a *beit din* (rabbinic court)."

"What do you have to say?" asked Rabbi Landau of the other man, who appeared as if he were a wealthy merchant.

"What can I say," smiled the man, "when it is perfectly clear to everyone that this man is a bungling fool if he thinks that he is a merchant and I am a wagon driver. For these last few days he has been chasing me around the streets of the city, and I don't know how to get rid of him."

Rabbi Landau began to examine the two men, but both of them stubbornly held on to their arguments and it was impossible to clarify the matter. Finally, Rabbi Landau told them that they must return to him the next morning, and he would make a decision.

After they left Rabbi Landau called his assistant and told him that when the two men arrived the next morning, he should not let them enter his room under any circumstances, but tell them that they had to sit and wait in the next room.

Early the next morning the two men arrived. A half hour passed, an hour passed, and the assistant still did not permit them to see the rabbi. Two hours passed, three hours, and one of the men became so impatient that he tried to offer the assistant money to go and persuade the rabbi to see them. The assistant replied that this was impossible, there was nothing to do; the rabbi had said they must wait, and they just had to sit and wait.

Afternoon arrived, and the two litigants were sitting as if on burning coals, and they began to get very hungry. From the adjacent room they could hear the voice of the rabbi, who was sitting and studying, as if he had forgotten the whole matter.

When the tension became unbearable, suddenly Rabbi Landau opened the door and called out in a loud voice: "Driver – enter!"

The man who was dressed as a rich merchant jumped out of his seat and hurried to the rabbi. And the other man who was dressed as a wagon driver remained seated in his place.

In a flash, it became perfectly clear who was the wagon driver and who was the merchant.

WORDS OF WISDOM

INTEGRATED WISDOM

It is important that the wisdom in our mind be joined with the understanding in our heart. In other words, our wisdom must come not only from the mind, but also from the heart.

Rabbi Tzadok Hakohen of Lublin

FOOLISH OR WISE?

What is the difference between a wise person and a fool?

A wise person can, at will, act like a fool. But a fool cannot, even if he desires, become wise.

Rabbi Leibush Harif

"GOD MADE THE HEAVENS WITH WISDOM" (PSALMS 136:5)

With wisdom? Of course with wisdom! How else would God create the heavens – with a needle and thread?

The Creator made the heavens in order that humans can look at them, and realize by doing so the purpose of Creation.

Rabbi Menahem Mendel, the Tzemah Tzedek

LEARN FROM EVERYONE

"Ben Zoma said: Who is wise? One who learns from everyone" (Pirkei Avot 4:1).

"One who learns from everyone" is wise. Why? Because such a person is always learning, and whoever is always in the category of "student" is a very wise person.

Rabbi Simhah Bunim of Peshischa

WHO IS WISE?

"Who is wise? One who can see that which will be born [the future]" (Talmud, Tractate Tamid 32a).

In other words, wisdom is a matter of seeing. A wise person sees how things are created ex nihilo, and how every day the world is recreated.

Rabbi Menahem Mendel, the "Tzemah Tzedek"

THE FOUR CHILDREN OF THE HAGGADAH

"One wise, one evil, one simple, and one who does not even know how to ask" (Pesah Haggadah).

The opposite of the wise child is not the evil child, but the foolish one. The Haggadah should have said, therefore, "one wise, and one foolish." But it is better to deal with an evil child who is smart rather than a wise child who is foolish.

Rabbi Naftali of Ropschitz

This World and the Next

REWARD AND PUNISHMENT

Rabbi Shlomo of Karlin taught: "Some people keep the entire Torah and all the mitzvot, but have no pleasure in their service. After 120 years, when they stand before the *beit din shel maalah* (heavenly court), they are instructed to enter the Garden of Eden, since they fulfilled everything written in the Torah. But since they did not feel any pleasure in this world when they fulfilled the mitzvot, it is decreed that even though they may live in the Garden of Eden they will not feel any pleasure there.

"A tzaddik who lives in the Garden of Eden and doesn't enjoy it, if he is a fool, gets angry and asks, 'What's the big deal about the Garden of Eden?' He does not know that if the Garden of Eden is not inside him in this world, then he cannot enjoy it even when he lives in it in the World to Come."

ELEVATION OF THE SOUL

When Rabbi Yomtov Lipman Heller had finished writing his book *Tosfot Yomtov*, a commentary on the Mishnah, he spoke in the beit midrash about his work. In the context of his remarks, he discussed the source of the long-standing custom of studying passages from the Mishnah after the death of a Jew. "In my youth," said Rabbi Heller, "my teacher, the Maharal of Prague, explained that the custom was connected to the fact that the word *Mishnah* was made up of the same Hebrew letters as the word *neshamah* (soul), and by studying passages of the Mishnah the soul of the departed was elevated to higher levels of Heaven.

"There is another reason," continued Rabbi Heller, "for the custom of studying Mishnah on the occasion of a death. It is well know that the Sad-ducees, the second-century group who opposed the Pharisees and denied the authority of the Oral Torah (Mishnah and Gemara, or Talmud), also denied the doctrine of the resurrection of the dead. They also claimed that there was no

World to Come. Because of this when a Jew dies, it is important to remind the family and friends that death is only temporary, that there is another world. Thus we study the Mishnah, the basis of the Oral Torah, to proclaim the validity of the Oral Law and assert the certainty of the resurrection of the dead."

ANGELS OF TRUTH AND ANGELS OF FALSEHOOD

Rabbi Moshe of Pshevorsk traveled once to Cracow and discovered that there were wealthy people there who made pledges during the reading of the Torah to give generous amounts of *tzedakah* to the poor, but did not follow through on their pledge – or they lied and reduced the amount when they made the payment.

During *seudah shlishit*, the third Shabbat meal, when many of the wealthy of the city were in attendance, he began his sermon by saying: "It is well known that out of every mitzvah is born a good angel, and out of every transgression an evil angel, who destroys and demolishes. Up above, in the world of truth, there are not only angels of truth, but angels who lie, who are created by the evil speech of wealthy men who make pledges and do not keep them. Be careful of them! The angels who lie accompany every man when he comes before the heavenly tribunal, and they are liable to tell things about him that never happened."

WHAT SHALL I SAY ON JUDGMENT DAY?

Rabbi Zusha of Anapol taught: "I do not worry that when I reach the World to Come I will be asked, 'Why were you not like our teacher Moshe, of blessed memory?' I will be able to defend myself against such a question. But I worry and fear terribly that I will be asked, 'Why were you not like Zusha?' For that I will have no answer."

THE POWER OF A SIGH

Rabbi Yisrael Baal Shem Tov told this tale:

> Once there lived two neighbors – one a scholar, the other a blacksmith. They both arose early each morning for their tasks. The first

went to the beit midrash to study, the other to the smithy and the anvil. When it was time for breakfast, the two of them went home. On the way home from his work the blacksmith hurried to the beit midrash to run off a quick and brief prayer. Every day the two of them met, passing each other.

On the face of the scholar was a smile of satisfaction, and his eyes flashed a mocking glance at his neighbor. It was as if he were saying to himself, "I labor and he labors. I study several pages of Talmud, I bathe in a pure mikveh before prayer, and my prayers are deep and sincere, deliberate and carefully paced. And what does he do?"

On the other hand, the face of the blacksmith was covered with sadness, and his eyes reflected sorrow and pain. It was as if he were saying to himself, "*Oy*, my years are quickly wasting away. My neighbor is surely studying Torah diligently, and how am I filling my days? I am constantly standing by my anvil, always with the sledgehammer, horses, and horseshoes. What will be of me in the end?"

Years passed, and the two of them passed away, and were called before the heavenly tribunal to give account of their deeds in this world.

First the scholar was called to discuss his record. With firm steps he ascended the platform, and with his head high and with full confidence in his record, he said, "Esteemed judges, I come not as a poor and pitiable scamp. I studied much Torah, and I fulfilled many mitzvot. Every day before the cock crows I sat with my Gemara. I prayed fervently and was careful to observe all the mitzvot, no matter how small."

From the hidden treasury the advocates for defense took out a pile of the pages of Gemara that the scholar had studied during his lifetime, and put them on the right side of the scale. They also added the prayers and recitations of the Shema. Everything was examined and weighed, and there was no doubt: the decision of the judges was that there was a place of honor for him in the Garden of Eden. But before the chief justice of the court began to speak, the advocate for the prosecution raised his hand and said, "Notice in the hidden treasury the condescending, mocking glance that this scholar gave at the time he met the blacksmith." Saying this he placed the glances on the left side of the scale. The mocking glances were also carefully examined and weighed, and behold! The weight of that brief, condescending smile shifted the weight of the scale to the left, and the judgment came out against him.

The scholar descended from the platform and in his place ascended the blacksmith with shaking knees, his head lowered. In a low voice he said, "As an embarrassed vessel I am here before you, honored judges. I have not studied Torah, and my brief prayers were not consistent. My whole life, from early morning till late at night, I shoed the horses and greased wheels; life's burdens – to make a living and marry off my daughters – were constantly weighing on me."

When the blacksmith finished speaking, the heavenly angels brought forth the two packages that accompany every person during his lifetime. On the right side of the scale they placed the package of mitzvot, and on the left, the package of transgressions. This time too they examined and weighed every mitzvah and considered the nature of every transgression, as the scale vacillated back and forth.

At that point the advocate for the defense stepped forward and said, "In my possession are quiet sighs of *Oy*, which burst out of the heart of the blacksmith when he saw his neighbor the scholar. Sighs of pain that came because he did not merit the possibility to immerse himself in Torah like his neighbor. Let these sighs be presented in evidence and bring merit to this man."

It was indeed the sighs that tilted the scales to the right side, opening before the blacksmith the gate of the Garden of Eden.

SITTING TOGETHER IN THE GARDEN OF EDEN

Sukkot was two days away, and in Berditchev and all the surrounding towns there was not one etrog to be found. The tzaddik of Berditchev, Rabbi Levi Yitzhak, and his community were filled with anxiety. The rabbi sent several messengers to nearby cities, in the hope that they would meet a Jew with an etrog. The messengers went and searched, and finally found a wagon coming toward them in which there was a Jew with an etrog and a lulav in his hand. Thrilled at the sight, they stopped the wagon and spoke to the man with the etrog and lulav. Their joy was short lived. The Jew told them that his destination was nowhere near Berditchev.

The messengers did not give up, and pleaded with him to pause for a short while and speak with the tzaddik of Berditchev. The man obliged. When the rabbi saw the man with the etrog and lulav, he was filled with joy, and asked him to please remain in Berditchev for the festival, and by doing so make possible the great mitzvah of lulav and etrog for the entire community.

But the man refused. He explained that he had a family, thank God, a wife and children. Why would he deny them the privilege of the joy of the festival by staying in a strange place?

The tzaddik of Berditchev promised him that if he remained in town he would merit having great wealth and wonderful children. But the man refused to listen. "I don't want wealth, and, thank God, I make a very adequate living, and furthermore I have good, honest children." He would not remain there; he was determined to return home for the holiday.

When the rabbi saw how determined the man was he said to him, "If you stay here, I promise you a place in the Garden of Eden right next to me." When the man heard this, his inflexible position began to soften, and he agreed to remain. The entire congregation rejoiced, and the tzaddik of Berditchev and even the stranger were very pleased.

The man gave the lulav and etrog to the rabbi, and went to prepare for the holiday. At the same time the rabbi called his messenger and sent him to all the homes in the city that had a sukkah, and told them that no one should allow this man to enter their sukkah. They should not deprive him of the best food and drink, but under no circumstances to permit him to enter the sukkah. Why? No one understood the reason, and no one dared ask. When the tzaddik issues an order, one must obey.

That evening, after the prayers, the man went from the great synagogue to his inn, and went to the room assigned to him. He saw there a table set beautifully with candles, wine, hallahs, fish, and beautiful dishes and cutlery. But he was surprised. Why did they prepare such a beautiful table in his room? Is it possible that the innkeeper, who appeared to be an observant Jew, did not have a sukkah, since it was the law to eat in a sukkah on the festival?

He went outside to the courtyard and his eyes lit up with joy. He saw a large sukkah, in which the innkeeper and his family were seated, and they greeted the guest with a loud "Happy Holiday!" – but did not invite him to enter. He stood, amazed and taken aback. What was going on?

No one answered him. He went from sukkah to sukkah, but no one invited him in. What could be happening? Finally, he found out the answer. The tzaddik of Berditchev had issued a strong directive not to let the man enter any sukkah. Frightened and humiliated, he ran to the tzaddik. "What did I do to deserve this? What is my crime?"

Rabbi Levi Yitzhak explained, "If you really want to eat in the sukkah, you may, but on one condition: that you sincerely promise to relinquish your place in the Garden of Eden next to me."

When the man heard this new plan, he remained totally confused. On the one hand, how could he give up joy such as this, a guaranteed place in the Garden of Eden next to the tzaddik of Berditchev? And how could they have enticed him to agree to ruin his family's festival joy, to be separated from his wife and children, to roam around in a strange place for a reward that they would later force him to relinquish?

On the other hand, how could he agree to violate the mitzvah of dwelling in the sukkah, about which he was so fastidious his whole life. And how could it be that everyone would be dining in their sukkot, while he would be eating alone in his room?

Finally the visitor overcame his compunctions. He stretched out his hand to Rabbi Levi Yitzhak and announced in a loud voice, "I promise you, in all sincerity, that I will give up my place in the Garden of Eden, as long as the rabbi will permit me to dwell in the sukkah!"

That entire festival day the rabbi did not converse with the visitor. Only on Shmini Atzeret did he finally send for him. After sitting him down at the head of the table and extending to him much honor, the rabbi finally explained to him, "Please do not be angry with me, my son, for treating you so harshly. I did not want a Jew to acquire a place in the World to Come in an easy fashion, by trading and dealing with a handshake and a promise. To earn a place in the World to Come necessitates hard work. One can only enter the World to Come by merit of one's own good deeds. For this reason I wanted to test you, and see if you would stand up to the test. And now that you have, with God's help, demonstrated your strong commitment to the mitzvah of dwelling in the sukkah, to the point that you were willing to give up your place in the next world, I hereby give you back my earlier offer, and I promise you that we will live together, God willing, in the Garden of Eden, next to one another."

REWARD FOR MITZVOT

It happened once on Purim that one of the yeshivah boys in the city of Radin became intoxicated. In this state he came to speak to the Hafetz Hayyim and asked him to promise that he would be close to him in the Garden of Eden.

The Hafetz Hayyim replied, "How can I promise? Who know if I will have a place in the Garden of Eden?"

The young man refused to be put off so easily; for an entire hour he continued to badger the Hafetz Hayyim with his request.

Meanwhile the time arrived for the Purim feast, and the people standing in the room suggested to the Hafetz Hayyim that he should agree to the promise. But the Hafetz Hayyim stood his ground. "How do I know that I will have a place in the Garden of Eden, so how can I promise that I will be near him?"

However, time was passing, and the hour of the Purim feast was getting close, so the Hafetz Hayyim turned to the student and said to him, "I do not know if I will have a place in the Garden of Eden, but one thing I do know: that there is one thing for which I will be worthy of having a place in the Garden of Eden. That is that I have never spoken evil about another person, and I have never listened to gossip about another.

"If you will promise me that from now on you will not speak any gossip or slander, and you will refuse to listen to any, I can promise you that if I merit entry into the Garden of Eden, you will be there with me."

THE SOUL YOU GAVE ME, GOD, IS PURE

A friend of Rabbi Yisrael Salanter came to ask him a question of halakhah (Jewish law). Over the course of the conversation Rabbi Salanter kept sighing. Finally, his friend asked him the reason.

The rabbi replied, "The sleeve of my coat is torn and stained, and I am embarrassed that you are seeing me like this. I then realized: If I became embarrassed because my outward appearance, my physical property – clothing – was unkempt and soiled, how much more so will I be embarrassed when I am ready to enter the World to Come? When I did not repair all the tears and stains in my soul when I should have, what will they say to me at the end of my days on earth?"

WORDS OF WISDOM

DISTRACTED FROM THIS WORLD

In the past the *yetzer hara* (evil impulse) tried to distract people only from the World to Come. But in our day it is learning how to drive people away from this world as well. People spend all their energy making a living, and in chasing after money they have no time to enjoy even this world.

Rabbi Yaakov Yosef of Polnoye

About the Author

Simcha Raz is an Israeli author and educator. He has an MA in public administration from Hebrew University and rabbinic ordination from Merkaz HaRav Kook Yeshivah in Jerusalem. He is the author of many popular books on aggadic and Hasidic themes, several of which have appeared in English translation, including *A Tzaddik in Our Time* (1972), *Hasidic Wisdom: Sayings From The Jewish Sages* (1997), and *The Torah's Seventy Faces* (2005). His articles frequently appear in the Israeli press, and he hosts literary programs on the radio in Israel. He has received several literary prizes, and he was awarded the Israel Minister of Religious Affairs' Jewish Heritage Prize in recognition of his efforts in teaching Hebrew language and literature in Israel and throughout the Jewish world, including the former Soviet Union. He lives in Jerusalem with his wife, Colleen.

About the Translator

Rabbi Dov Peretz Elkins is an internationally known speaker and author, winner of the National Jewish Book Award. One of America's leading congregational rabbis, Dr. Elkins is rabbi emeritus of The Jewish Center of Princeton, NJ. He coauthored *Chicken Soup for the Jewish Soul*, among his thirty-five books and hundreds of published articles. His most recent book is *Jewish Stories from Heaven and Earth*. He has spoken and led training workshops for synagogues, federations, JCCs, and other Jewish organizations in North America, Europe, and Israel, and his books have been read by thousands throughout the world. He was a member of the Committee on Jewish Law and Standards of the Rabbinical Assembly. Dr. Elkins and his wife Maxine live in Princeton, NJ, and travel often to see their children and nine grandchildren.

Dr. Elkins's websites are:
www.JewishGrowth.org, www.WisdomofJudaism.org, and
www.Eco-Judaism.org.
He can be reached via email at DPE@JewishGrowth.org.